ROSE'S CHOICE

A heart-wrenching wartime saga
of love, family and secrets

CHRISSIE BRADSHAW

Chrissie x

VALLUM PUBLISHING

Published by Vallum Publishing

All enquiries to vallumpublishing@gmail.com

Cover design by: JD Smith

Dedication

To Betty, Mary, Douglas and Allan Johnson
and Patrick, Jackie and Eileen Bradshaw
who lived in the colliery rows during the war and
shared such colourful memories of that time.

PROLOGUE

1934

NEWCASTLE EVENING CHRONICLE

BIRTHS

Born at home on August 15th 1934
to John and Virginia Kelly of
1, First Row, Linwood Colliery
a daughter, Rose Virginia.
Mother and baby well

John Kelly cut the birth announcement out of last night's evening paper and tucked it inside the family bible beside the certificate of his marriage to Ginnie. He put the bible back into the drawer of the dresser before placing the rest of the newspaper and a few sticks of wood by the hearth ready to lay a fresh fire in the morning.

Dry crumpled paper in the grate, then sticks crossing each other and a shovel of coal would get their range going in no time tomorrow morning before he set off to the pit. He was on the early shift but he wanted to get the fire going for when

Ginnie and their firstborn came downstairs. Even though it was mid-August, the fire would blaze to heat the oven and boil water. Ginnie loved her early morning tea.

Quietly climbing the stairs, avoiding the creak on the third step from the top, John found Ginnie lying on her side with her hand resting on the baby's crib by the bed. He'd sanded and painted the crib as Ginnie knit an intricate white shawl during their last weeks of waiting.

His wife looked beautiful with her dark curls tumbling to her shoulders and she didn't even stir as he tucked her hand under the blankets and stood over his daughter's crib.

Ever so gently, he picked the baby up and cradled her in his arms drinking in her warm, sweet smell. He traced the back of his finger around the curve of her cheek. Her skin, so soft, reminded him of the petals of the roses that grew in his allotment and they had the same cream tint with a blush of pink. That rosebud mouth, now there was an exquisite shade that he would find hard to recreate on his paint palette. He would never capture such beauty with a pencil or a brush.

He took her over to the open window to catch the last of the day's light and some cool air. The clock on the nightstand broke the silence as it marked time ticking by and, as John watched Rose breathe, he marvelled at this little being. Would he ever tire of watching those changing expressions?

He stood by the window as the sun's last rays sank behind the Linwood pit wheel leaving it a stark silhouette against the peach-tinged evening sky. Soon, that wheel would turn bringing men to the surface and beckoning the night shift workers to the pithead. The mine never slept. John would follow the night shift at day break.

His attention was swiftly drawn back to the baby as she stirred in his arms. What was she dreaming about? Was her mind like one of his blank canvases? Was it waiting for experiences to fill it with colour and emotion? Would those experiences shape her hopes and dreams?

Tears blurred his vision as a surge of love and protectiveness coursed through his body. Rose Kelly was his flesh and blood and he wanted her to flourish in his care, to grow rich roots of confidence and courage. He placed his little finger in the centre of her open palm and, even in sleep, she gripped it. He hoped she would always grasp opportunities. He would be a happy man if his daughter was given the chance to see the world in all its wondrous colours beyond these dark colliery rows.

1

1944

Ten-year-old Rose Kelly could hardly remember the time when there wasn't a blackout at night and you could buy as many sweets as you wanted. The older lads and lasses talked about those days and how they would be back after Hitler was sent packing. Until that day, carrying a gas mask and a trip to their Anderson shelter in the middle of the night whenever they heard the siren, Wailing Willie, was part of life.

They might have to be careful with their sweets but they all ate well in Linwood colliery rows because of the allotments that grew all manner of fruit and veg. A strip of land was allotted to each house and the miners used their plot for growing food, keeping chickens and building sheds from whatever scraps of material they could find. After hours underground, pitmen liked outdoor hobbies like growing prize leeks or racing whippets and pigeons. Rose's dad used his shed for painting and storing his canvases.

Even though they had the allotments, a lot of a miner's pay went on food because he did a job that needed fuel in the belly and he dreaded being laid off sick. Miners were allowed a few extra rations because of their work but it all had to be paid for. Her mam was a really good cook of stews and pies and soups but Rose's favourite meal of the week wasn't any of those. Her favourite was Friday's dinner when she could have either her one rationed egg, fried, with chips and a slice of bread, or have some battered fish and chips from Charlie's.

Like many miners, her dad handed his pay unopened to Mam every week. She would tip it out and count the pounds he had earned then hand him five shillings as pocket money. He saved this and then spent a lot on art materials and brushes every now and then.

Folk said her mam and dad made a handsome couple and Rose had to agree. Dad was as fair as her mam was dark. Her mam was the bonniest of all the women in the colliery rows, as pretty as that Vivien Leigh in the films. She had chocolate coloured curly hair that she tied up in a scarf when she was working, kind brown eyes and a big smile showing white teeth. Rose had her mam's brown hair and her dad's green eyes and, no matter how hard her mam tried, she put everything in her left hand like Dad too. Cack-handedness her mam called it.

Mam's nice teeth were because she was strict about teeth cleaning and eating apples and carrots to keep them strong. They all knew she was scared of visiting the dentist or the doctor. It was losing her mam when she was a little'un that had left her with a terrible fear of the very folk who could help to make you better.

'We don't want any teeth pulled in this family if we can help it,' she'd say as she brushed at Rose's teeth with a bit of salt or bicarb when toothpaste was in short supply and Rose tried not to gag. It wasn't easy to have white teeth.

Every weekend saw her dad sketching or painting after he'd done the gardening jobs and her mam making do and mending so much that she deserved a medal from Mr Churchill. Old clothes didn't go on a scrap pile to make proggy mats for the floor as often. Clothes were unpicked to see if they could be altered or made into something new for Rose, her younger twin brothers or another bairn in the row. Their mam was very handy with a needle and careful with clothing coupons.

Their neighbours, the Elliots, had given up sharing the Anderson shelter with them. It now had a shelf and blanket arrangement that her dad called a bunk at the end of it for her and the twins, Stanley and David, to sleep on. Benches ran along either side and a shelf under the bunk held jars of water, some old crockery and an oil lamp, candles and matches. Their oldest proggy mat was on the floor and they had put a couple of blankets in there. Her dad and Mr Elliot's son, Larry, had sealed the panels well with that stinky hot stuff before covering it with soil, and the shelter hadn't leaked so it was dry but, goodness, it could get cold down there.

Mr Elliot thought the cold and being underground reminded his chest of the pit and made it worse. 'I don't mind dying in my own bed,' he claimed. 'When your time's up then it's up.' Mary wouldn't leave him so she stayed in the house too.

'Do you think they're daft Mam?' Rose couldn't understand the Elliots ignoring the siren.

'I wouldn't make their choice but our neighbours have lived through a lot. They lost two boys in the first war. That's why Mr Elliot said, "when your time's up it's up". Jackie was twenty and young Tom was twenty-two.

To Rose, that was all the more reason to stay safe. 'What about Larry? He's lost two older brothers and might end up with no mam or dad?' she asked.

'You're getting to be a real chip off the old block,' Mam answered. 'Let me get back to peeling these taties.'

'What does that mean, Mam? What old block?'

'It means you ask too many questions, just like your father.'

Rose went out to play with her best friend, Lottie. She had a hundred questions in her head. Maybe her dad did too. It was better if she didn't ask too many at once because grownups didn't answer them carefully when she asked too many. Like her mam, just now.

She should be like her mam who eked out the meat ration

with lots of veg. She would eke out her questions a few at time and keep the tricky ones for Miss Wakenshaw, her favourite teacher, or Dad.

Rose loved school and she always wanted to read but often she had to put her book down and help out by keeping an eye on her brothers or running errands. She didn't mind because it seemed to her that Mam never ever stopped working.

On Mondays, Mam helped Mary-from-next-door with her week's washing because Mary was nursing Mr Elliot who was proper poorly with his lungs. Mary had no daughters so Rose's mam stepped in. Her daughter-in-law, who was married to Larry, hardly came by even though she just lived in Burnside, the next village. She always sent Larry and the bairns over for Sunday tea and had a nice rest herself. When she listened in to their crack, Rose could tell her mam and Mary hadn't much time for Larry's wife, Kate.

That's why it seemed so strange when Kate and the two children burst into Mary's kitchen one Tuesday afternoon.

Most days after school Rose would pop to the Co-op and get Mary's rations for her, and that day, just as she was taking the shopping list and ration books from Mary, the door banged open. Kate didn't take her headscarf off or say hello. 'There's been a fall at Burnside! A dozen men are trapped. Larry's down there. Keep the bairns. I need to go to the pithead and wait.'

Mary's cheeks drained of their high colour and, as she sat on a stool, Rose heard a clatter from upstairs. Mr Elliot shouted down. 'What's that you're saying, Kate? What's happened?'

Rose rushed out to fetch her mam. Mary looked terrible and Mr Elliot shouldn't be out of bed.

'Mam, Kate's come with news about a fall at the pit, Burnside not ours. You'd better go next door.'

She hovered, not sure what to do, as her mam dried her

hands calmly. 'You stay here with the lads and take the pie out of the oven in half an hour. Don't worry if your dad doesn't come in. When they hear about Burnside, the Linwood rescue team will go straight over there to see if there's owt they can do.'

2

Rose was in charge of number one First Row for the first time. With a glow of pleasure, she took the pie out using a cloth to protect her hands just as her mam did, then she gave herself a quick talking to. This wasn't an occasion to get excited about or be proud of, men were in danger just a mile or so away. She shuddered at the thought of being trapped and in the dark.

After setting the table, she gave Stanley and David their dinner. The pie looked delicious but she just wasn't hungry. She kept the fire going, washed up and waited for Mam and Dad to come home.

Her mam came back with Kate's bairns. They were two and four and Mary wasn't up to having them because she had her hands full with Mr Elliot and keeping him from walking over to Burnside pithead.

As they waited for news, Rose helped her mam to un-ravel the wool of an old sweater and wind the curly wool into a big ball. 'This'll make warm balaclavas for the twins and a couple of pairs of winter gloves,' Mam said but she didn't seem to be in the mood to chat so Rose kept quiet. Stanley and David played a noisy game of hide and seek with the bairns until they were tired out and ready for bed. They shared a bed in a curtained alcove of Mam and Dad's room but it was a tight squeeze.

When the little 'uns were tucked into Rose's bed, her mam sat with her head in her hands.

'Are you all right? Shall I make you a strong cup of tea?'

'Yes, that'd be lovely.' Her mam looked up at her and tears ran down her cheeks.

'We have a war on but we canna forget that our biggest enemy is underground. I canna bear it for Mary. She lost two fine young lads in the first war, her man has the black lung from the pit and now... now her youngest is trapped down there. Hasn't she suffered enough?'

Rose took a cup of dark brown tea over, just how her mam liked it. I've left Dad's pie in the oven but it'll get dry. Shall I take it out?

'Yes pet, you make a good little helper. Cover it with a plate and leave it on the side because God only knows when your dad will come home. Larry's bairns are asleep in your room so you get into our bed, and I'll join you in a while.'

'I'll pray for Larry and for the other men and for no siren tonight.'

'You do that, sweetheart. Let's hope our prayers get heard and those two upstairs still have a father in the morning. Night night.'

Rose couldn't sleep in the big double bed. The covers were heavy on her legs and she imagined being trapped with miles of rock above her head not knowing when the next lot would fall. If anyone could dig the men out, it was her dad and his rescue team.

Next morning, they heard from Lottie's dad that the rescuers had cleared a way through the rock fall and her dad, with the rest of the team from Linwood and Burnside, was going in to try to bring the men up.

Rescue teams were made up of experienced pitmen who were trained in first aid and knew pit seams. They could administer morphine and set bones before stretchering the men the mile or more to the shaft. Rescue work was dangerous so Rose and her mam turned their worries to whether her dad would get out all right. She managed some porridge but her belly churned.

'Take this apple for break time.' Her mam slipped the treat into her pocket and gave her a hug before she set off for school.

When Rose reached the school yard, there was a crowd around Danny Dodd. His brother Joe worked at Burnside as a driver with the pit ponies, gallowas they were called, so he would have news.

'Joe came straight home last night, couldn't stop at the pithead for his shower but by, underneath the pit dust, he was shaking and white even after a bath in front of the fire. He had a lucky escape, I'm telling you.'

'What happened Danny?' Rose couldn't resist asking and Danny didn't mind going over the story again.

'Yesterday, Our Joe was pulling tubs along the Bottom Main seam with his little gallowa, Sparkie, and Sparkie just stopped. "Howay, Sparkie," he shouted but Sparkie wouldn't budge.

His marra, on Major, told him to get his whip onto Sparkie because he was holding them both up but our Joe doesn't use the whip on his pony. He just pats Sparkie on the head and whispers to him but the gallowa is having none of it and sticks his feet in. He isn't going to move.

Then they hear it, the creaking then a rumbling up ahead. They get them gallowas out of their limmers, the cart shafts you know, and then run like hell.

That's how they missed the fall. The tubs they were pullin' got buried and, if it wasn't for Sparkie, our Joe would've been a goner. They say pit ponies have a sixth sense and there's the proof. There's a dozen men trapped at the other side of the fall.'

'Is Sparkie okay?' Rose asked.

'Aye. The mine owner himself come by and told the lads he was pleased they'd taken the time to uncouple their ponies. Our Joe loves that beast.'

Rose reached into her pocket and took out her break time apple. 'Will you give this to Joe to give to Sparkie?'

Danny grinned and held out his hand. 'Aye, I might, or I might just eat it meself,' he teased.

'Don't you dare!' He had a cheeky grin, did Danny.

Rose understood that gallowas had an important role down the mine but she hated the thought of those plucky pit ponies never seeing daylight or running in a field. Some pits brought the ponies up during the mine's two week summer holiday closure but Linwood's shaft was too tricky so they went down at four years old and came up when they retired.

Dad said the stables were spotless and they were well-loved and looked after but it just didn't seem natural. His view was that gallowas were work horses who liked to do a good job and were respected for it by the miners. Rose once argued, 'It's animal slavery, Dad. The horses don't have a choice about going down the mine whereas you men do.'

Dad's answer had been to laugh and say, 'Aye, we have a choice alright. We can go down the pit or we can sit on our backsides and let our families starve.'

Kate still hadn't come for her bairns so it was left for Rose to entertain them, after school.

'She's weeping and wailing at the pithead while eleven other wives will be going about their business, looking after the home and keeping their tears for when their bairns aren't looking.' Mam's tone showed that she didn't approve of how Kate was carrying on. It wasn't the way of miners' wives, even Rose knew that.

She was in Mary's kitchen helping the two little'uns to model figures with a clump of old brown plasticine they'd found when the back door opened and a blackened face shouted, 'Mam! Dad!' Larry Elliot's teeth grinned as white as her mam's bedsheets out of his sooty face.

'Oh son, I canna believe you're here. I thought I'd lost you too!' Mary flung her arms around him and didn't mind the dirt.

Mr Elliot hobbled down the stairs 'Is that my bairn?' He was crying. Rose hadn't seen a grown man cry but Mr Elliot hadn't been well for a while. 'Lad, I'll happily go six foot under now I've seen you're all right.'

'Don't talk like that, Dad.' Larry gripped his dad by the shoulders. 'It'll take more than a few stones to keep me down that pit after my shift.'

Rose put the kettle on and ran to fetch her mam. They brought the twins back with them and Rose was glad she could stay to hear the tale of the fall and the rescue.

'A few men are hurt but just bones, nowt worse. Your John is helping to stretcher them out. I was one of the first out because I could walk and I told Kate, 'If you've been to Linwood and my folks know I've been trapped then I'm going straight there. They'll be worried sick.'

After a cup of tea and a thick slice of bread and dripping, Larry set off to Burnside with his two little'uns in the pram.

When they got back home, Rose could see her mam was quiet and something was troubling her. 'Shall I take the two lads up to bed, Mam?'

'Yes, pet... and say another prayer for your dad. Last night's must've worked.'

'The men are safe, Larry said.' She stroked her mam's hair from her face.

Her mam hugged her. 'You're right, but you never know when there'll be another fall.'

Rose imagined her dad reaching injured men before a doctor could see them, giving first aid and administering injections to those in pain and doing it in a narrow seam with a propped roof that could give way at any time. He'd be working out the best way to carry them out, and the safest. She was proud that, as well as hewing coal and painting pictures, he could save lives, but it didn't stop her stomach churning. Pride didn't stop the fear that it might go wrong.

Next morning Rose padded downstairs to find her dad there just finishing his breakfast slice. She rushed over to hug him. 'When did you get home, Dad?'

'It was the middle of the night, hinny and you were all fast asleep. I'm off to my own pit now.' Dad's eyes seemed red and tired.

'Will you not get time off? You haven't had a good night's rest.'

'No, Rose. I've had a couple of hours and there's no time off, even for good behaviour, at the pit.' He smiled and put on his cloth cap.

Rose hadn't really thought about the danger her dad faced when going to work, until these past few days. She had worried about him going to war and prayed every night that he wasn't called up but pit work could be just as dangerous.

3

It seemed to Rose that life was light and dark just like her dad's paintings. Some of his canvases were dark and showed the miners going about their work underground and some were filled with light and showed the men laughing as they left the pithead or the lads and lasses playing in the rows. She had dismal days of sitting in air raid shelters or queuing for rations and then listening to news of bombs and destruction and bright days of fun like a birthday party or Christmas or the Sunday School anniversary. She knew life was hard but it would be even harder if the Germans won the war.

They all thought they were winning with the Normandy landings but then the Germans had attacked London with new flying bombs they called doodlebugs. Raids were never ending with houses lost and people killed or injured every day. Would her family be wiped out by a doodlebug? Would she lose her home and have to face a life without any of the fun days? This year's summer Olympics had been cancelled but imagine having no birthday to look forward to and no Christmas, even if she knew Father Christmas wasn't real.

Sometimes, Rose wasn't so sure about Jesus or God either. How could God be on both sides of the war and if he was on their side surely they should have won by now? She didn't tell Miss Wakenshaw this. She enjoyed Sunday School and the stories but, when she mentioned it to her dad, he wasn't surprised.

'Sweetheart, you're a clever lass and it is right to question everything and then come up with your own set of beliefs. Ask questions and listen to all the different answers. We all have a mind of our own.'

'What do you think, Dad?'

'I'm like you, I'm never completely sure but I wish I was because faith is a big help during hard times. I think if you're not sure it's best to keep the prayers and the Sunday school going, don't you?'

'You're right Dad, and I like the singing and getting a book. We still receive a new one every anniversary, even though there's a war on.'

Rose liked the atmosphere of their chapel, too. When she entered, it felt peaceful and the high narrow windows created dancing light patterns over the wooden benches. The most beautiful thing in Linwood Colliery was their chapel's one stained glass window. It was above the chapel door and showed Jesus as a shepherd tending a flock of sheep. When the sun shone through it, the light from the coloured glass gave the whole chapel a magical glow

Rose enjoyed listening in, cocking her lugs her mam called it, to the talk amongst the grown-ups about what would happen after the war, after they won. Her dad was interested in social reform and how education would change.

'It looks like this new act of Rab Butler's will go ahead and the bairns will all be having a decent secondary education. That has to be a good thing, Ginnie.' He was reading his paper and drinking a mug of tea before going to his shift.

'I'm not so sure. It'll mean they are not working until they're fifteen. Rose can already read and write as well as me, David is good at his letters and Sanley is too when he puts his mind to it. They'll be eating us out of house and home and growing out of their clothes and it's hard with just one wage coming in.' Her mam was making the grey border of a proggy mat before getting to a lovely flower design her dad had drawn on the centre of the sacking.

'We'll manage. They'll get good jobs if they stay on at school. Our Rose is top of her class and Miss Wakenshaw reckons she will do well for herself if she stays on.'

Rose, who was supposed to be reading her book, listened intently. She would love to stay on at school. At fourteen, some lasses went away to work in big houses and some took a bus into the town to work in shops or got set on in the factories by the Tyne and just came home on a Sunday, but some stayed at home and helped their mams, that was if they had a big family. Their family wasn't big enough for her stay home and help out so working would mean moving away from the rows.

When she had to work, she knew exactly what she'd love to do and it would be nice to have a pay packet to help her mam and dad out. The trouble was she didn't know how to start applying for her dream job where she could work with animals.

Rose had uttered hundreds of prayers asking for a dog along with her 'Our fathers' but she had never ever had her own pet. Her mam was the trouble. If he *was* for real, God clearly listened more to Ginnie Kelly than to Rose, she'd worked that much out.

Her dad was no help either. 'Your mam has enough on when she's cooking and cleaning for all of us and keeping pit dust out of the house. My paints and easel can take over the place at times and a pet wouldn't be fair to her.'

'Just a rabbit for in the yard then, Dad? I'd collect dandelion leaves to feed her and clean her out. There'd be no worry about fleas and she wouldn't go near Mam.'

'Sorry Rose, it's not just fleas. Your mam thinks she's allergic – it means she gets the sneezes and itches around pet fur, even in the yard.'

'I know what *allergic* means Dad but I've noticed she doesn't sneeze with Mary-from-next-door's budgie. I think, with Mam, it's psychological.'

'Do you now? The budgie has feathers not fur.' Her dad grinned and ruffled her hair. 'Don't be giving your mam such cheek or you'll get a clip around the lug.'

'Just wait 'til Mam tries to make me have liver and onions again. I'm going to tell her *I'm* allergic and sneeze 'til I have to leave the table.' Rose skipped out of the door having had the last word.

Rose still remembered her trip to the circus, so long ago it seemed like a dream. It had been just her and her dad because the twins were babies and there must have been no war because she recalled bright torch lights.

When she left school, she would try to find work in a circus. She hadn't mentioned it at home yet because it would take her far and wide around the world and her mam and dad would worry about that because of the war. Rose practiced her circus girl skills by training the Smith's dog, Laddie, and teaching Mary-from-next-door's budgie new words.

In the holidays, when the other lasses knocked and asked if they could take babies for a walk in their prams, Rose offered to take the dogs out for an hour or two. The women in the rows were always glad to have a baby or whippet out from under their feet.

The school holidays had just started and Rose looked forward to the long days of summer as she sat behind the Anderson shelter in the Elliot's allotment chatting to Lottie and a couple of other lassies about whether to have a backyard picnic for her birthday this year or take bait boxes filled with party food to the Saturday matinee.

If she chose the film, her dad would pay for *five* of them to go to the Hippo for a new full length film after the morning pictures finished, and her mam would make their bait, but then she wouldn't have a cake and candles. It was a tough decision and views were mixed.

'Picnic and cake! Definitely, I wait all year for a slice of your mam's humdinger of a sponge cake.'

'Aye. Cake!'

'*Bambi* might be showing and, if we all see it together, we'll not spoil it for anybody who hasn't been.' Lottie looked pointedly at Betty who always told them the ending if she saw a film first. 'Let's go to the Hippo, I say.'

Betty nodded. She liked cake but she liked sweets and the pictures better.

The decision was postponed when they heard someone say, 'Are you there, Rose?'. Danny and Robbie were standing by the allotment gate with a new lad who had moved to Fifth Row. 'Come and see this. Poor little beggar.'

Rose and the gang sauntered over to the gate.

'This had better not be a trick.' Lottie looked suspiciously at Danny Dodd.

'No. No. I told Robbie and Dennis here that Rose Kelly is good with animals and we've found this pup by the line.'

'Dennis rhymes with menace,' Lottie giggled before saying, 'You lot shouldn't be near the line. Dennis the menace might not know because he's new but you've been told often enough. If the Sir finds out—'

'Shut up, man. It's the holidays anyway.'

Rose looked at the tiny pup wrapped in Danny's jumper. She gave a sharp intake of breath when she saw it was only weeks old and its tail was all crushed and bloody.

'What's happened to you?' she crooned as she stroked under the pup's tiny chin with one finger.

'Here take it. I think it's been run over by a wagon on the line or got trapped or something nasty.' Danny gently held the pup, still wrapped in his jumper, out to her.

'What'll I do with it?' she asked as she took it from him.

'I don't know. Nobody in Fifth Row, by the line, knew anything about it. That's why I brought it to you. You're the clever clogs around here. Let us know how he is, though.' Danny turned to catch up with the other lads who were heading back towards the line.

Rose was left with an injured pup who she couldn't take home. 'What'll we do with you?' she asked as the pup licked at her fingers.

4

Lottie came up with the plan and Rose had to agree it was a good one. She left Rose waiting with the others by the allotments while she rushed home to get directions from her eldest sister, Eileen, and take a tanner out of her piggy bank. Rose tried to give the pup a drink of water but the poor thing turned its head.

Lottie came back in no time with a box. They lifted the pup into the box, said goodbye to the gang and the two of them set off walking towards the main road. They were going to the vets in Ashington to get help.

Neither of them had made the trip to Ashington alone. Even going to the Saturday pictures, there were always older lads and lasses from the rows on their bus. Eileen had given Lottie an idea of where the vets was but said they would have to ask once they got to the bus station to make sure. She had warned Lottie to be back for tea or she'd have to tell the mams where the girls were.

The journey there was no bother. A mile walk to the bus stop then a bit of a wait for the bus and then the short ride to Ashington. They asked a shopkeeper and a couple with a dog about the nearest vets. There were two different answers and one set of directions seemed a lot easier so they set off to find Maxwell's vets just off Woodhorn Road.

'This is it. We're here.' Rose turned to see Lottie pointing at a brass plaque. She had walked past the green door because she was intent upon looking up above the doors for a shop sign.

'It looks posh. Do we knock or walk in?' Rose hesitated and would have turned around if it wasn't for the poor pup who had even stopped whimpering.

Lottie reached for the knocker and the door creaked open. She giggled and covered her mouth with her hand. 'I feel like Goldilocks going into the bear's house,' she whispered.

'Don't be daft.' Rose gave her a nudge but had to try hard not to giggle herself.

The door opened onto a long hallway with a polished wood floor and a staircase to the left. There were several closed doors along the right wall. At the end was an open door with a woman facing them from behind a desk. 'Come in girls, come in. What have we here?'

Lottie pushed Rose forward and she put the box, which had become very heavy considering the pup was so small, on the desk. 'We have a pup who has had an accident and needs to see a vet.'

'Did you make an appointment?'

Rose's heart lurched. This was just like a doctor's and she hadn't realised it would be like this. 'Sorry, we haven't. Some lads handed the pup to us and we hopped on a bus to find some help. I didn't think about an appointment.'

The woman looked in the box and quickly shut it again. 'Stay here, girls. I'll just see if Mr Maxwell is available.' She scooped up the box and passed them to go into one of the closed doors.

'I don't think we'll have enough money, Rose. It's posh here isn't it?' Lottie looked as uncomfortable as Rose felt.

As Rose nodded in agreement, a familiar wail started. 'Oh no!'

'Blimey there's the siren starting!' Lottie grabbed her arm. 'What'll we do Rose?'

The woman came back into the hall and beckoned the two girls. 'This way, quickly. Follow me.'

They saw the woman open what looked like a cupboard door under the stairs. Were they going to shelter in a cubby hole? They ran to the door and saw stairs leading down into darkness.

'Don't panic girls, I'm taking you to the cellar. We'll shelter there.'

Rose and Lottie did as they were told. Rose was more worried about being late and facing her mam than a raid. She hoped it wouldn't last long.

She blinked when the light went on. The cellar had electric lighting and was huge! One end had bunks, two easy chairs, a bookcase, gramophone and radio with a large rug on the floor. This had to be the poshest shelter ever.

'Blinking Nora!' Lottie must be thinking the same because she was even swearing politely.

Rose got the giggles. 'It's another world!'

'Yes, we're stuck down here and have to put up with it and make do while the raids are on.' The lady ushered them to the other side of the basement.

A desk and a set of filing cabinets were along one wall. A bench with a kettle and a primus stove filled another and there was a large square table with four good dining chairs. There were shelves and shelves of tinned food. They could stay here for the whole war.

'What a fantastic place, Miss.' Rose finally found her voice.

'It's no fun having to work here without daylight but we're safe. Now you girls behave because Mrs Maxwell will be joining us and she doesn't like noise.'

Sure enough, the cellar door opened and a lady came down the stairs. A proper lady like Bette Davis with a twin set and skirt and pearls.

'Oh goodness, Vera. Another raid. I was telephoning Mother to make sure Ruth and Frank were behaving themselves when the siren drowned me out. Who have you dragged in now?' She sounded like someone from a newsreel.

'They were about to see Mr Maxwell when the siren sounded, Ma'am.'

'Please ensure quiet. No click click of typing and no chat. I'm badly in need of a nap.'

The lady sat back on an easy chair and rested her feet on a footstool. She lay back and pulled a mask over her eyes. It was an eyeless bandit mask and Rose tensed as she heard a stifled giggle from Lottie.

The miss shook her head and put her finger to her lips so they all sat in silence for a while, hardly daring to breathe.

A gentle snoring started from the chair and Lottie's giggles started again but the miss let out a sigh and relaxed.

'She won't wake up now, that's Mrs Maxwell off for a while. She can sleep for England that one and I don't know what she ever tires herself with.'

Rose could see there was no love lost between the two women.

'Who are Ruth and Frank?' Rose was always curious.

'Ruth is a few years older than you and Frank is about your age. They are the Maxwell's children and they are staying with their grandparents for the summer.'

'Lucky them. I've never had a holiday, but Dad might take me to London after the war.'

'Lucky you,' Lottie's eyes widened.

Vera interrupted, 'Shush girls, you'll have to be quiet, no chatter. I'm not allowed to type and make a noise so you can help me to address envelopes by hand. Who is a neat writer?'

'Rose is but I'm messy,' Lottie admitted.

'Okay. Rose, you can write the addresses and you, young lady, can put the invoices into the envelopes and seal them. I'm Vera, by the way. I'm Mr Maxwell's receptionist, secretary and assistant.'

'Where is Mr Maxwell?'

'He hasn't come down because he is seeing to that scruffy little scrap you brought. He won't be down until it's out of danger or out of pain.'

'Might he die?' Rose whispered. They were all talking in low voices.

Vera's eyes softened with concern. 'I'm sorry, dear,' she said, 'but Mr Maxwell will decide whether he can help your pup or whether it is kinder to put the poor scrap out of pain... and put it to sleep.'

Rose thought about this. What a decision, but she did understand. The tail looked done for and its paw was limp, if the pup couldn't survive, it shouldn't be in pain.

'I understand, Miss,' she said.

'Call me, Vera.'

They finished the envelopes and had a cup of tea with a biscuit before the all clear sounded.

Mrs Maxwell woke up, '*At last!* How tedious these warnings are,' she said before going upstairs.

'Come on girls let's see the damage.' Vera led them back up to the hallway and they all peered outside. Thankfully, their street seemed fine.

'Vera, there you are!' A loud voice boomed and a tall man with a shock of grey hair appeared from one of the hallway's many doors. 'Oh, and you girls are here too. How did your pup get into such a state? I've had to dock the little chap's tail and I'm not sure how well his broken hind leg will heal. He's very young, I'd say he's just five weeks, have you got his mother at home?'

'He's not ours. He doesn't seem to be anybody's. Thank you for treating him,' Rose answered.

'He should still be with his mother. If not, you will have to leave him here for a week or so. You girls had better come in here and tell me who is going to pay for his treatment.'

Now they had to admit that they hadn't enough money.

Rose tried to swallow but her throat was dry. Crikey! They just had their fare home.

Rose and Lottie left the vets feeling relieved.

Mr Maxwell was a lovely man and had agreed to allow the stray to stay and to see if he could find him a home. He wasn't going to charge them either. Vera had mentioned how they had spent an hour on his paperwork and he winked at her as he asked, 'Shall we let them off, then?'

Rose's summer frock was filthy with mud and blood and they'd be late home but they had saved a pup so the trouble they would get into would be worth it.

Rose's mam went ballistic. She had been worried; she never imagined Rose going so far on her own, she had imagined her dead when the siren wailed and so on. 'Get into that bath now.' There was a bath by the fire and Stanley and David were sitting at the table looking shiny clean and tucking into slices of bread and jam.

Rose was starving. She'd missed tea and only had a biscuit since lunch-time.

The bath was screened off from the rest of the room by a blanket over the clothes horse. She climbed into the water, murky from two grubby boys and tepid. Her mam scrubbed her hard and washed her hair and dunked her in the water like she was her dad's pit clothes. She didn't dare to complain. When she was dry, her mam brushed the tats out of her wet hair and Rose bit her lip, knowing better than to squeal. Eventually the brushing got softer and her mam said. 'Tell me about it, then.'

After her hair was brushed and half dry, she sat beside the fire and her mam gave her a slice of bread and dripping and a slice of bread and jam with a mug of tea. They tasted so good and her belly stopped its yammering. 'Thanks, Mam,' she said when she'd finished and she kissed her cheek before going to bed.

A few minutes later, the door creaked open and her mam came into her bedroom.

'You're a caring girl, Rose and I'm proud of you but don't ever go anywhere without telling me again. Not when there's this flaming war on. It's just not safe and I have enough to trouble me without you causing more grief.'

'I won't, Mam and I'm sorry you were worried.'

She reached out and her mam pulled her into a tight hug before saying, 'Goodnight, pet.'

As she snuggled down to sleep, Rose could feel the top of her night gown was wet. Mam had been crying. She hadn't realised her mam had troubles making her sad. Mam hid her worries well behind a smile most of the time. She blinked back her own tears and vowed she would never give her mam any cause to cry like that again.

5

Rose woke up to the siren's wail and automatically hopped into her siren suit. She had a new one and so did Stanley but David, who was the smaller twin even though Mam tried to feed him up, had to wear her older one with the pink ribbon picked off and he hated it. She met her mam and the lads on the landing and they all trooped downstairs then grabbed their gas masks. Rose had tucked her pillow under her arm. The benches were hard after a while but pillows felt damp if they were kept in the shelter during winter.

Stanley fell asleep straight away but David had an earache so her mam climbed into the lower bunk to cuddle up with him and Rose lay on a narrow bench with the pillow tucked under her head. She'd fall off her perch if she fell asleep, she was sure.

Dad came into the shelter last and sat opposite. He kept his pit lamp on his head because, once they were all settled, he'd pick up the sketch pad he left down in the shelter and soon he'd start sketching with pencils and charcoal.

After the siren, it was silent. There was nothing overhead but they were all listening. Her mam and dad could guess where the action was by the distance of any noise. David stopped griping and her mam did a couple of little snores that set Rose giggling.

'Mam says she can't sleep in here but I think she likes our bunk,' she whispered.

'She's had a hard day, pet. You try and get some rest on that bench. It's narrow but your just a spelk yourself.'

'I am not! I'll roll on the floor if I move.'

'Rest your eyes then.' Mam would've told her to rest her tongue but her dad didn't seem to mind questions or chat when he worked. 'Dad, why did you start painting?' she asked into the shadows.

'Now there's a tale. I suppose I did it because I needed something away from the pits, and your mam doesn't care for animals in the house so I couldn't have a whippet or a lurcher.'

'All I've ever wanted is to have a dog... or a cat.'

'You know, while there is a war on, it's irresponsible for anybody to take on a new pet. We need to feed the country,' Dad reminded her.

'What about when the war is over?'

'Not in our house, you know that, too.' He laughed before whispering, 'Your mam says she's allergic but really she has a fear about animals carrying fleas and you'll never sway her.'

Rose swallowed hard. This was the time to break it to him. 'Dad, when I grow up, I'm joining a circus. I'll take in all the strays and train them to do tricks... and I'll de-flea them so Mam can visit.'

'Yes, pet.'

Hmm. Her big plan for the future didn't get the reaction she expected. Dad was too engrossed in his sketch.

Rose watched his left hand move across the paper as he captured David and Mam cuddled up together. It was quiet except for the soothing sound of the charcoal as it travelled over the pad. They never had art at school because there were no paints left and last year's miss wasn't anything like Miss Wakenshaw. She didn't like mess of any kind in the classroom.

Dad went to an art group once a week except when he was on the wrong shift.

'Dad, tell me about your night classes. Can they teach *anybody* how to draw really well, like you do?

'Tell you about the night classes?' He carried on shading but she could see he was thinking about her question. 'Night classes can be about anything, Rose. When I first went along, it was to learn something about the world that wasn't to do with coal. I was an expert on coal and nowt else so I wanted to stretch my mind a bit and broaden my knowledge. Geordie-from-Fifth-Row got me into it. The Workers' Education Association were running classes and we thought it was worth the bus fare and the tanner subs to have a night out and learn something new.'

'What was your favourite class?'

'Evolution – all about Darwin and how the Bible's idea of Adam and Eve was just a tale to explain creation.'

'Is Adam and Eve a tale like Father Christmas?' Rose asked.

'*I* think so but you'll have to read about it and learn more then decide for yourself.'

'I guessed Father Christmas was just made up from old tales. I just knew it!'

'Don't you tell the twins. He's real for little'uns.'

'I wouldn't. Anyway, you were telling me about your classes at the hut.'

'The painting and sketching started just after we had a proper professor come along to teach us about art appreciation. Most of us, we just couldn't get it.'

'Get what?'

'Get what the professor was on about when he talked about the artist and his work. I nearly dropped out but I liked seeing the rest of the lads. Then, one night, he staggered in with a load of art stuff . "You're all going to learn about art through doing it," he said. That was it, we were off.'

'Off drawing and painting without being shown what to do?'

'Aye. We just drew what we saw. Mind you, we never expected our work to be used in exhibitions along with Julian

Trevelyan's paintings. We didn't know the prof's pal Henry would praise our efforts. We didn't dream we would be in the news.'

'I've always known you were a painter as well as a pitman. I can't imagine you without your paints, Dad.'

'Neither can I, not now I've started.' Her dad put his charcoal down and ruffled his hair as though the whole thing surprised him.

Rose's eyes grew heavy and she slept.

A shrill whistling sound woke her up. 'Dad! What is that?' He grabbed her and held her tight. It became silent, there was a shudder, then darkness. They couldn't get out of the shelter. There was something blocking the exit. Dad lit a candle and held it towards Mam who was rocking Stanley and David with tears running down her face. 'This is no world to bring children into. Look at what Mary had to face during the first war and look at us, no better off years later.'

'That's enough, Ginnie! Your job is to look after these precious bairns of ours, right now.' Rose had never heard her dad speak so harshly to anybody let alone her mam. It did the trick though, her mam seemed to come out of her panic. She gave her dad a brisk nod instead of the mouthful that Rose was dreading. They heard voices and knew someone would get them out.

By the time the exit was clear, Mam and Dad were talking normally and had a smile for Lottie's dad and Mr Elliot.

'I'm glad to see you two,' her mam hugged Mr Elliot. 'Is Mary okay?'

'Aye, she's got the tea masting for you, Ginnie. Go straight in. The houses are all right.'

Drinking cocoa with a slice of toast while Mam and Mary shared a pot of tea and talked about the bleedin' Germans and that traitor Lord Haw Haw who had been taunting them on the radio earlier that night, Rose sent up a prayer of thanks. She wasn't sure about Adam and Eve anymore but she was certain that God had to be up there somewhere, watching over them.

Somebody certainly had watched over Linwood because, in the morning, they saw the crater stretching into three allotments. It was like a giant had stamped its foot, made a dent and then kicked down and burned Ronnie's cabin just outside of the pithead.

Three end allotments that didn't house a shelter and a wooden lock up hut that served as a shop for chocolate and 'baccy' for the miners but had nobody in it. It had been a lucky miss for the folk from the five rows.

The bomb site was already teeming with lads and lasses collecting shrapnel before they went to school when Rose waved her dad off to his shift. She heard him greeted with, 'I see Bert Green has turned over that end allotment at last.'

'Aye, he's dug it a bit deep mind you,' her dad laughed.

Lottie's dad joined them saying, 'Have you heard about Ronnie getting rid of his old stock from the hut at last?'

'Some of that baccy was there before the last war. He'll be rubbing his hands and writing to the war damage commission.'

At Linwood colliery, it was business as usual and pitmen would make a joke about anything.

6

School started in September and Rose had a new teacher. The sir was strict but he knew a lot and was more interesting than last year's miss. He'd been in the first world war and had a stiff leg and, because he was an expert on planes and told good stories, the boys liked him too.

The first week, he explained how Brussels had been liberated and how it was a real victory because the Belgian government could leave England and return to their own country. They studied maps and learnt a lot about Europe and Rose decided he was almost as good as Miss Wakenshaw. He gave Rose the hardest sums ever but she got most of them right.

The dark autumn nights usually meant it was pitch black outside, unless there was a bright moon, but this year, the blackout rules had been relaxed so they could have dim lights no brighter than natural moonlight. It was strange to see the shadows of the rows and the pithead's stark black wheel instead of total blackness. Her dad started a painting of a shift trooping to the pithead in this half-light and she recognised a lot of the men, Geordie, Mr Dodd, Lottie's dad, Eddie-who-played-the-accordion. He got their expressions just right.

Just before their blackberry week holiday, after Sunday school, Miss Wakenshaw came to talk to her mam and dad.

She explained that, although Rose was in Mr Thompson's class now, she'd come to see them because she knew them best.

'I'd like to talk to you and Mr Kelly alone for a moment,' she said.

Her mam invited her in and sent Rose upstairs with Stanley and David because it was a grey sort of day and too rainy to go out. 'Read the twins one of your comics, Rose.'

Rose took them up to her room, sat them on the bed with a pile of Beanos and tiptoed quietly to the top stair.

'What are you doing, Rose?' David looked up from Pansy Potter's adventure with a frown.

'Shush! I'm listening to find out what the miss wants. You two stay here.' She stepped over the creaking third step and ventured as far as the middle of the stairs. The door was open so she could hear the conversation.

'I don't know if you are aware, but we're preparing for the changes in education that will go ahead with the new education act that was passed in the summer. In time, our colliery elementary school will become a primary school for the younger children up to eleven years and the older children will go to one of three types of secondary school.'

'Yes, I'm glad the act got through,' her dad said.

'It's through but it is going to take some time for Northumberland to organise its secondary schools. We have a sparse population and the older pupils will have to travel. It will be all settled for David and Stanley's year group. I'm here today because Rose's class is just on the cusp of this change.'

'What do you mean by that, Miss Wakenshaw?' her mam asked.

'Rose will just miss sitting the new test. The eleven-plus, as it is called, will be used to decide which of the three schools they go to. Rose will just miss sitting the test so she will stay on at the colliery school as they do now and then change to a new secondary school when they are up and running.'

'We understand that. We've talked about the extra

schooling this entails and we don't think Rose needs it. Well, *I* don't.' Her mam sounded firm.

'And *I'd* like the lass to learn as much as she can.' Her dad sounded firmer.

'Rose will have nothing to learn at the colliery school before she's much older, you're right there, Mrs Kelly. She is bright and loves school so what I'm here to suggest is that we put Rose in for a scholarship.'

'A scholarship?' her mam echoed.

'Yes, a scholarship for the girls' school at Morpeth. They have to take a quota of free scholarship places nowadays and they'll become a grammar taking eleven-plus pupils in the future so, if Rose passes the scholarship exam, she can be there from the first year and become one of the first from our elementary school to go on to higher education.'

'Could she pass?' Dad asked.

'I wouldn't be here if Mr Brown the headmaster, Mr Thompson her teacher and I didn't think so Mr Kelly. We all agree that she is a good candidate. My elder sister teaches at the high school and it is such a good school. Rose will flourish there.'

'We'll have to think about it and talk about it together, Miss Wakenshaw but we will give it some thought.' Rose's dad sounded very serious.

'Of course. It's a big decision. There are no fees with a scholarship but, of course, there is the expense of a uniform and the bus fare too.'

Her mam asked, 'Don't those lasses stay on even longer, until they are sixteen?'

'Yes, they take their school certificate exams at sixteen and some stay on to take their higher certificate and go on to university at eighteen.'

'We've never had the likes of that around here. It's a big ask of a parent not to see a pay packet until that age. I'm expecting Rose to take her head out of her books and help more around the house in a year or so.' Her mam wasn't keen, she could tell.

'You're thinking short term Ginnie, and anyway, our lassie isn't here to be our work horse. She has a chance of a good start in life; the chance we never had. After the war, she will have such opportunities if she has a decent education.'

Would Dad persuade her mam? Rose crossed her fingers on both hands.

'I'll leave you both to think about it and then you can let the school know if you want us to enter her for a scholarship exam.' Miss Wakenshaw's voice was clear as she headed for their back door.

As Rose slipped back up the stairs to see what Stanley and David were up to, her mind whirled. Sitting a scholarship, going to an Enid Blyton kind of school like St Clare's with a uniform, that was just as exciting as joining the circus! Would she pass such a test? Would her mam and dad want her to try?

7

After Miss Wakenshaw's visit, the grown-ups talked about the scholarship and about how secondary schools would be the option for everybody after this year's education act. They talked about it a lot. It wasn't just her mam and dad; her mam and Mary-from-next-door talked about little else but trying for a scholarship when they had finished with Mr Elliot's chest and the war.

She hadn't even sat the test but her earwigging informed her that mam was worrying about the uniform cost and whether Rose would get 'above' herself. She knew what that meant. It meant behaving all hoity toity like Maureen Potter from Fourth Row ever since she got engaged to someone in the air force.

Then, in November, a new enemy came to Linwood. Lottie's little brother Sid was the first to come down with it. Early, on a cold but sunny Saturday morning, a few of them played 'tuggy-on-high' outside of Lottie's back yard when the doctor, from Ashington, visited.

After a while, Mrs Simpson came out. 'Lottie, you get inside and Rose, you go home now and tell your mam our Sid is proper poorly and going to the isolation hospital. All of you get back to your own rows and you'd better not call around until I tell your mams we're clear.'

Rose ran to her own back door thinking it made a change

to relay a bit of news that wasn't about the war. The look on her mam's face told her it was serious.

'It's not a bit of fun and a way to stay off school our Rose. This is all we need in the rows.'

'What is it, he's got then, Mam?'

'We used to call it the strangling angel when I was a lass. Its rightful name is diphtheria and it comes and goes. There's a vaccination programme going on because it's on the rise again but, you might guess, there's been no sight or smell of the vaccine around here.'

Rose hadn't heard of any of the folks in the rows going down with the strangling angel but, now she knew it wasn't just a cold, it was no laughing matter. Isolation meant poor little Sid being taken away to stop it spreading and she wasn't to go near the house or see Lottie.

One of Sid's pals from Third Row was next and there was talk about the vaccine coming around to them all soon. Their school ran as usual but the teachers kept the windows open and had them out in the fresh air at playtime. If anyone had a sore throat or cough, they had to call the doctor out straight away and stay off school. A few lads and lasses had the doctor to them but it turned out they were 'putting it on' and got into trouble because a doctor's visit cost money whether you were ill or not.

The week after Sid Simpson went into isolation, Rose and Douglas Fletcher were going to do a practice scholarship paper in the headmaster's room to see if they were ready for the scholarship next term. Rose was excited when the day of the test came. There were two papers. One before lunch and one after and only two of them were doing the test. If she did well, Rose might sit for the girls' high school and Douglas Fletcher, the pit under-manager's son who lived in a big house beside the pit yard, was definitely going to sit for the boys' school.

'Are you nervous, Douglas?' Rose whispered as they were sent into the headmaster's room to sit at two separate tables and complete paper one.

'I'm not worried about the test, it's just a practice, but I don't feel well. Mam didn't believe me. She said it was just nerves and I had to come.'

The paper had lots of straightforward arithmetic and then lots of mathematical problems about men digging holes and the time it took to travel from one place to another. Rose didn't falter and got right to the end. She looked up and saw Douglas with his head on his desk. He seemed to be asleep.

'Sir!'

Mr Brown looked at her over his glasses. 'No talking until the test is over, Rose.'

'I've finished Sir, but look at Douglas. He said he didn't feel well.'

Mr Brown walked over to Douglas and shook him by the elbow. 'Douglas, lad what's wrong?' A groan told them both that Douglas wasn't right. 'Rose. Go quickly to Miss Wakenshaw and send her to me. You stay and watch her class of infants. You're a sensible girl so read them a story until you hear the bell and then send them out.'

Rose read the story of 'The Gingerbread Man' to the five-year-olds until the bell and then sent them home for their lunch. If she wasn't a circus girl or a vet, she'd like to be a teacher. She took herself home and ate her lunch as she told her mam and Mary-from-next-door the tale of her morning.

'I hope it's not the strangling angel and you've been sitting with him all morning.' Mary held her apron to her mouth in horror.

'Calm down, Mary. Rose has another test this afternoon and the lad might just have exam fright.'

Rose returned to school and answered comprehension

questions and then had spellings to correct and punctuation to put right. This was her favourite paper and she was sure she got everything right.

At the end, Mr Brown said, 'Rose Kelly you have been an exemplary pupil. You have been calm and looked after the infants and you have returned to work hard on your second paper. If anyone deserves to win a scholarship, it is you young lady.'

Rose flushed bright red. Mr Brown never praised his pupils and this was praise indeed. 'Thank you, sir. May I go now?'

'Go back to your class until the bell goes and let us keep quiet about Douglas's collapse until we know what his doctor says.'

'Yes, Sir.'

Douglas was whisked off to the isolation hospital and Rose's mam boiled everything she had worn on the day of the test. She gave her a dose of horrible tonic every morning before school but, a few days later, Rose woke up in the night feeling hot and her throat was aching. She knew immediately.

She tiptoed to her mam's side of the bed but didn't climb in. 'Mam.' She patted her shoulder. 'Mam, wake up!'

'What is it, pet? There's no siren tonight.'

'You'll have to send for the doctor, Mam. I've got the diphtheria.'

8

Rose woke up and, as her eyes got used to the dim light, she realised she was in a strange room. The ceiling seemed closer than her room at home; she was in a high bed with a rail around it and the sheets tucked tightly around her. Her head ached and her throat was dry and raspy. Where was she? What was going on? She couldn't remember how she had got here. Had they been bombed?

Her mind drifted to an air raid at a party. It had been hers hadn't it? Pictures of how happily the party started filled her thoughts.

It was August and the back yard walls of number one had been freshly whitewashed by her mam and Mary-from-next-door. Balloons, tied to the back gate, bobbed about in the breeze and a blanket on the ground couldn't be seen for food. Beside a mound of sandwiches, there was a plate of iced buns with a candle on each in place of a cake because of the rationing and a bowl of trifle decorated with the last spoonful of Mam's sugar sprinkles.

Her mam had mashed the corned beef for sandwiches with a good dollop of brown sauce just how she liked it. 'It doesn't need butter and it makes a tin go a lot further. *We* don't need advice on making do and eking things out. We've been doing it all our lives.'

Because it was a party, her mam had cut the sandwiches into little triangles instead of half slices. She still left the crusts on though and all the girls ate them because everyone knew it was the way to get curly hair when you were older. Straight lank hair meant you hadn't eaten your crusts as a lassie.

The butter, sugar, bacon and ham had been rationed all year and they had managed fine but her mam was upset because, from last month, the tea was rationed and she loved a strong cup of tea. Rose noticed how often her dad said he didn't fancy a cup and she often said it too. They'd hate Mam to be without her tea.

Dad, who was starting work at midnight, returned from the allotment in time for the lighting of the candles. Just as he opened the gate, Wailing Willie started up. The siren? Not on her birthday? Hell's Bells!

'Hell's Bells!'

For a moment, Rose thought she'd sworn aloud and waited for a clip around her ear from her mam even though it was her birthday, but it was her dad echoing her thoughts.

'Blast!' he continued, 'We've done this time and time again but never with five extra lassies and a party going on. I hope you've brought your gas masks!'

It was ingrained into them, of course they had. They trooped into the shelter with a plate of party food and their gas masks as Mam grabbed Stanley from Mary-from-next-door and the two women ducked in and shut the door.

'Where's Dad?' Rose asked.

'We're like sardines as it is. Your dad and Mr Elliot are going to sit in the cubby hole under the stairs until the alarm is over.' The girls budged along to make room for everybody.

An almighty racket told them all this wasn't any false alarm and there was fighting in the sky above them. This was for real and her dad wasn't with them. Fear coiled around Rose's stomach and she had to fight to keep her party tea down.

Lottie was crying for her mam and she felt ashamed. At least she had her mam and her brothers with her.

'Time for a party sing-song,' Mary said and she launched into the song about Cushie Butterfield. They all joined in and then took it in turns to shout out their favourites.

Still the noise went on but, after that first few minutes, it seemed further away.

'I think they're heading for the dockyards or the bridges over the Tyne again, do you, Ginnie?'

'That'll be it. They've been intercepted as they were passing over here. Maybe they'll not reach the town. I haven't heard a bomb dropping though and they'll get rid of them somewhere.'

Rose sent up a silent prayer, 'Not on us, or on Dad and Mr Elliot,' and hoped it was answered.

'Can we still go to the pictures tomorrow, Mam?' Stanley piped up. They'd been promised this treat on the day after Rose's birthday.

'We'll have to wait and see, sweetheart. Her mam stroked Stanley's brow and muttered, 'If the picture house is still there.'

David sat up in shock. 'Hitler canna bomb the picture house. It's not fair!'

Only four at the time, the twins didn't know yet that life wasn't always fair.

It was quiet but they had to wait for the all clear. Her friends finished off their picnic and sang 'Happy Birthday' to her and then they looked through old Beanos by torchlight.

At last the welcome sound of all clear signalled they could leave the cramped six by four space and walk into daylight. Mams and Dads hurried from other shelters to collect their girls.

Her balloons were still bobbing on the gate, Mr Elliot and Dad were waiting to greet them and Mam said it was time they all had a cup of tea. That was the day when Mr Elliot claimed he had enjoyed being in the cubby hole so much that he wasn't going to the Anderson shelter again.

News headlines telling a tale of German bombers flying from bases in Norway and Denmark and of dog fights in the sky as British fighters fought them off. Floated through her dream.

'Who won yesterday, Dad?'

'The German bombers had to retreat so we won but not before a good few bombs were dropped on Newcastle and Sunderland.'

'The pictures of bombed houses look awful, don't they?' The photos sent shivers along Rose's spine.

'It's a crying shame and something we never want to get used to, pet.'

'I'll never forget this birthday, Dad,' she said. He grabbed her for a hug and when he let go, she saw anger in his tear-filled eyes.

Rose woke with a start and brushed tears from her own eyes with the back of her hand. Such vivid memories. How old had she been then? Six candles? How old was she now? Her head was so fuzzy.

A woman walked by the bottom of her bed. As Rose craned her neck to see her, she became aware of other beds in the room, all in a line. A figure strode into the room and, from the white headdress and apron over a blue uniform, Rose guessed she was a nun or a nurse.

She wiggled her fingers and toes. All there. She tried to sit up and the woman came closer. 'No pet. Don't try to sit up yet. Here, Rose, I'll give you a sip of water.'

Rose sipped the water gratefully. Her carer knew her name and the watch pinned to her apron meant she was a nurse. Where was she? How long had she been here?

9

Rose tried to ask a question but she couldn't find her voice. She lay back on the pillows, darkness claimed her again. and she was near her dad's allotment with Lottie and some others.

A pair of white butterflies dancing over the fence towards her dad's cabbages catching her eye, Danny Dodd piping up. 'The whole country is going to fight the enemy, soon. The Germans, they're called. They've beaten Poland, but they canna beat us. We'll have to use guns and bombs on Germany or else we'll all be captured and, if we are, me dad says they're a bunch of bad beggars.'

Dad saying, 'There's talk of war, but talk is just talk. Nobody can be sure about whether war will be declared or not, pet. I've seen one war and hope there's not another one. You can tell Danny Dodd it's nowt to get excited about.'

Dad mixing a sludgy colour, painting men working underground with shadows of grey and black. The smell of oil paints and rags soaked in turps that clung around him when he was painting. 'Dad? Dad are you here?'

Rose drifted in and out of consciousness and, as well as the lucid memories, she had terrible dreams. She shouted out at strange creatures and felt as though a snake was coiled around her neck and choking her. She was burning then shivering with an icy chill and she wanted her mam. 'Mam! Where are you?'

10

'Mam... Dad, I can't find you!' She must have shouted out loudly because her first memory on waking was someone wiping her down with tepid water and promising, 'You're at the isolation hospital and in safe hands, Rose. You'll go home soon, you're on the mend now and you'll be able to see your mam and dad in a little while, pet lamb.'

A hazy memory surfaced. She'd been caught by the strangling angel that was doing a round of the rows. 'Stanley and David, my little brothers, are they all right? I didn't pass it on did I?' she croaked.

'There's no Stanley or David here and you've been isolated for two weeks so they won't have caught anything from you.'

Two weeks? Rose could hardly believe she'd been in this bed for such a long time. There was a lot she wanted to ask but she was so, so tired. She thought of asking how Douglas was. 'How is...' She was asleep before she could form the words.

Rose slept a lot at first. She had to stay in the isolation hospital for six long weeks. No visitors allowed. No questions answered either. 'Just you rest,' was the answer to everything. Mam and Dad sent her letters and she was so glad to hear from them but she couldn't write back in case of germs. Rose had so many questions to ask about what was going on at home but she could only read the news her family had written.

Her dad came all the way to the hospital on Saturdays to wave at her through the window of the ward. Mam hated hospitals but she came before Christmas and stood as close to the outside window as she could with a scarf around her mouth. They handed over a bag of fruit to the nurse but they couldn't leave presents. In case of infection, she wouldn't be able to take them home.

'Your presents will stay wrapped until you're well again, sweetheart,' Mam mouthed through the glass. Rose gulped back tears as they turned to go.

A Christmas tree was set up in the corner of the ward and carols by candlelight on Christmas Eve were a real treat. In the early hours, a nurse came and put a stocking by all of their beds. Rose couldn't sleep and heard crying from two beds along. She tiptoed over to little Doris Grieves and got under the bedclothes to give her a hug. Doris was only five and, if being away from home at Christmas was miserable for Rose, she could imagine how desolate this little girl felt.

Rose missed the twins and her mam and dad but she was ten whereas poor little Doris... she cuddled her and told her about the Christmas when she was five until Doris fell asleep with her thumb in her mouth and left Rose with those memories of a happier time.

Rose remembered shivering as she sat up on Christmas morning to feel for the lumpy stocking at the end of her bed and the thrill of discovering he'd been! She pulled her curtain aside and it was still dark. The window was covered with an intricate lacing of frost on the inside. Oh, but it was cold. She crept into her mam and dad's bedroom and slipped in between them.

'Our Rose, your feet are like blocks of ice!' Her dad sat up. 'Has he been then? Old Ho Ho?'

'Yes! He's been and he's filled my stocking, Dad.'

'You stay here for a minute or two, no peeping into that stocking, and I'll get the fire going downstairs. You can open it in the warm, when we've woken the lads.'

'I'm awake, I'm awake now… Rose, has he really been?' Stanley scooted into bed beside Rose as their dad pulled on trousers and a shirt.

'I'm awake too.' A yawning David joined them.

They all cuddled up to their mam while Dad went downstairs.

'No peeping, Dad said.' Rose nudged Stanley.

'Feeling isn't peeping. Is it Mam?' Stanley asked.

'Yes it is! It's peeping with your fingers so stop it.' She tickled Stanley to stop his prodding.

As the sky turned a steel grey, Rose could see their breath, rising into the air as if they were coal trains. It was so cold, but she felt warm inside. Today would be just grand.

After Sunday school, they'd had a roast chicken dinner and Christmas pudding and Rose's last treat was revealed at bedtime.

'Your dad is looking after Stanley and David because they're too young to sit through a full film and I'm taking you to see *The Wizard of Oz* next week. It's going to be in colour. Imagine that!'

She'd been Doris's age, she'd believed in Father Christmas and they had just gone to war, but Mr Hitler hadn't spoilt the Christmas of 1939 at all.

Not like the strangling angel had spoiled this one.

11

Rose tried to cheer up when she found an apple and a bar of chocolate in her stocking on Christmas morning but the day dragged. What were her brothers doing? Were they going to Sunday school with Maisie and Betty? Her mam and Mary-from-next-door would be running around their sculleries like linties by now.

The Christmas dinner was served on the long table at the end of the ward and they pulled the crackers they had made earlier in the week. They had meat and veg followed by a pudding but Rose's mouth watered at the thought of the big plum duff at home. It wasn't a patch on Mam's and Mary-from-next-door's feast. Would her dad find the silver sixpence again?

After their pudding, a bell chimed and the ward doors opened to reveal a fat old man in red. The younger ones squealed with delight and Rose smiled and accepted a gift from his sack, even though she could see his beard was cotton wool. She opened her present and found it was *Betsy-Tacy*, a book she had read at school when she was six. She remembered her manners and smiled and said 'Thank you' then put it to one side to read to Doris. Ah well, she wouldn't be able to take it home anyway in case it carried germs. The tight hard lump in her chest grew as the afternoon dragged on endlessly.

'Special delivery for Rose Kelly.' A smiling nurse brought

a bundle of letters into the ward and handed them over. 'A young lad dropped these off for you, Rose. If you go to the window, I've told him you can wave to him.'

Rose dashed across to the window. Who was there? Who had brought him? Her jaw dropped when she spied Danny Dodd's cheeky grin. He put his hand on the glass to peer in and she couldn't help but cover it with hers. Someone from the rows had come! Their eyes met and she saw kindness there before he pulled an awful face then cycled over the grass into the grey blustery afternoon. Danny had brought her messages from home. How had he got into the grounds?

The nurse stood behind her laughing at his antics. 'There are no buses today. He told me he cycled all the way over so you could have some letters to cheer you up. It took him longer than he thought to find his way in. All the gates are locked. He's quite a character, isn't he?'

Rose turned. 'He used to be the cheekiest, naughtiest lad in Linwood but I think he's growing up to be more sensible. He likes animals and he's funny.' She shuffled through her mail, a sketch of her and her brothers sitting by a Christmas tree from Dad, a few lines from Mam, even a messsage from Mary-from-next-door, a drawing of their Christmas tree by the wireless signed by Stanley and David and a card from Danny. She opened it and was surprised by the very neat writing. 'Merry Christmas to Rose from Danny. Get well soon.' That Danny Dodd could be a wild lad at times but he had a warm heart.

At long last, the day came when Rose could return home. An ambulance would deliver her right to the door. The doctor said she must stay off school until half term but she was not contagious and could go home to finish her recovery. Rose found it hard to say goodbye to some of the nurses but to one or two she felt like saying good riddance. You'd think all children's nurses would like children but they didn't! She gave Doris her Betsy-Tacy book and was sorry to leave her but she couldn't wait to see her own little brothers and Mam and Dad again.

12

1945

Home was strange. It seemed so colourful after the green and cream of hospital walls with its nurses and bedding of stiff bleached white. There was a roaring fire, the smell of broth and newly baked scufflers and a clash of colours from proggy mats and cushions and Dad's pictures propped along a wall.

Mam greeted her in her best pinny and sat her in a comfy chair propped with cushions. It was quiet, not the fuss she had expected, because Stanley was at school and Dad was working days. David was off school with the sniffles and Mam was keeping a close eye on him because diphtheria was still doing the rounds. It had struck the Grieves family in fourth row.

'The twins were playing with those Grieves lads at the weekend and they were all as right as rain,' Mam told her. ' I've boiled all their clothes but I'm keeping David at home because he has a bit of a cough. She made him stay uptairs in her bed so he wouldn't spread germs to Stanley but he wasn't poorly enough to call the doctor. Rose was given strict instructions just to say hello from the doorway.

Mam's face was familiar yet looked different. Over the weeks, her features had blurred in Rose's imagination and now she was rediscovering them again.

'My you've grown, hinny, even though you have been poorly. We need to get some meat on your bones though.' Mam cooled a bowl of soup by stirring it at the door and tested the temperature before handing over the bowl with pieces of broken up scuffler floating on the top. Mam always cooled the twin's food and made sure her dad's wasn't so hot it burned his mouth but Rose, being a girl, was usually expected to manage for herself. She was getting special treatment today.

The soup tasted delicious. 'This is like manna from heaven, Mam.'

'Ah you're back and you're still a funny 'un with your sayings.' Her mam's dark eyes were shining with tears but she looked happy. 'My lassie is home at last,' she said and planted a kiss on her brow. Blimey, Mam must've missed her.

'Is Mary-from-next-door calling in, Mam?'

Her mam took the bowl from her and shook her head. 'Not today, Rose. She's letting you settle in first. We thought that would be best.'

Rose found the early start to the day tiring and had a sleep in the armchair by the fire until Stanley ran in from school and dived onto her.

'I'm glad you're back, Sis. Mam needs somebody else to keep an eye on because she doesn't miss a thing that I do wrong.'

'Leave your sister alone and wash those hands or you won't be getting a slice and some jam.' Mam flicked her tea towel at Stanley who winced.

'See what I mean. This house hasn't got a germ in it 'cos we all have to be hospital clean now you're home. It hasn't stopped David from catching summick, though. I reckon he's a germ magnet. Can I go up and see him Mam?'

'Stop your cheek or you'll get a proper clip across the lug our Stanley. I'll have you know this house is always clean and

I'm glad to have Rose away from the hospital because it must be full of germs.'

'Can I go up to David?' Stanley was heading towards the stairs.

'He could do with some company but sit on the floor by the doorway, don't go too near because I don't want you off school too.'

The lump that had been in Rose's chest most of the time she was in hospital dissolved. This is what she had missed, the colour and crack of her own kitchen.

Dad came in and whisked her up and into the air as if she was a feather. He swung her around and her head nudged the main lightshade.

'Careful, John! The bairn is just out of hospital and we don't want her back in.' Her mam stopped laying the table for tea to feel Rose's brow with the back of her hand.

'You're not too big for a shuggy, are you?' he said before plonking her onto his knee. 'We'd better do as your mam says though and keep you quiet for a bit. How are you, pet?'

'I'm better just being here, Dad. Hospital isn't a good place to be when you're not well.' Her mam and dad both laughed so she did too. She was home.

Rose must have fallen asleep listening to the radio because she was aware of being carried up the stairs by her dad. Her bed warmed by a hot water bottle, felt soft and familiar and she almost drifted off again but Mam's voice caught her attention.

'To think we nearly lost her, John. I've never been so glad to see a living soul. I think we did right in not telling her the news today, do you?'

'Certainly. Hearing bad news doesn't change it and our Rose has had enough to contend with for one day.' Blackness and muffled voices told her the door had closed. She was wide awake. What bad news had they kept from her?

Reading a copy of *Anne of Avonlea* under the covers by torchlight, she tried to distract herself with the story.

JOHN KELLY

At daybreak, before going on his shift, John Kelly looked in at his sleeping bairns. The twins had outgrown the alcove in the main bedroom last year and they all shared the second bedroom now so, while Rose had been in hospital, Ginnie had rustled up a curtain from some old material she had tucked away and he'd curtained off the bedroom into two sections. He'd painted a pink rose-patterned border around the top of the wall by Rose's bed. Now she could rest and read without the twins disturbing her.

From the doorway he could see his little lads sleeping top to tail in their single bed. David had slipped away from the watchful eye of his mother in their bedroom to be with his brother at some point during the night. Those lads hated being apart. Stanley, eight years old with rosy cheeks framed in dark curls like his mother's had his blankets kicked off. David's slighter build made him look younger and he clutched Cubby the tatty bear he hid under the bed every morning when he pulled his 'big boy' attitude on along with his shirt. David was a reader like Rose whereas Stanley was a happy lad and no scholar even though John tried to push him to learn. He didn't want either of his lads going down the pit and schooling was the way out so he'd carry on pushing.

They'd felt so lucky when their boys hadn't caught diptheria from Rose but now Ginnie had a fresh worry because of them playing with the Grieves lads. Two of them were in the isolation hospital.

John felt David's brow, slightly warm but not a high fever. He didn't blame Ginnie for fussing over him like she did. He couldn't imagine what the Fletcher's were going through. Mr Fletcher, his under-manager had lost Douglas, his only child, to the disease. Why hadn't the vaccine reached Linwood before now?

He pulled the curtain aside to find Rose fast asleep with a book on her pillow and the torch she was allowed to use for half an hour beside it. He picked up the book and saw it was one of her favourites and set in Canada. Rose's escape from the grime of the rows was through reading and his was through painting.

Over the years, he'd watched his girl blossom into a caring, questioning, clever young lass and his dreams for her now were exactly the same as they'd been when she was born. He still wanted Rose to flourish in his care and grow rich roots of confidence and courage. He hoped she would always grasp opportunities and there would be more like the one that had been offered but snatched away by her illness.

Sitting for a scholarship to a good school would have been Rose's gateway to a different world but, she'd missed out on sitting the exam. They'd have to break the news to her when she was feeling stronger.

He had almost lost her but she had fought to survive and here she was, that was the important thing. Just as he'd promised her all those years ago when she was a babe in arms, he vowed to move heaven and earth, to mine coal until his back broke with the effort, for his daughter to see something of the world beyond these dark colliery rows.

13

It was daylight when Mam brought Rose a glass of milk and a slice of bread and jam and set them down on the cracket by the bed before opening the curtains.

'What time is it, Mam? I was just going to get up.' Rose shuffled to a sitting position.

'You'll do no such thing. You need plenty of rest, the doctor said.' Her Mam had her hands on her hips.

'Mam, as we got better, we got up and put our clothes on for breakfast at the hospital and then we had a bit of schooling. We didn't lie down all day. Honest.'

'It's still a bit chilly downstairs, pet. When the fire heats the room up, you and David can come down and read for a bit.' Her Mam put the tray on her knee and turned to leave.

'Mam, what's the bad news? I heard you and Dad, last night when you put me into bed.'

There were tears in Mam's eyes as she sat on the end of the bed. 'You are far too good at earwigging, Rose Kelly. There's nothing wrong with your ears, anyway.'

Rose pushed her tray away and grabbed Mam's hand. 'What's happened?'

'We thought it was for the best, pet. We wanted you to have a good rest first but we weren't going to hide it from you for long.'

'Has somebody died, Mam?'

Mam nodded, ' The black lung took Mr Elliot just after Christmas. His chest couldn't stand another winter.'

'Oh no. How is Mary? Is that why she didn't come in, yesterday?'

'Yes. She's spending a week or two at Larry's but she is coming over to see you at the weekend.'

Rose cried for Mr Elliot and for Mary-from-next-door and Mam hugged her and crooned, 'There, there. At least he's at rest now and he had a good innings considering how bad his chest was. He didn't go early like some.'

'You mean like his sons, Mam?' Rose wiped her eyes.

'Yes. Like a lot of people's sons, pet.'

She cuddled her mam and felt a bit better.

But the day got worse. After dinner, Dad sat her on his knee and explained how Douglas Fletcher had not recovered. Complications from the strangling angel of diphtheria had taken him.

'That's why your Mam is hovering a bit, over you and David. We know you're better but she's frightened of complications.'

That night, she thanked the Lord for keeping her safe but couldn't help asking why he hadn't helped Douglas. Douglas Fletcher's mam and dad must be broken-hearted. He was their only bairn and he had been a really nice lad.

Next morning, Rose learned that Mam and Dad had sent for the doctor for David during the night. That bleeding angel had struck them for a second time and David had been carted off to the isolation hospital. How had she slept through it all? Poor David, he'd miss home more than she did.

For the whole week, a sadness hung over Rose making her limbs heavy and her movements slow. She was pleased to be home, but David was ill and Douglas wasn't ever going home and his death made her guilty and miserable. She had a Christmas book to read. It was still in its wrapping when she got home but even seeing that it was the brand new 'Five Find-Outers' story couldn't cheer Rose up. *The Mystery of the Disappearing Cat* lay unread and Rose didn't feel hungry at all, not even for chip shop chips.

Lottie was allowed to visit. 'Hi. Rose! You look awful, you're as white as Marley's ghost. We thought you'd be next you know, after Douglas. I said a lot of Hail Marys for you and our Sid and you've both been saved. I'll pray for David this week. Poor Douglas, I should have mentioned him, but you'd think his own family would have been praying hard. They're chapel like you. He had a massive funeral at the chapel and Miss Wakenshaw said a beautiful poem but his poor mam couldn't even go. She's mad with grief they say.

Rose wished Lottie would shut up nattering. She almost wished she was back to the routine of the isolation ward. She felt weary until the word 'pup' caught her attention.

'What did you say about the pup?'

'You're not listening, Rose! I *said* the vet, Mr Maxwell called just before Christmas with the abandoned pup. He had our addresses remember. The pup was all better and he was wondering about a name and if either of us wanted it. *My* ma said, "Not bleedin' likely" and so did yours. He was sorry to hear you were ill and said he might keep him.'

'What's he like? Does he limp?'

'Mr Maxwell?'

Rose giggled. 'No, the pup.'

'I knew I'd get you smiling,' Lottie beamed. 'He's a fluffy black ball with a stump of a tail but his leg is mended, no limp. He is well behaved; he sits and walks to heel and everything. Mr Maxwell thinks he's got a bit of poodle in him because he doesn't cast hairs and he's bright.'

'I wonder what he's called him. Oh, I wish I could see him! He won't visit again, I bet.'

Mam looked in. 'What are you so excited about? You've found you're tongue at last, I see.'

'Lottie was telling me about the pup, Mam. I missed him!'

'Lottie! I told you to let that tale lie.'

'I know but I forgot meself Mrs Kelly... sorry.'

'I'm glad to hear some good news at last. Don't be vexed with Lottie, Mam.'

Mam nodded but she still said, 'It's time you went home now, Lottie. Rose still needs her rest.'

'Okay. See you in the week?' Lottie followed Ginnie downstairs and Rose heard her asking, 'Does she know about the scholarship yet, Mrs Kelly? Have I not got to mention that either?'

'Sssh! Don't mention it yet, Lottie.'

Scholarship? Rose slumped back onto her pillows. What were they keeping from her now?

14

She wheedled the secret from Stanley by giving him a chocolate bar and promising she wouldn't tell on him. He whispered, 'The scholarship exams were last week and nobody from our school sat them because Douglas... you know... and you were in hospital.'

'Thanks for telling me, Stanley. Will you tell Mam I don't want any dinner? I'm tired.' Rose lay down on her bed, turned her back and faced the wall.

So much for her dreams of Enid Blyton schooldays. She knew she was lucky to still be here what with the strangling angel and the war, but no new school, no pets and her brain just didn't enjoy reading any more. That settled it. Tonight she wasn't even going to pray.

In the blackness of night, Rose woke up feeling guilty. Falling asleep and forgetting her prayers was one thing but she had turned her back on Jesus tonight. She shivered as she got out of bed and her feet touched cold lino. She found her bedside rug, knelt and clasped her hands tightly together.

'Sorry our Father and Jesus, but I'm flaming angry with you both. Douglas was a kind boy. The Germans are bombing good people. I have prayed for a pet and neither of you listen to anything I pray for. I'm sorry I'm so annoyed but will you please bless Mam, Dad, Stanley, David and Mary all the way over at Burnside and keep our David safe or I'll be more angry.

I promise to go to Sunday School when I'm better. And stop Mam from worrying, Amen.'

Mam worried about her not eating and not wanting her books but Rose felt tired and sad all the time and just wanted to lie in bed.

David had taken a turn for the worse. A boy on a bike came with a message for Mam and Dad to visit the hospital and Mary-from-next-door stayed to look after Rose and Stanley. Mary was worried. Her shoulders were tight as she made pot after pot of tea to keep herself busy. Rose had bitten her lip sore and neither of them had a thing to say.

When Stanley came home from school, he wanted to go to the hospital.

'It's parents only so you can't but there is something you can do.' Rose persuaded him to write him a letter as they waited for news.

Stanley lay on his front by the fire with a pencil and paper. 'Is it soppy to say you're the best brother in the world and I'm sorry for laughing at you for still cuddling up to Cubby at night?' David twisted the pencil between his fingers and searched Rose's face.

'David would never call you soppy. Anyway, I've seen you sneak Cubby into your bed while David has been away.' Rose answered.

'That's just in case Cubby is lonely without David. I know I am. I'll tell him I'm looking after his tatty bear.' Stanley stuck his tongue out as he composed another sentence. 'Maybe Mam and Dad should have taken Cubby in to be with David.'

'They would have taken him in but he'd have to be destroyed afterwards for germs. Best to let David know he's in your safe hands, eh?' Rose was relieved to see this answer pleased Stanley and he continued with his letter.

All night, Rose tossed and turned. Her parents had never

been allowed to visit her so David must be proper poorly. Her heart sank at Mary's red-rimmed eyes next morning. Mary had used the phone box in the village to speak to the hospital and she had been told that Stanley was to stay off school until his parents came home.

Rose didn't dare ask Mary the one question in her head because she dreaded hearing the answer but felt an icy chill that the range couldn't warm and knew in her heart that Stanley's delight at a day off school would be short-lived.

She was right. David's weak chest couldn't withstand diphtheria and he had slipped away in the early morning. Mam and Dad looked like ghosts themselves as they relayed the news.

'Can I pray to David like we do to Jesus?' Stanley asked.

Mam burst into tears and left the room but Rose took Stanley's hands in hers. 'You can close your eyes and talk to him whenever you want to. Think about it as though he is in another room. Last term, I copied out a verse or two from a poem that said just that. I'll read it to you tonight before bed, if you like'

Mam came in drying her eyes on her pinny. She was holding Cubby bear and Rose's heart jumped in fear. Mam hated germs but she couldn't destroy him! 'I'd like to hear those verses too, Rose. Maybe Eddie will read them in the chapel when... when' Mam burst into a fresh bout of tears.

'What are you doing with Cubby, Mam?' Rose had to ask.

Mam clutched the bear to her. 'I'm giving him a hug then giving him a good boil with the sheets just in case. He'll dry as good as new.'

At bedtime, Rose read part of the poem, "Death is Nothing at All" by Henry Scott-Holland to Stanley. He asked her to read the part about laugh as we always laughed again.

After she'd finished, he confided, 'I want to say sorry to David for a lot of things. I was mean sometimes and I hid

Cubby all the time. I wish I hadn't.' Stanley's eyes were laden with unshed tears and Rose pulled him to her.

'Brothers do daft things. David knows you love him.' Stanley sobbed and clung to her. 'It's okay to cry. You'll feel better for it.' She held him tightly and tears coursed down her own cheeks. Stanley was a tough little nut but he'd always looked out for David. He'd be lost without him. Why had she been saved when her little brother and Douglas hadn't?

After a while Stanley's sobs subsided. 'Thanks, Rose. I'm glad I've got you here. You remind me of David because you're kind like he was.'

'You remind me of David because you're a little imp like he was and remember he liked to fight just as much as you. It's what brothers do.' She stroked Stanley's brow.

'Let's not fight, Rose. Not ever. I'd give anything to see David again. I'd even give him my best steely marble to keep.'

On a grey wet Tuesday, David entered their little chapel for the last time. He was carried in by Dad and Mary's son, Larry, and folk gasped at his brightly coloured coffin.

'He's just a bairn and won't want flowers, Ginnie,' Dad had explained as he took out his paints as soon as the tiny plain coffin arrived at the house and Rose had to agree. John Kelly said farewell to his lad in the way he knew best. He painted a cast of David's favourite comic characters around the sides and, on the lid, between Koko and Eggo, he'd added Cubby the bear. Once it was dry, he'd carried it himself to the undertaker's hearse and accompanied it to the hospital.

Rose clutched her mam's hand and kept an arm around Stanley. She knew that, safely tucked inside was an envelope from Stanley containing the letter he'd written and his best steely marble. Since Cubby had been boiled along with the sheets by Mam, he was no longer hidden under the bed but had pride of place on top of Stanley's pillow. 'Rose, I hope

David thinks the steely is a good swap for Cubby. Cubby is the next best thing to sharing my bed with David,' Stanley whispered. Rose clasped Stanley closer to her and couldn't speak.

Her little brother would be the second child to be buried in the village and, for a small boy, he left a huge gaping hole in all of their hearts.

The funeral passed but Rose still had no appetite for food or for reading. She stayed in bed as much as Mam would let her. Why was she here when David hadn't been saved?

The diphtheria vaccine finally arrived in their area for all children up to fourteen. Of course the villages were delighted, imagine being free of the strangling angel for good, but the Kellys wished it had arrived sooner and Rose was sure Mr and Mrs Fletcher would be thinking that too.

Her mam went around to see Mrs Fletcher quite regularly now. They'd both lost a son but Rose thought it was more than that, it seemed to her that her mam had made a friend.

15

It was only a Saturday and an ordinary one at that but Rose's mam made her get washed and dressed, pulled her hair into tight plaits and told her to put her Sunday school dress on. 'Must I?'

'Yes, you must. You're fading away and need food and fresh air.'

'But *this* dress? We must be having visitors, Mam. Is Mary coming over today?'

'No, she's coming for tea tomorrow but I want you to look nice. It's… it's a bit of a surprise.'

'Do *I* know the surprise, Mam?' Stanley piped up.

'No you don't, pet. And you keep those shoes clean too.' Stanley's hair was slicked back.

What was this about? Dad was still around. 'Why aren't you at the allotment, Dad?'

He looked up from reading the paper. 'That's for me to know and you to wonder about, hinny.' He gave a wink and went back to his paper.

Rose picked up her new Enid Blyton and had just started the first page when there was a loud knock at the front door. Who would use the front door?

'I'll get it, Mam.' She rushed to open the door and there stood Mr Maxwell and a black ball of fur with a smart red collar and lead. 'Hello, you have a visitor, Rose,' he said. 'This is Lucky. May we come in?'

Rose blushed to the roots of her plaits and looked at her shiny polished shoes. 'Sorry Mr Maxell but you can't. My mam won't have an animal in the house. Can you go round to the back yard and I'll meet you there?' She knelt down and bent her face into the dog's fur to hide her embarrassment at keeping a visitor on the step. The pup licked her excitedly.

'Rose Kelly, where are your manners?' Her mam dashed to the door. 'Come on in Mr Maxwell. I don't know what our Rose is thinking of leaving you on the doorstep.'

'If you're sure?'

'Of course I'm sure. Do come in.'

They all went inside and Mam, who had taken her pinny off, put a plate of newly baked melting moments on the table with a fresh pot of tea. It all slotted into place. This visit had been planned. It was the surprise.

The pup sat obediently at Mr Maxwell's feet as they all sat around the table and Mam poured tea while Rose handed around the biscuits. She frowned at Stanley who was just about to take two at once. He should know better at his age.

Dad broke the silence. 'Rose don't get too excited, but your mam and I have discussed it and, if you feel well enough to walk and look after a pup, you can have Lucky here as your own pet.

'*Really?*' She looked from Dad to her mam and then to Mr Maxwell.

'Yes, really,' Mr Maxwell answered. 'Your mother and father have persuaded me to give Lucky up because, although my son Frank and I are rather fond of him, you saved his life so I'm willing to hand him over. As long as you bring him to me if he is ever ill.'

'But, Mam what about your allergies and… you know… fleas?'

'Mr Maxwell says there are no fleas on this dog and he

doesn't cast hair. It's the poodle in him, so we can bath him regularly and give him a brush and trim.'

'Yes, yes, yes!' she hugged her mam and then Dad before turning to say, 'Thank you Mr Maxwell.' She bent to pat the little dog who was sitting up to attention and he gave her a paw. 'I think he's asking for a piece of biscuit. Can he Mam? just this once?'

'Rose Kelly, there will be no feeding at the table and no going upstairs. They are the rules.'

Rose cuddled up to Lucky hardly believing he was her own pup. She knew how much it must have taken for her mam to agree to a pet in the house. Mam wanted Rose to get well and she thought that Lucky was the answer. If Mam could do this for her then she could eat her dinners and become strong again to please her mam.

'Rose Kelly has a dog.'

News spread like pit dust around the lads and lasses in the rows and next afternoon Danny Dodd knocked for her. 'Can I see how that little scrap is doing?'

Rose called for Lucky and Danny crouched down to greet the pup. 'I knew you would fix him properly, Rose. He really was a lucky beggar to come to you!' As he stroked Lucky he whispered, 'You got me a clip around the lug for losing a jumper little fella but you were worth it.'

He stood up and kicked at a stone for Lucky to chase. 'Shall I come by and walk him after school? Just 'til you're feeling stronger, like.'

'No need Danny. I'm well enough to walk him or Dad will, but thanks for offering.'

'See ya then.' He walked off and blew her a kiss. 'Sorry about your David and I'm glad the strangling angel didn't get ya!' he called over his shoulder.

Rose blushed for the second time that weekend.

Later in the afternoon, Mary-from-next-door came from her son's house at Burnside to have a wander through her own house and then have a cup of tea at number one. Rose was reading with Lucky asleep at her feet as Mary chatted to Mam about living with her daughter-in-law.

'It's lovely to see Larry and his bairns every day but it's a squash staying there. I'm in with the bairns and up with the larks every blessed morning. I can have the fire lit and their breakfast over with before I see her ladyship.'

'Don't the pair of you get on any better, then?' Mam asked.

'Do we heck as like. I bite my tongue but she knows I think she's wasteful. Ginnie, you should see the amount of skin she takes off her taties!'

Rose giggled at the outrage, the thin peeling of potatoes was a matter of pride to her mam and Mary. Her giggles meant the game was up. 'Rose take your dog for a walk or read your book upstairs and stop cocking your lugs or you might hear something you don't want to!'

Every day she felt a bit better. Lucky was always at her heels and she was teaching him tricks, her mam fed her up like a Christmas turkey so her clothes didn't hang as loosely anymore and she loved reading again. Rose really wanted to go back to school but Dad said there was plenty of time for that. He suggested she should write a letter to the sir asking for a few pages of arithmetic and another to Miss Wakenshaw asking if she could borrow a book or two.

Stanley took the letters to school for her saying, 'You're daft in the head, our Rose. I wish I was off school. You wouldn't catch me *asking* for sums or extra reading.'

'You should take a leaf out of your sister's book and you might do a bit better at school, Stanley.' Her dad winked at her. She knew Dad was proud of her even though she had missed her chance of taking the scholarship exam.

Miss Wakenshaw called to see Rose one Sunday after chapel and they discussed the 'Little Women' series of books that she had devoured. 'I've brought you one or two books by the Brontë sisters, Rose. It is advanced reading but I think you'll like them and they will keep you going until you get back to school at the end of the month.'

'Thanks, Miss Wakenshaw.'

'Now, I'd like a word with your mother so perhaps you could leave us for a while?'

Rose was curious but she couldn't listen because her mam sent her with Lucky over to the allotment to ask her dad to pull some carrots for dinner.

When she got home, she was given the job of peeling the carrots and watching out for Stanley who was outside fixing old pram wheels on a bogie with Sid because her mam remembered she needed an onion from Dad's allotment.

'Shall I run back, Mam?'

'No pet. I could do with a breath of fresh air.'

Rose knew it was an excuse to chat to Dad about whatever Miss Wakenshaw had said. Mam *never* left the Sunday dinner to go to the allotment when she could send her or Stanley.

Something was going on and they didn't want her to know. What could it be?

16

The letter came during the half term holiday. The typed address to Mr and Mrs J Kelly looked very official and her mam placed it behind the clock on the mantlepiece until her dad, who was working nights, got up.

'Why don't you read it, Mam? It's addressed to you too.' Rose asked.

'Because I'm not impatient or a nosey parker like you.' Her mam carried on with her day's work of boiling sheets, and pegging up line after line of washing because it was a dry, breezy day for February.

'I could read it for you, if you like, Mam.' Curiosity about the sender of the thick white envelope got the better of her.

The remark earned her a flick of the wet pillow case in Mam's hand, 'I *can* read, I just don't have time.'

'Sorry, Mam.' It was time she took Lucky for a walk otherwise she would be given a job to shut her up.

She hadn't meant to be cheeky but her mam was always busy with cooking, cleaning and sewing so she usually got Dad to read her bits out of the paper or listened to the news while she was knitting. Her mam liked to do two or three things at once and you couldn't really do that if you were reading.

Lucky and Rose got caught up in a game of skipping with Lottie, Betty and the gang and she didn't get back until tea-time.

'It's good to see you with some roses in your cheeks, lassie.' Her dad was up and sketching at the kitchen table. On the table was the opened envelope.

'Did you have a good sleep, Dad? Were we quiet enough?' Rose kissed his stubbly cheek. He didn't shave if he was going to work.

'Aye, I did. I got up to some good news for a change too.'

'The letter? I knew it looked important! Didn't I say that, Mam?'

Her mam smiled, rare since they'd buried David, and dried her hands on her pinny. 'You did, hinny. Shall we tell her, John?'

'I think she can read it for herself. You said she was itching to read the letter. Here you are, pet. Tell us what you think of this.'

Rose took the letter and read it. She had to read it twice and it still didn't make sense. 'How?' she asked.

'There are quite a number of people who have put in a word for you, Rose. That's how.' Her dad hugged her.

Dear Mr and Mrs Kelly

We have pleasure in inviting your daughter, Rose Virginia Kelly, for an interview with a view to joining the September '45 intake at Morpeth High School for Girls.

We have a limited number of scholarship places and a study of Rose's school work and several references indicate that she is a suitable candidate for one of these places.

If you are interested in taking up this offer, please bring Rose to attend for interview on Friday March 24th at 2.00 p.m.

There had been a lot going on that Rose hadn't had a clue about. The sir from her primary school, who gave her such difficult sums, knew the headteacher and had been singing her praises. Miss Wakenshaw's sister, who worked in the English department, had also talked to her about Rose's love of books. Mr Maxwell, who had saved Lucky, was a governor at the school and asked the headteacher what was in place for pupils who were ill at the time of the scholarship exam. The headteacher was persuaded to look at Rose's practice paper from November and at her school books and had decided she was a potential scholarship girl. Now, she had to get through the interview.

Miss Wakenshaw explained how the interview at the school may result in a formal offer of a place. It was an opportunity for the headteacher to decide whether the school would suit Rose and whether her family would be supportive of Rose and her schooling.

'If I've learned anything these past few weeks, it's to take every chance you get. I hope Rose gets a place. *You'll* have to go with her, John. I can't go and talk to the headteacher there.'

Rose, her nose in a book, was half listening to her mam and dad chatting after dinner.

'I canna change my shift, lass. You'll just have to dress up smartly and let Rose talk her way in. It'll be no bother.'

'That's all right for you to say. You and Rose have a way with words. I haven't.'

'Don't put yourself down, Ginnie. Nothing but good sense and truth leaves your lips. Be yourself and you'll be fine, bonnie lass.'

It was a dry but chilly March day when Rose and her mam walked to the main A1 and took the bus to Morpeth. The school was a walk from the bus station, on Newgate Street. A brass plaque beside large arched wooden doors declared they were at Morpeth High School for Girls.

'Do we ring the bell or open these big doors, Rose?' Her

mam, so smart in a powder blue fitted coat and a little felt hat, had a touch of lipstick on and looked beautiful.

Just as they were about to press the bell, a teacher came along the street with a line of girls wearing short bottle green skirts and carrying hockey sticks. 'Can I help?' she asked.

'We're here for an interview and wondering whether to ring or open the door.' Rose explained.

'I'll show you the way… stop the chatter now we're near school, girls.' The teacher opened one half of the door.

Rose and Mam stepped into a lovely garden filled with trees and shrubs with daffodils and small blue flowers scattered on the lawn. It was surrounded by old buildings, some stone and others dark brick. The blank wall and door from the street opened into a different world and who ever would have guessed all this was behind it? The teacher pointed to a building along the garden's pathway. 'If you go through the main door there, you'll find chairs and meet the head's secretary.'

'Thank you,' Rose said as she squeezed Mam's hand tightly.

'Can you play hockey?' the teacher asked.

'I've never tried but I'd like to.'

'Good oh! Come along girls.' They walked off in a different direction.

'Wasn't she posh?' Mam whispered.

'Good oh!' Rose giggled.

It was a nightmare. The longest few minutes she had ever experienced. After shaking hands with the headmistress, Rose was tongue-tied for the first time in her life. Her mouth was dry so she could hardly say, 'Good afternoon'.

The interview began and she couldn't remember the last book she had read, she couldn't think of a hobby she enjoyed and she felt herself blushing right from her ears to her toes. She wanted to be anywhere but in front of this formidable woman with white pin-curled hair, a large bosom and piercing blue eyes. She couldn't meet her gaze any longer and looked down at her shoes. The clock on the bookcase ticked slowly on as her cheeks burned and she thought, *please ground just swallow me up.*

Her mam stepped in. 'I think Rose is feeling overwhelmed today, Ma'am. We were admiring the beautiful building and grounds and I think she has lost her tongue for once.'

'She isn't usually this... reticent?'

'She would normally tell you how much she loves the Brontës and why *Jane Eyre* is her absolute favourite and she would tell you all about her dog training ability, but I do think this beautiful room of yours has left Rose speechless. You know we're from a working class home and she hasn't much experience of grand places.'

Rose looked up. 'I've seen them in pictures though. My favourite architect is Gaudi.'

'Is he now? Tell me why.' The headmistress broke into a smile. After that, Rose found her voice and the interview flew by.

As they stood up to go, Mam said, 'I do like the painting behind your desk, Ma'am. It's rather like a Monet but I don't recognise it.'

'Oh, thank you! I'm flattered but I don't have a Monet. *I* painted this as a girl. I don't have much time nowadays but I do like this painting of my childhood garden.' The headteacher's face was flushed with pleasure.

'It's a wonderful way to express yourself. My husband, John, paints. He's a pitman but a painter too and he's had some work exhibited in London.'

'I saw an article about the Ashington painters! How wonderful to have one of their daughters at the school. After Rose starts in September, perhaps he can come and talk to the higher level art students?'

'She has a place?'

'Oh yes. She has potential and I can see she has a supportive family who will help her get the most out of her opportunity.' The headmistress shook hands with them both and they left.

'You were great, Mam!' Rose said when the gate closed behind them.

'Wasn't I just? Your dad showed me the Monets in a book. That was a piece of luck. Wait till your dad hears what I've landed him with; a talk on art to the young ladies!' They linked arms.

'Rose, what does reticent mean? I hadn't a clue!' Mam asked.

'Me neither, I'll have to look it up when we get home.' They both laughed.

'A cup of strong tea and a scone next, eh?'

'Yes, please.' They headed for the Clock Tower Tea Room. 'Thank goodness I got in, but Mam, it was you who won the headmistress over!'

17

Rose's scholarship victory was nothing compared to the other victory of that spring . At last, Europe was being liberated city by city and it looked as though they were winning the war. The papers reported that Hitler had committed suicide and, after that, it seemed it was only a matter of time before the war would be over.

Rose was horrified to hear of Goebbels' suicide with his wife and how he had killed his six children too. Children like her were not to blame for the flaming war. It was unbelievable how mean some adults could be when they couldn't have things their own way.

People started preparing for VE day, sure it would arrive in May. The Germans admitted defeat and, at last, they could celebrate victory in Europe. Churchill announced that the eighth of May was a national holiday and what a street party they had in the rows!

Every row had its own long line of tables and chairs out in the street and all the best china came out. There were mountains of sandwiches and pies and pickles. Fresh eggs from Mr Dodd's chickens as well as dried egg powder were used to make fancy cakes decorated with whatever sweet treats they had saved. Mam used cocoa powder to make a chocolate cake with buttercream icing and shredded flakes from a precious chocolate bar on top. That cake disappeared in a jiffy! The lads and lasses got ice cream and jelly and the grown-ups had a sherry or a beer.

The rows were red, white and blue with homemade bunting and everyone who had a flag hung it from their bedroom window. They all had paper union jacks to wave and the colourful Linwood pit banner declaring 'Education, Democracy, Humanity and Liberty for All' was brought out and placed at the pithead.

The brass band members congregated by the banner and then marched along the rows while a few young pit lads held the pit banner high. Rose, Stanley and the other Sunday school lads and lasses followed the band with Eddie-who-plays-the-accordion and they sang a few songs too.

The party went on forever and the street was bright all night. After dark, hymns gave way to 'Knees Up Mother Brown' and the grown-ups joined in a Hokey Cokey around the street. No more blackouts! Rose stood in the glow of First Row's street light thinking she would remember this special day forever.

Her dad was sitting on their step with his sketch pad. 'What are you standing there for lassie?' he asked.

'Just thinking.' She walked over to look at his sketching. 'Dad, today's party will make such a happy street painting.'

'It will, pet.'

'Is this your happiest day ever?' she asked.

'Nearly, but it can't match the day I married your mam or the day I saw you curled up like a rosebud just after you were born,' he said. 'That's why I chose Rose for you. Your mam hankered after Mary Virginia but she came around to Rose.'

'What about the twins? Wasn't their birth a happy day?' Rose asked. She loved being one of her dad's happiest memories but she wanted to be fair.

'Stanley and David? Your mam picked their names. David was so small she named him after David who took on Goliath and Stanley, he was a funny-looking little beggar, he got her father's name. I was happy they were healthy but, by then, I knew babies meant noise and worry.' Her dad's eyes showed he was joking with her. They sat for a bit longer and he gave her a sip of his beer.

'Mmmm, thanks Dad.' It was awful!

18

Later in May, Mr Maxwell called by to congratulate Rose on winning her school place and to see how Lucky was doing. He was impressed to see Lucky dancing around Rose on his two back legs and how he would follow her with his front legs resting on her back and would turn in a circle.

'You two will be joining a circus next,' he laughed.

'It was my plan to join one day, until I passed for Morpeth High. Now, I think I'll look after sick animals like you, Mr Maxwell.'

His eyes lit up. 'There'll always be a receptionist job for you at my practice when you qualify, Rose.'

'Not a receptionist, Mr Maxwell! I'm going to study hard to become a vet, just like you.'

Mr Maxwell raised his eyebrows. 'Good for you, Rose. I wish you every success.' As Mam handed him a cup of tea, he said, 'I've brought some outgrown school garments along, Mrs Kelly. They belonged to Ruth, my daughter. She is going into the final year and we have no other daughters, just Frank my son, so my wife packed up her outgrown uniform and we would be grateful if you could use them for Rose. "Make do and mend" is still going on and I know that the outfitter, Raymond Barnes, has been short of some school items because of the war.'

Rose watched Mam's face, she was in two minds. Mam didn't like receiving charity but she hated waste. 'How kind of you Mr Maxwell. We have some money put by but the uniform list *is* very long. It would be a great help to me, and our clothes ration book.'

'Excellent! Stanley, will you collect the package from the car when I leave?'

Stanley nodded eagerly and Rose knew why. He was thinking maybe he'd get a penny for sweets.

When Stanley staggered in with the box, they found it contained enough bottle green pinafores, cream blouses and sports skirts and jumpers to kit out three or four lasses. There were two blazers, different sizes, with the badge and a felt hat, a very battered one after five years of wear. The older girls who were taking their Highers changed to berets. There were hockey socks and boots in two sizes and a tennis skirt. Most of the things she needed were in that box and Mam was delighted. 'I'll steam and press these so they are like new, Rose. I'll make sure they fit nicely too. I think Ruth Maxwell must be a bit tubby.'

They tried on the hat. It was a sad affair. 'It's fine, Mam.'

'No it's not, Rose. That Maxwell lassie has not taken care of her hat. We'll go to Raymond Barnes on Grey Street and get you kitted out with your own new hat. Your dad has given me some of his painting savings and I'm buying you new bottle green knickers as well, I wouldn't use the tatty ones in here for dusters. I'll knit you a yellow and green striped scarf for September, you'll get a proper satchel for your birthday and that will do you.'

Rose turned the list her mam had been ticking over. 'What about a hockey stick and bag, Mam?'

'Oh crikey, there's more on the other side of the page, what a list for one lassie!'

Over the next couple of weeks, Mam set to work making the clothes look smart and they were hung away until September.

All too quickly, the day came when she left elementary school. Mr Brown called her onto the stage at the end of assembly and presented her with a hockey stick and a proper hockey bag in the Morpeth school colour of bottle green. The teachers had put together to get her something and Mam had told Miss Wakenshaw the only thing she needed was a hockey stick. The whole school cheered after the sir said 'This scholarship place is a triumph for our school. Use Rose Kelly as a good example of what can be done with hard work.'

Her face was aflame and she was a bright crimson rose when they left the hall.

After the bell signalled home time, Rose walked through the hall and revisited all of her old classrooms. The school had seemed vast on her first day but she had grown into it. Would she grow into all of the buildings of her new school as easily? She took her cardigan and shoe bag from her peg and walked slowly into the girls' yard. She would remember every crack of this play area and all the memories it held.

Miss Wakenshaw caught up with her. 'I saw you taking a last look around. It's not easy to leave old faces and places behind, Rose, but you have a bright future to look forward to. This country is going to see such changes, whoever wins the election, and there will be plenty of opportunities for young people.'

Rose hugged the miss. 'You are right but it's sad to leave a happy place for something unknown. Thank you for all the books and for everything, you're the best teacher ever.'

That summer, Mam seemed more set than ever on making Rose her helper in the house. Stanley could go out and play but she couldn't pick up a book without being asked to strip a bed, iron some plain items like pillow cases and aprons or peel some veg. Washing pots was never-ending and she was fed up with housework as much as she was fed up with hearing about the election. It was the first general election in her lifetime and after years of war talk, now the grown-ups were talking about who should govern the country. At first, Rose had enjoyed earwigging to find out what the adults were thinking but it had gone on for weeks and she had lost interest in the 'what ifs'.

The pit folk of Linwood were behind Clement Attlee and his 'Let us face the future together' programme of change. Mr Churchill had gained some respect in the colliery rows during the war years because he had been decisive and led them to victory but that was thrown back on the slag heap when he stated Attlee's proposals would require some form of 'gestapo' to carry them out.

'That bleedin' Churchill, he's back to his tricky ways again. Trying to frighten folk into sticking wi' him.' Lottie's dad was chatting to Mr Dodd over the allotment fence.

'Gestapo! That was under the belt and folk don't believe him.' Mr Dodd was digging up onions. 'The forces, men like our Billy, are all for a change. I reckon Attlee will get a lot of their votes but we'll hadda wait'n see.' He handed a few onions to Lottie's dad and, noticing Rose and Lucky, he asked. 'Could your mam use a few onions, hinny?'

Rose nodded and took a few back to the house. From reading Dad's paper, listening to the radio, her mam and dad, and the gossip on the street, she decided a Labour win would be best for the country. It would bring about changes such as a welfare system, a national health service and it would nationalise the mines and give her dad better working conditions. Who could argue with that?

The funny thing was, on the Thursday when Attlee won the election, everybody seemed shocked except for Rose. They were happy about it but couldn't believe Attlee had achieved such a landslide victory.

'I bet even Clement Attlee himself is shocked,' her mam said to Mary-from-next-door.

'Not as shocked as Winston! He thought he could ride on his success but too many voters in the country are not convinced he can lead in peace time.' Mary, who had been helping Ginnie to finish a proggy mat, put her progger down and searched for a handkerchief. She dabbed at her eyes. 'If only a national health service had been here for my Tommy. I wish he could have seen this day.'

The last victory of 1945 was the victory over Japan on Rose's birthday. An era of world peace had begun. She unwrapped the satchel she had been promised and couldn't wait to fill it with books. This year's birthday treat was taking Lottie and her other friends to the cinema and they were going on their own. *Blithe Spirit* was showing at the Hippo and had a séance in it, but it was a comedy with a U certificate so they were allowed to go. There were supposed to be exciting special effects and a ghost, and her mam would pack them a small bag of sweets each. Sweets were still rationed so they'd been saving the coupons for ages.

After summer she had September to look forward to and starting Morpeth High School for Girls. She would face a new school and new challenges while the country was facing a whole new way of working.

19

Rose had a walk then a long bus ride before she reached Morpeth bus station and started another walk up Newgate street. It was a bright, gusty morning and her teeth chattered uncontrollably. Was it nerves or excitement? Rose couldn't tell. She was part of a swarm of green all heading towards the High School.

Once inside the grounds, the morning was every bit as nerve-wracking as she thought it would be. It was just like being in one of the school stories she had read with everyone milling about and catching up after the holidays and there were girls of every age. The sixth form, almost women, wore a skirt with a sash instead of a pinafore, and the prefects, who wore an enamel badge on their lapel, seemed like teachers as they rounded up the first formers and put them in lines.

Everyone in her line was new and in Form 1A, named after Miss Alexander, their form mistress. Together, they found their way around school and learned school rules. There was quite a mix of girls. Some were very well spoken, as she had expected, but a lot were tradesmen's or farmer's daughters and talked with the Northumbrian country lilt. She hadn't come across any other pitmen's daughters with a broad colliery dialect like hers and felt out of place at first.

Rose listened and learned. She realised most people talked the way books were written, like Miss Wakenshaw, and, as her confidence grew, 'wor hoose' became 'our house' and 'divent' became 'don't'. Some girls were catty but she found her own set of friends. Her best friend was Brenda Anne Charlton, a farmer's daughter from Rothbury and they were part of a larger group of 1A pupils who played out at break, swapped homework notes and kept each other company over lunch.

She travelled home on the bus by herself, nobody else took her route, and it gave her time to do her reading homework or snatch a few pages of a novel she'd borrowed from their huge school library. Rose loved that library! First formers could spend one lunchtime in there and that was her favourite day. She carefully chose two books every week and Miss Dove, the librarian knew her name already.

One sunny October day, her friends chose their books and hurried outside to walk around the gardens but Rose stayed behind. She liked to visit every section before leaving. Turning into the alcove containing history books, she came face to face with a trio of older girls who were lounging around a table with a pile of French magazines in front of them.

'Buzz off, Pippi,' one of them called. The new intake all got labelled Pippi Longstockings. The girl had a grown up curled hair style and her pudgy face scowled at Rose.

Sixth formers could use the library every day so Rose didn't stay to argue. As she turned to go the same shrill voice called over, 'Wait there Pippi. Are you the pitman's daughter? The one who Mummy sent all my cast offs to?'

Rose blushed as she turned back towards the three. 'I'm Rose Kelly. Is your father Mr Maxwell?'

'Yes, that's him. Always looking for a charity case. We don't know what to do with him. It's strange to meet someone who's wearing my old gym knickers. Hope your mother darned the holes!' She turned to the others and let out a false laugh.

Ruth wasn't a prefect so she had nothing to do with Rose up until now. Why was she being so hurtful? Rose's face burned and she knew her cheeks would be aflame so she walked quickly to the shelves near Miss Dove's desk to compose herself. She blinked back her tears.

That girl was despicable. In the rows, there were many hand-me-downs passed about and it was drilled into her to *never ever* comment if someone was wearing one of her old dresses or skirts. Where she came from, it was the height of bad manners to point something like that out and would earn you a quick clip around the ear. She couldn't believe Mr Maxwell's daughter could be like that.

Why hadn't she held her own? She wouldn't let anyone in the rows get away with that sort of cheek even if they *were* older than her.

She blew her nose and marched back to where the three were still sitting. 'Excuse me, Ruth Maxwell.'

'What do you want now Pippi Holeybritches?' Ruth swung back on her chair.

'I just wanted to say that, thanks to the kindness of your father, my mother *did* take in a box of your cast offs. Unfortunately they were all like big sacks on me and my mother thought your panama hat, held together with a *safety pin* was a damned disgrace. As for your holey gym britches, she wouldn't even use them for dusters. If you must know, your old uniform *is* being put to good use. Most of it is making a proggy mat for us to wipe our feet on at the back door!'

Ruth stood up and Rose thought she was going to hit her but she was ready for that too. Ruth must have thought better of it because she brushed past her and left the alcove.

'Well done Pippi!' one of the girls said. 'Ruth is a hanger on, she isn't a friend because she can be such a bitch. Good for you, sticking up for yourself.'

The other girl added, 'Ruth is kidding herself if she thinks you'd fit into her old duds. She was a little pet elephant in first year. Do you remember?' she nudged her friend and they both laughed.

'Will she report me?' Rose asked.

'She wouldn't dare, bullying isn't allowed. Watch your back though, she's mean.'

When Rose took her hat from her peg that afternoon, it was drenched. Someone had dunked it in one of the cloakroom wash basins. She dried it as best as she could with paper towels. Her brand new hat! It cost a fortune.

'It must be that Ruth Maxwell, what a nasty piece of work she is,' Brenda said. Rose had told Brenda about her spat in the library.

Rose didn't tell Mam or Dad or Lottie about Ruth's bitchiness but she did tell Lucky. 'I'm so glad you are not living in that house with that bitch of a girl, Lucky.'

Rose didn't see much of Lottie during the week because of the long bus journey, walking Lucky and homework but they usually went together to the pictures or looked around the shops in their nearest town, Ashington, on a Saturday.

One Saturday, Lottie met up with her at the corner of the street and, as they walked to the bus stop, she asked, ' Rose, has your mam said anything to you?'

'About what?'

'About *anything*?' Lottie looked like she was about to burst with some news.

'Come on get to the point, Lottie. I know you're itching to tell me.'

'Have you noticed anything?'

'Like what?'

'Like your mam being sick or anything?'

Rose stopped in her tracks. 'No, I haven't. What's the matter? Is she ill?'

'Don't dare to say I told you, but no she's not ill. I heard her talking to my mam on Thursday and I've had to keep it to myself since then.'

'What? What did you hear?' Rose's impatience made her want to shake Lottie.

'Your mam told my mam that she's expecting.'

'Expecting? You mean a bairn?' Rose hadn't seen that coming.

She couldn't concentrate on the new Lassie film. When was Mam going to tell *her*? She couldn't drop Lottie in it so she would just have to wait and notice what was going on around her a bit more.

Were they having a baby because they'd lost David to the strangling angel? Crikey, where would they put the baby? The tiny alcove in Mam and Dad's room was where the twins had slept when they were tiny so the crib would have to go back there. It would be a tight squeeze at number one but they'd make room. Would Mam and Dad be able to afford her fares and uniform? She couldn't bear to leave her new school now she'd settled in.

Wasn't it obvious, once you knew something? Mam wore her blouses over her skirt and she kept her pinny on most of the time but she was definitely more round around the belly. She wasn't sick but she looked pale and dozed off in the chair after tea after asking Rose to do the washing up. She caught Rose looking at her a couple of times but she still said nothing.

It was a week later when Dad told her. He took her and Stanley for a walk through the fields during blackberry week and they collected three cans of blackberries. They walked back towards the allotments, the sunset a stunning flamingo pink.

'That would make a great painting, Dad,' Stanley pointed to the horizon.

'You're observant, you've got the eye of a painter, Stanley.' Dad ruffled his hair.

'Have I?' Stanley grinned and held Dad's free hand.

'You know, you two bairns have made your mam and me so happy and proud in so many ways. There's nothing better than seeing your lassie doing well at school and your laddie playing for his school football team. A family is life's greatest blessing.'

Great start, Dad. I know what's coming next, she thought before asking, 'Is it so good that you'd think of having another one, Dad?'

Dad caught on. 'You know?'

'It's not hard if you're observant.'

'What does she know, Dad? I'm observant, you've just said, but I don't know what you two are on about.' Stanley looked from Dad to her.

'We're going to have a brother or sister, Stanley,' Rose said.

'Cripes, I'm not keen on that idea. I loved being a twin but don't want a crying baby. Do we have to?' Stanley pulled a face.

Dad gave him a soft clip around his lug. 'Yes we do and don't you go saying that to your mam, do you hear me?'

When they got back, Dad threw the blackberries into a big basin and added water and a sprinkle of salt. The salt made sure any hidden maggots were killed and they'd float to the top.

'We'll make a blackberry pudding and some jam with those tomorrow, Rose. You should be able to remember the pudding recipe yourself by now.' Mam said. She had prepared singin' hinnies and was ready to cook the scones on a flat griddle over the fire. 'Have you two heard our news?' the brightness of her voice confirmed she had given Dad the job of sharing the news.

'Yes Mam and, if we have to have a baby, I'd like a brother. He won't be half as good as David but I'll try to like him.' Stanley hugged her.

'The baby isn't replacing David, son. Nobody could take his place in my heart,' Mam quickly turned and brushed at her face with the bottom of her pinny.

'You're quiet Rose. What would you prefer?' Dad squeezed her shoulder.

She couldn't say she'd rather have a kitten or another pup. 'I'm not bothered as long as it doesn't cry all the time. When exactly is it due?'

'Not until March. We have plenty of time to get used to the idea,' Mum said as she turned the scones on the griddle and they started their high pitched 'singing'. That meant they would soon be ready to eat with a bit of butter or jam.

20

Hockey was played on the boys' school fields. The girls' school was old and had beautiful grounds but no fields of their own because sport was quite a new thing for girls. It meant they had to march along Cottingwood Lane and pass King Edward VI boys' school buildings on PE days.

Rose stopped to stroke a big ginger cat who was soaking up a rare patch of November sun and had to run to catch up with the disappearing crocodile of green. She tripped over her loose bootlace just as she reached the wrought iron entrance gates. One knee was lightly grazed but the other had been gashed by something sharp and was bleeding. Of course she found no hankie in her gym knicker pocket. It hurt too, she bit her lip and held back the tears.

'What's happened to you?' A tall boy with a shock of blonde hair was looking down at her.

'What does it look like?' She blurted out and the tears wouldn't hold back.

He crouched down and produced a white laundered handkerchief. 'Don't get upset. I'll mop this up and see what the wound is like underneath. All this blood will clean it out anyway.'

She watched him work methodically. He cleaned her leg, applied pressure to the cut so it stopped bleeding and then fashioned a bandage out of the bloody handkerchief. 'That's the best I can do until we get you to a first aid box.' He held out a rather bloodied hand, she took it with her very muddy hand and he pulled her to her feet.

'Thank you so much. I'll be able to find my games mistress now.'

'Link my arm and I'll help you over.'

'Shouldn't you be at a lesson?'

'I've been to the dentist for a filling so I've missed most of the afternoon anyway,' he explained. 'How did you get left behind from your group?'

She told him about seeing the cat and losing sight of her class and he laughed.

'I'm like that with animals too.' When they got to the edge of the playing field, he said, 'I'll leave you here and get back to my lesson.'

She remembered her manners. 'Thanks, once again. I'm Rose Kelly.'

'I'm Frank, Frank Maxwell. Get that cut properly cleaned and you'll be fine.'

Mr Maxwell's son? He was nothing like his bitch of a sister.

Mam and Mary-from-next-door were turning two old flannel sheets. They cut them in half and put the threadbare middle to the outside and the less used outside to the middle with a flat seam.

'There'll be a few more years in these now, Ginnie. Do you have any of your own that need turning?'

'No. I've got one that's thin in the middle but I'm cutting it up to make a few cot sheets before March.'

Rose was in the scullery peeling potatoes and carrots to add to the knuckle of ham her mam had simmering on the range.

'That's wise. You can never have enough sheets for a new-born, Ginnie. If they're not being sick on them, it's the other end.'

Rose shuddered at the thought. Their house was going to be full of nappies and sheets and a wailing baby.

Mary said, 'There's quite a lot of babies being born now the war is over. It's a boom, so the papers say.'

'I bumped into Dorothy Fletcher, she's another one expecting at the same time as me.'

'Douglas's Mam?' Rose asked, 'Isn't she a bit old to be having babies?'

'She's just a bit older than me… still in her thirties, I think. They've tried for a bairn a few times but she miscarries early. She's hoping she keeps this one. It's been hard on her losing Douglas. I feel for the woman, I've had two of you to keep me going.'

Rose hugged her mam. This baby might make her less sad. Poor Mrs Douglas, Rose hoped she would have her baby too. It wouldn't take Douglas's place but she always looked so lost nowadays.

Next library day, Rose asked Miss Dove where she'd find a book about having babies.

'The one for lending is one of the most thumbed books in the library, Rose. It's always out but there is an identical one in the biology reference section too. I'll keep the one you can take home to one side when it comes back in. Is there anything special you want information on?'

'Everything, Miss Dove. From the beginning to giving birth… and losing babies. My mam is expecting again and she's no good at talking about these things so I'm better off reading for myself.'

'I see. I know just the book and, Rose, if you do have questions, you can always ask me.'

What a revelation! Everything became clear and Rose learnt the right terms – intercourse, conception, miscarriage, full term, contraception and menstruation were all set out clearly. She read the reference book every week and made notes. 'You're going to be an expert by the time you get to the end of that flaming book,' Brenda moaned. 'Come on out and get some fresh air before we're back to our lessons.'

At last, the lending edition was returned and it certainly was tatty. Miss Dove taped some pages back inside before handing it to her. She took it out until after the Christmas holidays so she could read everything again slowly and make sure her mam knew what was happening to her body.

'I don't need to know what the baby looks like at five months, Rose, I can feel the beggar!' Her mam's reaction was not what she expected. She hadn't liked answering how many times you needed to have intercourse or when she had started her menstruation either.

'Honestly Mam, you're going through this pregnancy like it's a game of blind man's bluff. Your eyes are firmly shut and you're staggering through each stage by accident!'

'I had you and I had the twins and the only thing that was an accident was falling for a third time. I do not need you to keep me right, hinny.'

'Accident? Was it an accident? Perhaps you need to read the chapter on contraception, Mam.'

'*Perhaps* I'll toss that book on the fire if you keep talking like that, Rose. It's not done to talk of such things at your age.'

'It's learning, it's biology, Mam. Anyway, you and Mary-from-next-door talk about "such things" plenty.'

'We are grown women. Seeing as you're on about all this, I've put some towels in your underwear drawer for when your... you know. It might not happen for a while, but they are there.'

'You know?' Rose was exasperated. 'Mam, the term in this book is menstruating or a period and it happens in your teens so I'm a year off that.'

'That's enough of that, Rose. Not everything needs to have a flaming posh name.'

Before Christmas, the whole school had two long walks to St Mary the Virgin church, though the head and some senior teachers whizzed up in cars. The school carol service was being held there this year and there was a rehearsal that took half the day and then the actual service.

The fourteenth century church was so ornate and different to Rose's tiny chapel at Linwood with its one stained glass window. On the day of the service, bunches of holly, Christmas roses and candles made the whole atmosphere magical. Rose was in the junior choir and was proud that Mam came to watch in her best blue coat, a hat and a fur muff she'd borrowed from Mary-from-next-door.

At the end of the service, they chatted to Brenda's mam and Rose spied Mrs Maxwell and Ruth coming out of the church. Mam was easily as smart as Ruth's mother. Of course, the Maxwells passed by without so much as a nod. Rose led her mam to the graveyard without letting on who the Maxwells were in case Mam was upset at being snubbed.

'Look Mam. Here it is.' Rose pointed to Emily Wilding Davison's family plot. It was quite grand and her gravestone bore the suffragettes' slogan 'Deeds not Words'. A marble flower urn, laid in tribute to Emily said, 'Emily Wilding Davison, Died June 8 1913 Valiant in Courage and Faith'.

Rose regaled her mam with the story of Emily running in front of the king's horse at the Epsom Derby as they walked towards the bus station.

She stopped mid-flow when she spotted Mrs Maxwell's fur coat and Ruth's bulky shape just in front of them. They had met up with Frank. He was as tall as his mother and had stuffed his cap in his pocket so his fair curls were blowing all over the place. As the Maxwell's crossed the street to get into a car, she caught Frank's eye, ' Hey, Rose, Rose Kelly... Merry Christmas!' He waved.

'Who are they?' Mam asked.

Rose blushed. He'd remembered her name. 'Frank Maxwell, the vet's son and his mother and sister.'

The Co-op had bananas in store! Rose wasn't sure if she remembered them or if she knew them from pictures but Stanley certainly hadn't come across one before. Mam had brought two home for their Christmas eve supper. They all had cocoa and a slice of buttered toast with half a banana spread on top. It was what Rose thought of as an Enid Blyton supper... and was delicious.

Stanley and Rose went up to bed and Rose was allowed to read for half an hour. Stanley shuffled about getting ready for bed and said a quick prayer before whispering, 'David, I had a banana and you'd really like them, I think. I'll miss not being able to wake you up in the morning but I'll be thinking of you, promise. Cubby's in my bed so don't worry about him. Night night.'

Listening from behind the curtain, Rose's chest ached to hear Stanley's whispered words. She put down her book and wept into her pillow. No baby could make up for David's loss.

21

They got through Christmas. Mary went to stay with Larry and the family so it was just the four of them.

The baby in the crib at chapel softened Rose's heart towards another baby and she thought she might try knitting some mittens or booties. As she looked around at the paper chain streamers that the little'uns had hung around the lectern of the chapel and the tinsel star above the crib, she had to admit, even though it only had the one stained glass window and wasn't as fancy as St Mary's, this was her favourite place for worship and singing.

Her present was a tennis racket, brand new and not even on her list. She'd been a bit worried about asking for one once the hockey season stopped but now she could practice against the wall and not be too clumsy when summer came. She'd been told the girls trooped along to Carlisle Park courts and played there and she'd walked by those courts. They looked huge.

Mam landed Rose with a few of Mary's Christmas cooking chores and got tetchy when she wasn't speedy enough. Why couldn't her mother see that she wasn't cut out for kitchen duties? After dinner, they all sat back to let their feast digest and Mam and Dad chatted about Dad's mining work. They were hopeful about the future. Dad explained to her and mam that, when the mines were nationalised, he was sure the vote for nationalisation would go through, he'd have a better wage, better work conditions and a better pension.

'When you get the new family allowance, it'll be for Stanley and the bairn so that ten shillings'll keep things ticking over until Stanley starts work.'

'What about me?'

'The allowance isn't for a first bairn, hinny,' Dad explained.

'I meant about work.'

'You'll not work for a long time. At least, I wouldn't want you to. Stanley here, he wants to follow his dad so he can.'

'Aye! I hate school. I really want to work with the gallowas.'

'You'll start picking at the pithead first of all. Maybe you'll have a gallowa when you've proved yourself.'

'Proved what?'

'That you're a hard worker, laddie.'

Rose was trying to cast on. She had been given a ball of white wool and some number nine knitting needles from her mam. 'Mam, can you just cast on for me? Knitting is not my forte.'

'How can it be a fort?' Stanley asked as Mam sighed and held out her hand.

'Pass it here.'

'Stanley, use the dictionary and tell me what you find,' Dad pointed to the large book with a magnifying glass on top of it on the sideboard.

Rose grinned as Stanley got up saying, 'I wish I'd kept my mouth shut.'

They settled around the wireless to listen to King George's Christmas message before tea. It was cheering. Life without a war going on would be grand if they hadn't lost David, Douglas and Mr Elliot.

Mary-from-next-door came back the day after boxing day. 'Eh Ginnie lass, I've just heard that poor Mrs Douglas isn't expecting. She's miscarried again... Christmas and all.'

Mam stopped stirring the broth she was making from the Christmas carcass. 'You know Mary, God has a lot to answer for leaving mothers without bairns and bairns without mothers.'

Rose stopped her knit one, purl one. 'It's not God, Mam. Either the baby wasn't forming properly or Mrs Douglas has a weak cervix. Her doctor would know. You can't blame God for a weak cervix!'

'I don't know what a cervix is, but I flaming well *can* give him a piece of my mind! Stop getting above yourself our Rose!'

Rose got back to her knitting. This baby was making her mam a bit quick-tempered and they had another three months to go. 'Mam, what bairns have been left without a mother?'

'Plenty. I was for one and my sister was left to bring us little'uns up. It's a terrible thing to lose your mother when you're young.'

Mam was wiping a tear with her pinny now. She'd better shut up and knit.

Before she left, Mary pulled Rose to one side, 'Could I have a look at that book your mam was telling me about Rose?'

'Of course, but I thought you'd know all about the labour and stuff already.'

Mary-from-next-door had brought many of the bairns in the rows into the world over the years and, even at seventy-odd, she was regularly in demand to help the registered midwives. Mary-from-the-Co-op, Betty and Maisie Johnson's mam, had gradually learned the ropes and often helped the women in the rows until the midwife called but Mary-from-next-door was the local expert.

'I want to see the pictures, hinny. I've always just delivered by feeling so an idea of the inside would be handy. I want to read about how you lose a bairn, by accident I mean not the other and I want to read about those "c" words you mentioned.'

'Conception and contraception? I think you're a bit old for that Mary.'

'And I think you're a bit young for such cheek, lassie.' Mary gave her a push and laughed.

'Bring it around, quiet like. I don't want your mam to think I'm encouraging you. She still thinks of you as her bairn.'

When she'd gone. Rose mulled over Mary's words. 'Lose a bairn by accident, not the other, what did that mean? Later in the week, she'd take the book and ask her. Mary-from-next-door might answer more questions than her mam.

After New Year, Rose called in to number two and it was Mary who explained to Rose how some lasses got in the family way and then tried to 'lose' their bairn. 'Nobody in the rows does that dirty work, mind you Rose. We take in our bairns and give them a good home or they go to an orphanage.'

'I thought that orphanages were just for children with no parents.'

'Nobody to parent them. A parent is the person who loves and looks after you it doesn't have to be the one who gives birth to you.'

'You've given me something to think about there, Mary.'

'Now there's a thing,' Mary chuckled.

'Don't you think it would be better, in 1946, to teach young people about contraception rather than leave them ignorant?'

'You've given me something to think about too, Rose. You see, *my* church and Lottie's, so don't go talking to her about contraception, doesn't believe in such artificial things.'

'I think God has enough to be doing without bothering himself about that sort of matter,' Rose said.

'Eh, lass your talk, contraception in one breath and God in the next, it's too modern for me.'

Rose took that as a clue to leave Mary-from-next-door and save some questions for another day. Time to wrap up and take Lucky for a walk.

22

1946

Icy cold sleet was coming horizontally at their faces as Rose and Lottie ran to catch an early bus from the Saturday pictures. They were drenched through so Rose popped back home to change into something dry and collect her knitting before going to Lottie's house for tea. She was taking ages with those baby booties and thought she might knit a line or two while she chatted to Lottie and her mam.

The back door opened quietly with no ecstatic greeting from Lucky to announce she was home. Stanley must have him out for a walk.

'Are they *sure*, Ginnie?'

'Not sure, but it's obvious to me.' Her mam and Mary-from-next-door were chatting.

'Twins, heaven forbid!'

'*Shush*, there's the door closing. Who's here?'

'Hi Mam.' Rose popped her head through the door to find her mam and Mary working on the proggy mat for the bedroom.

'You're back early, hinny.' Mam looked up and smiled.

'I'm soaked to the skin so I'm just getting changed, picking up my knitting then I'm off to Lottie's.'

Rose started up the stairs. Had she heard correctly? Are they sure? It's obvious… twins. Could Mam be having two babies again? Midway, she turned to go back down; she had to ask. 'Mam, what were you saying to Mary when I came in? What was obvious? What was that about twins?'

'I wish you wouldn't listen in to private conversations, Rose! It's women's talk.' Mam tucked a bit of stray hair behind her ears and her neck flushed pink.

'I couldn't help it. You were saying it as I came in. I couldn't shut my ears.'

'You've always had flaming good hearing, lassie,' Mary looked flustered too.

Mam stood up to stretch her back and Rose thought she looked big enough for triplets never mind twins. Her ankles were swollen and her feet puffed over her slippers.

'Trust you to get the hot end of the poker our Rose. If you must know, I was telling Mary that it's good news for Dorothy Fletcher. She thought she'd missed at Christmas but she's still expecting so it must've been twins. That can happen.'

'That's a relief. I thought it was you for a moment.'

'*You* think too much and mind you, just keep this news to yourself. Dorothy is nervous about it all and she's just told me because we lost the boys together and now our dates are near each other. She won't want you broadcasting her business.'

'Mam, I'd never do that!' Rose was affronted.

'Perhaps not, but it's as well to warn you. No gossiping when you're along the row at Lottie's.'

Rose left. As if! How could Mam say that when she was chatting away telling other people's business to Mary?

Her mam had chosen a home birth and her dad argued hospital might be better. The midwives were kept busy in the densely populated town of Ashington. It seemed like lots of babies were being born now the war was over. The midwives found it hard to get to the rows in time unless it was a long labour and they didn't like cycling along to Linwood at night, either. The discussion simmered on for days.

While Rose and Mam were knitting and listening to the radio one night, Dad broached the subject again.

'Babies can't be relied on to come at a convenient time, Ginnie. You might be hanging on for a midwife. Have you seen the number of bairns being born now the war is over?'

'I want to be at Linwood, John.' Mam's needles were clicking three times faster than Rose's.

'A ride to the hospital and a few days rest would do you the world of good, pet.' Dad was painting the crib that had served her and Stanley and several babies from the rows before that. He'd sanded it down and was putting on a coat of pale cream.

'I've had the last bairns here with the midwife and Mary-from-next-door and I'm quite happy to do it again, John. Don't interfere in women's business. I've seen the district nurse and she's happy enough.'

'Does she know how quickly you had the twins, though? You needed stitches.'

'It's all in my notes so stop mithering me.'

'This house is full now as it is. Hospital is much better.' Dad was pushing his luck.

'My plan is to leave Rose here with Stanley, you're likely to be at work, and I'll have the bairn in Mary's spare bedroom. She's got everything prepared as well as any hospital and she'll get someone to call the midwife.'

'Are you sure love?' Dad knelt in front of Mam and clasped her hands in his.

She kissed his cheek. 'It's all taken care of John.'

Rose finished the last row of the second bootie. 'Look, I can cast off now and then sew this up.' She didn't want to knit anything else, it was frustrating work and she preferred her books.

In the middle of March, Mam started her labour right on a Friday teatime. She told Rose to warn Mary-from-next-door but to say nothing to her dad when he got up because she wanted him to go on his shift without a worry.

As soon as Dad was down the row, Mam picked up her big shopping bag. 'You stay here with the doors locked and go to bed. You have Stanley to look after and Lucky to keep you company and, by tomorrow, I might have a little'un to bring home.'

Rose gave Mam a hug and a kiss and locked the back door after her waddling figure. They didn't usually bother but Mam wanted to know they were safe.

She listened to the radio and read then turned off the light and sat by the dying embers of the range but she didn't take herself off to bed. She was nervous for Mam. The library book had been returned but those pictures of childbirth floated around in her head.

She'd left the curtains open and, before drawing them for the night, stood on a dining room chair to look into the Elliot's back yard to see if the midwife's bicycle was there. No. Where the heck was she? Could Mary manage on her own? She might need help. There was always Mary-from-the-Co-op to call on. As she was climbing down, she saw the gate open. A dark figure entered the yard and turned Mary's door handle.

She couldn't see much but it wasn't a woman, too tall. It seemed to be a man in a hat, a trilby.

Had they called for the doctor? Dr Bob was short and stout, it wasn't him. Was Mam okay? She said a prayer and went up to bed. She'd never sleep.

She must have gone out like a light because next morning she woke to the sound of Mary-from-next-door singing as she rattled at the range. 'I've put you and Stanley an egg on to boil and soon you can call around to see your mam and new brother,' she said as soon as Rose entered the kitchen.

'A boy! I knew we'd have a boy! I talked in my head to David about it and he said he wouldn't mind.' Stanley followed Rose into the room punching the air.

'Is Mam okay, Mary? I saw somebody come along late at night. Was it the doctor?'

'Doctor? No, pet. You're mistaken. The midwife got herself here at five this morning when we were all done and dusted and she's checked the bairn and your mam over but we didn't need Dr Bob.'

'But I saw somebody, a man, in your yard.'

'Were you dreaming pet? You'd have to be standing on that table to see into my yard,' Mary laughed.

'I was… not on the table but on that chair on tiptoe and I saw the door open.'

'What a lassie you are! You didn't see anything but shadows, pet and don't go upsetting your mam with tales like that on this of all days,' Mary warned.

Rose began to doubt herself. Could she have imagined it? She'd been tired but she was sure she'd seen a figure.

Dad came in and turned straight on his heels to go next door and see Mam and the baby.

'We'll let your dad meet the bairn first and then you two can go along.' Mary started a fry up of bacon and an egg for when her dad came back in.

'Your turn,' Dad said as he sat down to his breakfast. 'Time you met your brother, Terence.'

Young Terence Kelly was a red, squalling scrap with no hair, flailing fists and a frown. Rose picked him up and loved him, immediately. 'Oh Mam he's perfect.'

'Isn't he?' Mam smiled.

'Wherever they go, babies bring their own love.' Mary wiped tears from her eyes.

'Let's get you three home and leave Mary in peace.' Her mam looked tired but happy. Now they were back to five again.

23

1947

On her thirteenth birthday, Rose wanted a change from celebrating in the colliery rows. She had grown to love tennis and could hire a tennis court quite cheaply at Carlisle Park in Morpeth so her parents agreed that tennis and a picnic with her friends would be the order of the day.

The mid-August day dawned clear and the sun had already created a puddle of warmth for Lucky to lie in as Rose excitedly helped Mam to pack three bags with cake, sandwiches and drinks for a picnic. It was a lot to carry but they would spread the tea out on the grass afterwards and it would be better than her back yard picnics of the past. Rose invited Brenda and a couple of other school friends and Lottie, of course.

Terence, who'd grown into a lively toddler, was left under the watchful eye of Mary-from-next-door, and Stanley's present to Rose was the promise of a long walk with Lucky so it was just Mam, Lottie and Rose who set off for the bus to Morpeth lugging heavy bags as well as Rose's racket.

Lottie couldn't play and didn't want to try so she helped Mam find a shady spot for the bags then sat on a grassy bank by the courts and just watched. The other girls took turns to play foursomes and, when it was her turn to sit out, Rose noticed that Lottie was not her usual self.

'Why are you so quiet Lottie? Is it too hot out here for you? We can go in the shade, by the bags you know?'

Lottie, stringing daisies into a chain, looked over at the girls on the court. 'I'm fine, Rose it's just…'

'Just what Lottie?'

'Lottie snapped the chain and faced Rose. 'This is too posh for me. They all speak differently! *You* speak differently when you're with them. I'm not comfortable.' She wiped a tear from her cheek. 'I shouldn't have come!'

'Don't cry! You *always* come to my parties, don't be like that. They're nice girls if you give them a chance.'

'I'm going for a walk.' Lottie jumped up and strode off.

Rose wanted to go after Lottie but she was due to partner Brenda in the next game. She decided to follow Lottie.

'Leave her, Rose.' Mum, dozing with her back to a tree, had heard them. 'I'll go and talk to her in a minute, hinny. You go and join in the tennis and then we'll serve the tea.'

Rose still hovered, she wanted to run after Lottie and wanted to join in the next game. 'She's my oldest friend, Mam and she's in a huff with me.'

'Lottie won't want you drawing attention to her so it's best if I go,' Mam said.

Lottie seemed to cheer up after Mam talked to her and the picnic was fun but Rose was worried about upsetting Lottie so she made sure she chatted to her and sat by her.

They chatted happily on the journey home and Lottie called a cheerful 'goodbye' when they reached her row. Rose could, at last, ask Mam what she'd done wrong.

'You're between two worlds, pet. I guessed this would happen. You have friends who use different words, play tennis and the like and dragged Lottie into that world. She didn't feel part of it.'

'Do I talk and act different Mam? I just think I'm me?' Rose was confused.

'You might not realise it but, yes, sometimes you do. You're not all la-di-da but you talk differently and you need to do that to fit in at that school. You've been mixing with a host of different people for two years now and Lottie hadn't noticed how you've changed so she got a shock.'

Rose thought over what Mam had said and had to admit that she always made an effort to turn into the 'old Rose' when she met Lottie on a Saturday. Mam was right, she was between two worlds and she loved them both.

Lottie wasn't well the next Saturday. Mrs Simpson came to the door and said, 'She doesn't want to go out today, pet. She's got something hanging on her I'm sure because she's just mooched about all morning.'

The Saturday after that Lottie had work to do for her mam. She stood at the door and made this an excuse for not going out.

Rose took Lucky for a walk over the fields and, as she came back, she saw Lottie walking along the road with Betty and her gang. They looked like they'd got off the Ashington bus because they were wearing their good clothes and carried shopping bags.

She swallowed the hard lump in her throat. Is this how Lottie had felt on her birthday? So what if she liked tennis and sounded her 'ings' at the end of words? She was still from the rows and, if *she* could move between two worlds, you'd think a true friend would try to understand.

It was getting late but the days were still long and she didn't want to go back home so she walked down to the burn for some time to herself. Hell's bells, Danny Dodd was there fishing. She didn't want to talk to him, of all people.

'What brings you here, Rose? You and that dog will frighten the fish off.' Lucky rushed to Danny and pushed his side into him quivering and yelping, waiting for a pat or a treat. Lucky loved Danny. Did he remember who had rescued him or was it the dog biscuits he always seemed to carry?

'We'll get out of your way. Come on Lucky.'

'No, no, it's okay, they'll have darted off by now. Come and chat for a bit, I could do with some company.'

Rose sat down beside Danny. 'How's work going?' she asked.

She knew Danny, glad to narrowly escape the raising of the school leaving age, had been working for a year. To everyone's surprise, he hadn't followed his brother Joe down the pit; he was a delivery boy for Williams, the big bakery in Ashington.

'I love it. I'm out on my bike and in the open air and I visit all the local villages. It's flexible, you know. I can arrange my own rounds and it leaves a bit of time for other interests.

'Like fishing?'

'No, I just come here for a bit of peace and quiet, sometimes. I mean business interests. I dabble… make a bit on the side, Rose.'

'What do you mean?'

He touched his finger to the side of his nose. 'Nothing dishonest but maybe not strictly legal.'

Danny could tap his nose all he liked but it wouldn't be a secret, not in the rows. If it was happening in Linwood, her dad would know.

'Are you still enjoying all your schooling Rose? You must know a hell of a lot by now? Can you speak French?'

'*Mais oui*, Daniel.'

'Eh?' He frowned.

'I'm saying "yes" in French you doylem!' Rose laughed and stood up. 'I have to go now, Danny.'

'Okay, see you around.' He gave her one of his mischievous grins.

'Danny…' She fiddled with Lucky's lead.

'Aye, what is it? Spit it out.'

'You don't think I've got above myself do you?' Her faced flushed pink.

'Above yourself? Speaking French and speaking nicely like

you do is something to be proud of and you never push it in folk's faces or forget your friends so don't worry about that.'

'Lottie doesn't think that. She's dumped me good and proper.'

'Keep your head up and be yourself. If Lottie Simpson canna like you as you are it's her loss, I say. I remember Miss Wakenshaw once telling me, when I had a falling out with Robbie, that you can have friends for a reason, a season or forever so time will show you what Lottie is.'

'Did she? Thanks Danny.' Rose left and felt cheered. Words of wisdom, philosophy from Danny Dodd, well from Miss Wakenshaw. Danny was growing up. They all were.

After leaving Danny, she walked over to Dad's allotment to see if he was still painting. The sky, silver streaked with a warm pink, would turn dark in an hour so Dad would be packing up to go home shortly.

'Hello sweetheart. Have you been to the Hippo with Lottie today?'

'No, Dad. She made an excuse then I saw her with other lasses. She has better fish to fry.'

'What fish is that then, hinny?'

'Betty Johnson and her gang.'

'And she left you to spend the last Saturday of your summer holidays on your own?'

'Yes. Apparently I'm getting "too up mesel".' Rose managed a good impression of Lottie.

'Lottie said that?'

'No, but that's what she thinks. It's ever since I invited her to my tennis afternoon.'

Dad put down his brush. 'Some people manage change better than others and friendships change over time.'

'I know. I've got good friends at school but it's a travel to see them and friendships aren't always forever that's what Danny and I were talking about.'

'Danny?' Her dad was cleaning his brushes with a rag and turps. Rose loved the smell.

'Danny Dodd, I met him by the river and he was trying to cheer me up.'

'He was a right little tyke when he was younger but now he's quite the lad, doing well at the bakers. He's still got a reckless streak though.'

Rose took the clean brush from her father and passed him another to clean. 'What does he do on the side, Dad? He hinted but wouldn't say.'

'It's not much of a secret, pet but it could get him into trouble with the bakers. He's a runner.'

'A runner?' Rose knew it wouldn't be athletics.

'Aye. He's working for the Shepherds as a bookie's runner.'

'I'm not sure what you mean Dad.'

'That's cos we're not a betting family, pet.' He packed up the last of his brushes and added, 'Pull up that cracket and I'll tell you how bookies and their runners work.'

'It's only legal to bet on a horse when you're at the racetrack or if you have a betting account with a bookmaker and bet by phone. Lots of folk fancy a little flutter but canna get to the track and haven't an account so they place a bet with a bookmaker's runner.

The runner takes cash bets, puts them in a special bag with a lock and timer on it so there's no cheating and then takes the bets to the bookie. If a bet wins, he goes and pays the winnings.'

'Runners are breaking the law, then?' Rose asked.

'Some are and some aren't. You *can* place your bet in your own house and it's perfectly legal but placing or taking a bet in a public place, like the back room of the 'tute or the pithead baths is illegal. It's gambling in a public place.'

'Does Danny do that?'

'Not that I know of. Older runners have the Linwood 'tute and the baths. I reckon that Danny takes bets from the houses he delivers to and calls in to a few others in work time too.'

'So Danny's kind of running is legal?'

'Aye, it is but calling here and there when he should be delivering loaves of bread might get him into trouble with Mr Williams. He's running during work time.'

'I see. Maybe he's checked with Mr Williams first. I'd love to go to the races to see those thoroughbred horses.'

'It's not for me. Some people are happy to have a little flutter but I've seen men lose their whole wages.'

'I wouldn't want to bet. I'd go to see the horses and make sure they were well treated.'

'You'll be wanting a horse next.' Her Dad smiled as he added colour to his brush.

'I wish.' Rose got up to go. 'See you later.'

24

The next Saturday, Rose didn't bother calling for Lottie. She finished her homework and read until late afternoon when Mam asked her to go to Norris's across the road for a quarter of boiled ham because she liked theirs better than the Co-op.

It was just after five and the shop was packed. Mrs Norris was rushed off her feet.

'I thought queues for groceries had finished after the war. Haway Mrs Norris I'm ganna be late making Ned's dinner.' Mrs Potter from fourth row loved to moan.

Mrs Norris explained that Mr Norris was at a football match and had promised to be back by five for the pre-closing rush. She was serving as fast as she could and there were still orders to make up in the back.

'Shall I help by getting the goods off the shelf for you?' Rose asked.

'Would you hinny? Thanks a lot.' Mrs Norris flashed her a smile.

Rose stayed until closing at six. After the sign was turned to show closed, she helped make up the orders for Mr Norris to deliver the minute he got in and made Mrs Norris a cup of tea.

A bell signalled the shop door was opening and Mr Norris walked in wearing a black and white magpie's scarf and a guilty expression. 'Sorry I'm late, hinny. I couldn't get out of the town. We won 4-2 against Leeds, mind you. We'll be out of the second division and into the first at this rate. Give me them orders and I'll take them around the rows now.' Mr Norris looked flushed and Rose thought she could smell beer. Maybe he had been waylaid by more than traffic.

'Folks might want this stuff for their tea, Henry! It's not the first time this has happened. If you are going to go regularly to the home games on a Saturday, we need another hand and I say that this lassie here would be ideal.'

Rose hurried home and, as soon as she opened the back door, Mam called out, 'You've been more than an hour getting that ham, did she have to kill the pig?'

'I got a quarter of ham and a Saturday job, Mam. I'm working at Norris's.'

At first, Rose helped out at Norris's corner shop on home match days, every other Saturday. She made up orders, stacked shelves and kept Mrs Norris going with cups of tea. When they found out she was good with figures and could help Mr Norris with the book keeping he hated, she worked every Saturday.

She offered her mam her pay packet every week but Mam didn't want the money so it helped to buy any school materials she needed and paid for a day or two out with her Morpeth chums in the holidays. The best thing about the work was it stopped her feeling lonely at the weekends without Lottie.

On Sundays, she still went to the chapel but Lottie was catholic so they didn't meet up. Now she was thirteen, she had her own little class of pre-schoolers to tell stories to and look after. When you added her increasing load of homework, Lucky and little Terry, who tried to follow her everywhere, into the mix, her weekends were always full and the months flew by.

25

1949

The Easter holidays came around bringing some early sunshine and Rose was full of the joys that a lovely spring day could evoke. There were hyacinths blooming in a pot on their window sill and, outside in the yard, crocuses and daffodils were poking their heads out of an old wooden tub her dad had painted a vibrant green. Spring had arrived bringing a splash of colour to Linwood colliery.

She had arranged to meet Brenda and two other girls for their first game of tennis of the year so they could practice before they played during the summer term at school.

They enjoyed an afternoon of fun and carry on as well as the tennis and, when it was over, Rose took a stroll through Carlisle Park with Brenda. It was a mass of daffodils and shoots were appearing in the flower beds planted with intricate designs. Warmer days were on their way and, by summer, the grounds would be a riot of colour and the paddling pool would be filled for youngsters to splash in.

At the back entrance to the park, by the river, they watched one or two people going out in the boats and waited for Brenda's dad to pick her up in his truck.

When he appeared, Brenda gave her a hug, 'Bye, see you next week for the summer term.'

Rose waved until the truck was out of sight and set off for the bus station.

She stopped to see what films were showing at the Coliseum. Rose visited there with her school friends now instead of going to the Hippo at Ashington. She did miss Lottie but all she got from her these days was an embarrassed nod if they passed.

She had enjoyed *Hamlet* starring Laurence Olivier last year even though half the play had been cut to make it film length. The screen brought the play to life and she hoped it would be the same for *The History of Mr Polly* starring John Mills. It was due to be released soon and she couldn't wait to see if it was as good as the novel.

Disappointed there was no poster advertising it yet, she turned away and caught sight of a woman in a striking green coat. Was it Mrs Fletcher, Douglas's mam? She had a summer coat like that and her mam had often admired it but thought light green wasn't practical around pit dust.

Rose walked past the sweet shop to take a second look and make sure it was definitely Mrs Fletcher, she hadn't seen her in ages. It had been quite a while since Mr Fletcher became under-manager of the Gloria mine and the couple moved, so of course this would be their nearest town. Folk in the rows said Mr Fletcher applied for the transfer to a different colliery because there were too many memories of Douglas at Linwood and nobody could blame him.

The woman wheeled a pushchair and stopped further along the street. It *was* Mrs Fletcher. She'd walk along to say hello to her and her little girl. Word had spread about the Fletcher's having a daughter, Joy, shortly after they moved from Linwood. As she approached, Mrs Fletcher put the brake on the pushchair and popped into the greengrocer's.

There was someone being served before Mrs Fletcher inside the shop so Rose strolled to the front of the pushchair.

She bent down and said, 'Hello there,' and the child turned her head to reward her with a dazzling beam.

Rose took a step back, her fingers trembled as she raised her hand to her mouth. *How? Who?* The same chubby cheeks, the same golden curls, the same sweet smile; Joy Fletcher was the image of their Terence. She could be... she could be his...

Mrs Fletcher came out of the shop and her eyes widened at seeing her. She pulled at the top button of her coat hand and swallowed rapidly. 'Hello, Rose. What are you doing all the way over here on your own?'

'Meeting friends. I'm at school here.' Rose could hear the tremble in her own voice.

'Of course, the scholarship. Well, lovely to see you but we're in a rush today.' She fumbled with the brake, trying to release it, and was about to leave but Rose put a hand on her arm.

'When's her birthday? Your daughter's?'

'It was in March. Now we really have to go.' Mrs Fletcher's knuckles were white as she gripped onto the bar of the pushchair.

Rose still held on to her arm and she felt Mrs Fletcher try to pull away but she had to ask. 'Mrs Fletcher, what date?'

Mrs Fletcher didn't answer, she pulled her arm from Rose's grip, 'I really must go!' She scurried away towards the Clock Tower and the main street.

She didn't need to answer. Mrs Fletcher's ashen face and trembling hands had said enough. What have you done, Mam? Bile rose into her throat and she darted down the side alley by the greengrocer's. She was violently sick.

After she was sick, Rose's heart stopped pounding and she felt less dizzy. She needed to wipe her mouth and felt in her tennis skirt pocket for a handkerchief but couldn't find one. She'd dropped her bag at the entrance to the alleyway, did she have one in there?

The spring sunlight was bright after the darkness of the alley and it took a while to focus on a figure crouching beside her bag.

'That's mine!' She reached down to claim it and came face to face with Frank Maxwell.

'I know it's yours, I read the name tag.' Frank's wide grin slid from his face and no wonder, she must look a real mess. 'I say, Rose, you look a bit green. Are you ill?'

She reached into her bag and avoided his gaze. She couldn't find her blasted hankie.

'Here.' Frank handed her a handkerchief and she gratefully took it and wiped her eyes and mouth.

'Thanks Frank. I dashed into the alley to… because I wasn't well.'

'I can see that. Come on, let's get you a glass of water or a cup of tea.' He picked up her long hockey bag that had to double as her tennis bag, took her elbow and walked her in the direction of the Clock Tower Tea Room. Rose didn't object, she couldn't think straight .

Once seated, a sip of water helped Rose's brain to clear. 'Thank you, Frank. I must return your handkerchief. This is the second one I've borrowed.'

'Ah yes, the gashed knee.'

'Your other one's been laundered and at home all this time but I wasn't sure when to give it back to you.'

'I'm not counting a couple of handkerchiefs, Rose.'

A cup of tea and a lemonade arrived. Rose had been icy cold but now she flushed. 'Oh crikey, Frank. I don't have any spare money, just my bus fare home.'

'I ordered so I pay, don't worry, Rose.'

She sipped her tea and still felt light-headed. It was as if she was here in body but not in mind. Her mind had frozen. She couldn't go over what happened with Mrs Fletcher and she couldn't make small talk. Frank chatted away about helping his father at the vet's practice over the holidays.

Rose excused herself to go to the ladies' and washed her face and re-plaited her hair. She looked a bit better but couldn't look into her own eyes, she didn't want to see what was inside her head. If she thought about... the events... she'd go to pieces.

When she returned, Frank had already paid the bill. 'I'm meeting Dad in a moment and I'll ask him to give you a lift home. You can't get a bus after being sick. It's my guess you've overdone the tennis today and become dehydrated.'

Rose was happy to let him think that but there was no way she would accept a lift home. 'I'm much better now, Frank, and you're very kind but I'm perfectly okay to get the bus and I would be embarrassed if you told your father I was sick in the street.'

'If you're determined, at least let me walk you to the bus.' He opened the door, carried her bag and walked her to the station chatting easily about his plans for the rest of the holidays.

At last the bus pulled in and Rose could sink into her seat. She looked out of the window and tentatively raked through the scorching memories of the afternoon, coming face to face with Terence's double and Mrs Fletcher's panic-stricken eyes. She tried to come up with a more logical answer but Mrs Fletcher's fierce possession of the pushchair told her she was right, her own gut told her she was right and she couldn't get little Joy's beaming face out of her mind.

Why had her mam done such a thing? How could she? She needed to know.

26

Stanley was starving and mithering Mam for a slice of bread, Terry was hanging onto her mam's legs and asking for one too and Lucky was bouncing around begging for a walk. Nothing had changed but everything was different. It was as if there was an invisible wall between her and the familiar scene.

'Rose, pet, can you take the bairn and Lucky for a walk and get them out from under my feet so I can finish this shepherd's pie before your dad walks in.' Mam looked flushed with cooking but as happy as always. How *could* she be?

Grabbing the lead and heaving a protesting Terence into his pushchair, she left the house. When would she have a chance to talk this over with Mam? Certainly not tonight when Dad was about.

Rose left her dinner, went to bed early then tossed and turned all night. She raked through her memory of the lead up to Terence's birth three years ago. Mam talking about twins in the kitchen with Mary-from-next-door. For the life of her, she couldn't recall that exact conversation. Mam had been annoyed that she'd overheard her talking about twins. She said something about Mrs Fletcher miscarrying and then it being twins with one still growing, possible but how likely was it that her daughter was so like Terence?

What remained clear in her memory was that shadowy figure at Mary's door, on the night Mam went into labour. Who was it? Why had Mary led her to believe she was mistaken? She decided that Mary was in on the deception. She drifted into a fitful sleep of crying babies and shadowy figures and woke with a start thinking she was back in the isolation hospital. Her bedclothes were drenched with sweat and she shivered.

The encounter with Mrs Fletcher and Joy was on her mind all of the time but she couldn't bring herself to mention anything to her mam. She was sure her dad had no knowledge of what had gone on and, as the days passed, the very idea seemed unbelievable, even to her. Could her mam give up a baby? Had she been mistaken? Could two bairns look so alike and be unrelated? Maybe she should take another look?

It was as if her mind refused to believe what she had seen and she battled with her own certainty and then her doubts, Rose could hardly eat or sleep or look at her mam.

'What's the matter, hinny? There's something troubling you. Is it school?' Dad asked her one evening.

Rose shook her head and tried to force some stew past the hard lump of despair that wouldn't dissolve. She couldn't meet her dad's open and trusting eyes and she hated her mam for making her feel like this.

Rose told Mam she would be late after school because she was playing tennis with her friends. It was the first deliberate lie she could remember telling her. She had to see little Joy again and she hoped and prayed to God that she'd been mistaken last month.

After school, she took the bus to the Gloria colliery. It was a pit with colliery housing surrounded by countryside, as small as Linwood, six miles out of Morpeth. She entered a small shop beside the bus stop to ask directions to the under-manager's house.

'Straight ahead just to the left of the pit baths. There's two management houses here. The Smiths, he's the manager, have the one with the nice lawn and flowers and the Fletcher's, he's under-manager, have the one with the slide and swing in the garden.' The young girl sold her a bar of chocolate but was more interested in her own reflection in the mirror behind the shelving than in Rose so she made a swift exit.

Both houses had walled gardens but there was a slope at the back of them and Rose found a spot where she could see into the gardens and remain hidden by shrubbery. She sat on the scratchy grass, hugged her knees up to her chest and waited. Joy had a lovely garden to play in. A swing, a sand pit, a slide and what looked like a play house painted white and yellow.

After an hour, Rose's legs were cramping and nothing had happened. The low sun in the sky told her it must be well after five and she would have to catch a bus soon. She stood to stretch her legs and then darted back down as the back door of the Fletcher's opened.

Out ran Joy tugging on Mr Fletcher's hand. He lifted her onto the swing and she squealed with excitement as he pushed the swing higher and higher. Rose wasn't close enough to see Joy's face so she crept slowly to the stone wall then edged her way to the gate to peer through the wooden slats.

The little girl was now playing catch with her daddy. Rose was mesmerised. She had the same curls and light-footed run as Terry but maybe she had overblown the whole thing. This little girl belonged to the Fletcher's.

Before she turned to leave, the ball came rolling right to-wards the gate. Rose drew in a breath and remained frozen to the spot as Joy ran to pick up her ball. 'Got it! Got it, Daddy.' Joy's voice, her green eyes, the dimple in her cheek, the little gap between her front teeth were Terry Kelly to a T.

Rose had almost willed herself out of believing it but she couldn't. She leant her back against the wall and closed her eyes, rubbing them as if she could erase the truth. She had a sister who had been given away. She had a mother who had done it. She knew a secret that she didn't want to know. What could she do?

27

'You're late our Rose. I've put your tea in the oven. A nice corned beef pie and mushy peas.' Mam wiped her wet hands on her pinny and stepped towards Rose.

Rose avoided her hug and dropped her school bag at the foot of the stairs. 'I'm not hungry. I'm going to take a glass of milk upstairs and do my homework, if that's okay.'

'No Rose, it's not. I'm having none of that. You'll eat something and have a hot cup of tea before you disappear up those stairs.'

Rose sat at the table and picked at the pie that Mam placed in front of her.

'What's the matter, hinny?' Mam sat opposite her, her brown eyes clouded with concern. 'Your dad and me, we're worried sick.'

Dad was at work until morning, Stanley was allowed to play out until half seven now the nights were lighter and Mam had just taken Terry up to his cot. It was now or never.

'I met Mrs Fletcher and her little girl, Mam. They were shopping in Morpeth.'

Mam's smile didn't reach her eyes. 'Oh did you now. When was that?' Her voice seemed over bright.

'In the Easter holidays, when I played tennis with Brenda.'

A guarded look came over Mam. 'You're a long time saying.'

'I *couldn't* because I didn't know what to flaming well say!'

Anger bubbled through Rose's veins making her feel hot and impatient to get to the truth.

Mam stood up and moved in front of the fire. She rested her hands on the mantlepiece. Was she dreading what would come next?

Rose made herself carry on. 'The little girl in the pushchair, Mam, she was the double of our Terry.'

Mam stared into the fire with her back to her, 'Well they're the same age. Bairns do look alike at that stage, pet.'

'No, Mam, the absolute spit of him like a *twin*... his sister.'

'Nonsense. Don't you go saying stuff like that our Rose. How could that be?'

'Oh, Mam if you're just going to stand there and blatantly lie then I don't want to talk about it.'

'Rose... it's that imagination of yours.' Mam turned and smoothed down her pinny but she didn't meet Rose's eyes.

Rose moved away from the table and faced her mam. 'That's what I thought until I went today, after school, for a second look. Now I'm sure I didn't imagine you talking about twins to Mary-from-next-door, I didn't imagine the man who visited you and Mary when you were in labour and I didn't imagine the look of panic on Mrs Fletcher's face when I met Joy. Today, I didn't imagine it, I *saw* Terry's twin with my own eyes.'

Her mother slumped in the chair by the fire and rubbed her arms as if she was cold. 'Did you go pestering Dorothy and that bairn, today?'

'Nobody saw me but I saw her... Joy.' Rose bit hard on her lip to stop the tears. All her mam was concerned about was upsetting Mrs Fletcher. Hell's bells! A rage built up ready to spill over and she tasted blood from her biting.

'Mam. I didn't think you'd lie to me. You must've lied to Dad too. How *could* you?'

Her mam looked up, her eyes as dark as coals and glassy with unshed tears. 'I could because I had to and it's for the best. How was I to know the twins would look alike? Stanley and David weren't alike and they were both lads. Seeing as you know part of the story, I'll tell you the lot but it goes no further than us. If you ever tell your dad, it'll destroy us, this whole family. Swear you won't?'

Rose swallowed hard. She had a choice. She could spill the beans to her dad and have a clear conscience but it would tear her family apart or she could keep Mam's secret. She wouldn't hurt her dad for the world. 'I won't tell a soul.'

'Your dad and I, we agreed to have our family early. We were happy to have you and the twins were a blessing. We had our hands full and didn't expect another to come along. Well, you know the ins and outs of expecting from that book of yours so I don't need to explain that some babies come as a surprise.' Mam tossed her head and laughed. 'One is a surprise and the idea of two at my age is a flaming shock.'

Looking into the flames licking up the chimney, Mam seemed to be in her own world. After a moment, she carried on. 'The midwife suspected twins so that's why I didn't go back to the clinic and I opted to have the baby at home. They're overrun and don't check missed appointments if you've had a couple of bairns. I met Dorothy Fletcher, who had just miscarried and was desperate for another... losing Douglas that way. We came up with a solution that suited us both.

When I went into labour, Mary held off calling the midwife; she rushed to the phone box and called Mrs Fletcher's private doctor, one she'd found in Jesmond. He helped deliver the twins and took one of them back to his clinic where Dorothy was already waiting. She paid a lot of money to the clinic and the birth was registered as hers. Nobody was meant to be any the wiser except for the four who were involved.'

'Not Dad? Not Mr Fletcher? Not me, the baby's sister?' Rose couldn't help butting in.

'No! It's women's business and I'm sorry if you've caused Dorothy any more upset. She's had a tough enough time, bless her.'

'What you've done must be illegal and it's taken a sister away from our family. I just don't understand your reasoning, Mam.' Rose's voice was getting louder and she gripped the arms of the chair to stop herself from getting up and shaking some sense into her mam. Anger and frustration exploded into tears.

'Happen you don't understand but let's be clear about this. Joy is Dorothy Fletcher's child and *not* your sister. Upbringing makes her a Fletcher not a Kelly.'

'Why her? Why her and not Terence? Did you choose the boy to replace David?'

'No I didn't do that, pet. I gave Mrs Fletcher the choice and she said she'd like a girl if I had one.'

'We could have made room for one more, Mam.' Rose blew her nose, she felt her anger draining away with the crying.

'That's not the reason I gave the little girl up, Rose. I gave her up because bringing up one child is hard work and trying to raise two would make the load too heavy for you.'

Had she heard right? '*Me*? Where do I come into this?'

Stanley opened the back door. 'Mam I'm starving can I have some bread and dripping before bed?'

Mam got up. 'I'll talk to you about my reasons after Stanley's in bed. I'm not the monster you think I am.'

After discovering a sister who had been adopted, Rose thought nothing could surprise her but her talk with Mam later on that night had left her deeper in shock. The conversation played in her head before she slept, it invaded her dreams and it was there like a heavy weight next morning. Rose wished she could turn the clock back to the spring day she played tennis in Carlisle Park. If only she'd hopped on the bus and come home without ever seeing Mrs Fletcher's bright green coat. Other people's secrets were a heavy burden to carry.

Once Stanley was asleep, Mam explained about her grandmother on her mother's side dying young of 'women's troubles' and how her own mother had become ill when Ginnie was eight. She had been diagnosed with cancer in her breast and had been determined to bring up Ginnie and her brothers and sisters so had undergone a radical treatment. Ginnie could remember her mam coming home after the removal of her breast and chest muscles and being unable to use her right arm.

'Mam didn't mind the pain or the loss of the use of her arm because she told us she'd be able to see us all grow up and marry. She didn't though, she went through all of that suffering and died the next year. My dad was sure that cancers grew once the air got to them and swore that she should never have been cut open. He said it shortened her life when she thought it would save her. I've had a fear of doctors and dentists interfering with me ever since. I could never have an operation.'

Then Mam had come to the worst part. They had lost Auntie Elsie to cancer of the breast when Rose was a little'un and Mam was expecting again. Mam had decided that she would finish her family after the boys arrived because she didn't want to leave young ones or give Rose the job of raising children and staying at home. Auntie Elsie had raised Mam and her brothers and had no life of her own.

'I was always checking and waiting to go the same way and, just before I found out I was expecting, I felt a little lump, our Rose.' Mam smiled and squeezed Rose's hand. 'I didn't need a doctor to tell me it was the disease that had plagued my granny, my mam and my sister. It must be a flaming family curse. I knew I wouldn't have a surgeon cut it out and let the air get to it like it did with my mam so there was no point in spending good money on a consultation.'

'Mam! Treatments change. We have the National Health Service now. Does Dad know?'

'Not yet, just Mary-from-next-door and Dorothy Fletcher... now you. You see, I was worried that I'd be too ill to manage and you would have to leave your schooling to nurse me and two babies.'

Rose's eyes filled with yet more tears. 'Mam you know I would! I love you Mam and would do anything for you.' She flung her arms around her mam.

Mam rocked her saying, 'One baby to a loving home desperate for a child just lessens the burden. I'm feeling fine and the lump is slow-growing. My prayers to stay around a bit longer are answered so God mustn't think I've done a bad thing.'

'Please see a doctor, Mam. You might be worrying over nothing.'

'I know my body, pet. I'll show the doctor sometime but I'm not being cut open. I just want to see you get your exams, Stanley start work and Terry start school. That's my prayer every night.'

The embers of the fire glowed red, Mam stroked her hair as she rested her head on her mother's knee and Rose forgave her. She silently said a prayer for Mam's health and said a goodbye to her sister.

'Mam, you should write to Mrs Fletcher and tell her not to worry about bumping in to me. I won't bother her or Joy again.'

'Maybe you can write it for me with your nice handwriting and good spelling and I'll sign it, our Rose. You can put it in the post tomorrow and stop Dorothy from fretting.'

Rose called at the post office after school and posted Mrs Fletcher's letter and she bought her mam a bar of her favourite Fry's dark chocolate with five centres. The burden of their secrets felt no lighter today but the choice to keep Joy a secret had been made. Maybe it would become lighter in time.

Maybe Joy's face would fade from her memory and maybe her mam would stay healthy for years. Maybe.

28

During the summer term, Rose walked to the furthest bus stop in Morpeth, just opposite the Sun Inn, with Frank Maxwell most days after school. It started when she waited for him by the Clock Tower to return both of his handkerchiefs.

'Frank!' she'd called then blushed so even the roots of her hair must have turned auburn when his friends laughed and nudged at him.

'You've got an admirer, Maxie. Nice looking too!'

Frank just shrugged his shoulders and strolled over to her with a welcoming smile. 'Don't let them embarrass you. They're just jealous.' The remark was loud enough for the lads to hear and they moved on still laughing and making comments to one another.

'I wanted to return these.' She held out two beautifully laundered and ironed handkerchiefs. One embroidered with a blue F and one with a maroon F.

Frank took them, paused and stuffed them into her blazer pocket. 'You keep them… for emergencies. I just hope you don't require a third.' He took her satchel and slung it over his shoulder along with his own. 'Shall we walk through the park and go to the last Morpeth stop? I like to do that when it's a warm day.'

'What about your friends?' Rose didn't want them to see Frank carrying her bag.

'They're long gone. It'll stop them ribbing us when we get to the bus station.'

That did it. 'Okay, we'll walk through the park.'

After that, Brenda left her at the Clock Tower and Rose and Frank met up most afternoons. He even waited there when she had library club and left school an hour later. 'I get my maths homework out of the way in the library and then walk along,' he explained.

They talked about school, home and their friends. Being with Frank was easy. Rose learnt a lot about his family. His mother was always ailing with something but liked to gad about. London was her favourite place to be. His father worked long hours because he loved it and it kept him out of his mother's way.

He thought his father and Vera, his receptionist, had a soft spot for one another and he was fond of Vera because she'd had more time for him than his mother when he was a young lad. 'Sometimes, I wish Dad had met her first. She'd be a great mum. Is that a strange thing to think, Rose?'

'It's just a thought, Frank. Maybe, your dad thinks the same. He wouldn't ever act on it though, would he?' She'd seen *Brief Encounter* and knew about unrequited love from some of the novels she'd read.

'Oh no, Dad and Vera are both too nice to split up the family.'

She discovered that his sister, Ruth Maxwell, who had made her first term a misery, had partied too hard at uni in Durham and had to repeat a year. Rose didn't tell Frank about her mean ways, after all she was his sister, but Frank admitted that he didn't understand Ruth at all.

'She doesn't like animals, can you imagine? She's always fussing in front of a mirror and wears too much stuff on her face and, every time she's home, we get tears and tantrums about absolutely nothing. She's hard work.' Frank shook his head then smiled, 'I think she'd be prettier if she just washed the stuff off her face and didn't eat so many chocolates but I'd be hung, drawn and quartered for suggesting it.'

Frank knew all about her dad and his painting and how Stanley wanted to work with the horses down the pit as soon as he left school and how bright and funny little Terence was. She didn't mention her mam and the rest. What could she say? My mother might be ill but she's ignoring it. I have a secret sister. No, she hated carrying Mam's secrets but she couldn't share them with anyone.

It was the end of term and Rose knew Frank loved going to the countryside and staying with his grandparents for the summer. 'Rose, would it be okay if I wrote to you? I'll miss our chats.'

Rose looked down at her shoes and shrugged. 'S'pose so.'

Frank frowned and tilted Rose's chin up. 'I can tell you don't want me to. Sorry I asked. It's only six weeks or so, anyway.'

Her bus was coming. 'It's not that I don't want you to. It's just I'd be embarrassed getting letters from a boy. We don't get that many letters and my family are nosey.'

'I'll sign off Frances, then.' His grin warmed her heart.

She jumped on the bus and thought, why not? 'Linwood… One, First Row!' she called out to Frank.

'Frances' wrote regularly and Rose enjoyed the summer of '49. She had a week on Brenda's farm and, for her fifteenth birthday, she got her long plaits cut to shoulder length at a proper hairdressers in Morpeth and a pair of shoes with a bit of a heel for weekends.

'You're as smart as a carrot in that dress and your new shoes. Your new hairstyle makes you look like quite the young lady.' Mam's smile lifted the tiredness around her eyes. She stood in the back yard and watched Rose set off to the chapel.

Terry wasn't quite mature enough to sit through the whole of Sunday school and would start when he was four. Stanley escaped whenever he could and didn't go very often.

Rose smiled, as she set off with a spring in her step, and tried to keep her best shoes out of the dirt. 'Smart as a carrot' was Mam's highest praise and usually reserved for Princess Elizabeth but not Margaret. Rose couldn't understand the simile but she knew the sentiment behind it and it lifted her heart.

She stayed behind to chat to Miss Wakenshaw who was getting married to a minister from the chapel in Gosforth later in the year.

'The service will be here in Linwood so all my class can take part and I'd like you to be a bridesmaid, Rose.'

'Thank you! I'd love to.' She'd never been a bridesmaid before. Her head was full of bouquets and long dresses when she bumped into Danny Dodd who was sitting on a wall outside of the 'tute.

He wolf whistled. 'You look a real bobby dazzler today Rose Kelly.'

Rose tried to hold her head up and move on like she'd seen other girls do but she couldn't resist stopping to say hello. 'What are you doing loitering outside the 'tute?' she asked.

'Hoping I'd see you. These are for your birthday... Rose's chocolates for Rose of the rows.' He handed her a wrapped box of chocolates.

Rose's mouth dropped open and she wasn't sure what to say as she took his gift. 'You shouldn't have, Danny. How many coupons...? But thanks.'

'I'll walk you home, shall I?' His blue eyes didn't look as cocky as usual.

She took a breath and recovered enough to resume their usual banter. 'I know my own way home from chapel, Danny. But I can't stop you walking along with me.'

Danny walked in step with her, broadly built but not tall like Frank. 'You're nearly as tall as me in those shoes, Rose.'

'That's because all those cigarettes you smoke have stunted your growth, Danny.'

'I do like a tab, maybe you're right.'

Rose reached her gate. 'Smoking's not good for you or your pocket.'

Danny winked, 'I'd better cut down then, eh Rose?'

'Don't cut down, give them up.' Rose smiled at having the last word and turned into her back yard.

29

Their kitchen was full of smoke; the potato pan had caught and Dad was trying to lift it off the range. Rose slipped off her heeled shoes, grabbed a tea towel and went to help asking, 'Where's Mam? Did she forget she had these on?'

'This is my fault, hinny. Your mam isn't well, she's having a lie down, and you were at chapel so I thought I'd make myself useful.'

'What's wrong with her?' Rose carried the pan to the sink in the scullery and tried to rescue the potatoes that weren't stuck to the pan.

'She's been coughing all night but, this morning, it was still troubling her and she's worn out. I've told her she'll have to see the doctor if she's nay better the morrow.'

'Where's Terry?'

'Stanley's taken him to catch tiddlers in the burn but they'll be back soon for their dinner and look what I've done... ruined it.'

'Sit down, Dad. I've saved most of these and I'll put some Yorkshire puddings in the oven with the meat and then we'll be ready for them.'

In spite of her mam's efforts to get her interested, Rose was still no cook. Her Yorkshires were more like pancakes and her gravy was on the watery side but they all managed to clear their plates.

'I didn't know Mam's dinners were so nice until I had yours, Rose.' Stanley's solemn face told her he wasn't trying to be funny. 'What's for afters?'

Afters? Mam usually put a rice pudding in the oven or made a fruit pudding or tart but she hadn't given it a thought. 'It's bread and jam today, for a change.'

'Well you canna spoil that can you?' He sat back and folded his arms.

'While I'm making it, you can stack all of these plates and cutlery in the sink.'

'Eh? That's women's work, our Rose.'

'It's 1949 Stanley, and there is no such thing as women's and men's work.'

'But…' Stanley started to object but must have thought better of it because he began clearing the table.

Mam got up later and assured Dad she felt better but she had a grey look and a hacking cough.

'You're still going to the surgery in the morning, Ginnie.' Dad didn't often put his foot down.

'I will, pet,' Mam sat by the fire even though it was a warm afternoon. The fire in the range was always kept alight for cooking and baking.

Mam usually baked a cake and a fruit tart depending on how their ration coupons were going. At the very least, she made scones on the griddle on Sundays but today they had toast and jam. Rose decided she would take more interest when her mam tried to show her how to cook. She definitely needed to watch her making Yorkshire puddings and gravy.

Rose waved Mam off as she set off for the doctors the next morning. She had instructions to make a start on the Monday wash with Mary-from-next-door and keep an eye on Terry. It was flaming hard work! Clothes to sort, linen to boil, the mangle to squeeze the water out of the washed clothes, rinsing the clothes and pegging out. All that with Lucky around her heels and Terry to keep amused had her exhausted.

Mam still wasn't back. Mary said nothing but Rose knew that she was concerned too. 'Your mam usually makes a pie with the leftover meat and a few potatoes on a Monday, hinny. I think we'll have to get cracking or your dad will be home to no dinner.'

A miner coming home to no dinner... that just didn't happen in the rows. How the hell did Mam make her pastry? She didn't use recipe books. 'I can't make a pie, Mary. Maybe a meat and potato stew? Mam should have been back ages ago.'

'Where's my mammy? I's hungreee!' Terry cried.

The dog whined at the door because he hadn't been walked and Rose burst into tears. 'I don't know where to start. There is still a dark wash to do.'

'I'll make the pie and give Terry a slice of bread and dripping. You walk the dog and pick some fresh greens from your dad's allotment and we'll be all finished by teatime.'

Thanks to Mary-from-next-door, they were. They had just pegged the last line of washing out when Mam walked in.

'Where've you been all day, lass? Sit down and I'll pour you a fresh cup of tea that we've just brewed.' Mary bustled about in the scullery while Rose took her mam's new summer mac to hang up.

'You've been busy here, pet. We'll make a little housewife of you yet. I had visions of a mountain of washing, no fire on and no dinner made.' Mam smiled as Rose handed her a cup of tea.

Rose could think of nothing worse than being a little housewife but she enjoyed the praise from her mam. Kneeling on the floor beside Mam's chair, she waited for her to explain where she'd been.

'Dr Bob sent me straight to the hospital for tests and an X-ray. I've been poked and prodded all day and I'm glad to be home. This tea is the best I've had all day.'

'What did they say, Mam?' Rose could hear her own heart pumping. She wanted to know but she dreaded it. It had been so long since her mam first told her she wasn't well and she'd pushed the knowledge right to the back of her mind along with her little sister. Both reared up in the dark of night sometimes but she stuffed her thoughts away in the morning.

'Nothing I didn't expect. I'm going the same way as the other women in the family. The cancer. It's travelled to my lungs and maybe elsewhere. I won't make old bones, pet.' Mam seemed so calm. No tears. Was she in shock or had she lived with the fear for so long that she really wasn't surprised.

Rose took her cue from her mam. 'We've prayed for ages now and it's worked. You're going nowhere until Stanley is at work and Terence has started school.'

Mary-from-next-door cleared the cups and bustled about with the pie and the washing and Rose sat at her mam's feet with her head on her lap. 'I'll tell your dad tonight when you're all in bed, hinny. He wouldn't want you to see him upset.'

Mam got up as usual next day. It was the last week of the summer holidays but, instead of having her head in a novel, Rose started a housekeeping notebook. 'I'm making notes on everything you do, Mam. Just in case you're too poorly and I have to make a pie or sew a button on or something.'

'Oh lass, I'm so glad to hear that. It's not in case, it's when, and I've been trying to show you for months but you didn't take the hint.' Mam took her through her dozens of daily tasks step-by-step.

The notebook was almost full and she had started a recipe book by the time the new term started. Mam's recipes didn't use scales because she hadn't any. It was handfuls, sprinkles, half bags of flour or table and teaspoons. She laughed at Rose's titles as she read them back. 'Ginnie's gingerbread, the loudest singin' hinnies in the row, gravy fit for a pitman's plate and stand-your-spoon-up-in-it soup were all recorded.

Rose asked Dad to add little sketches and the book was littered with pencil drawings of Mam making her food. 'I never thought I'd see a recipe book in this house but it's grand to see it all written down, Rose. Now we have to add a clootie fruit dumpling this week.

A dumpling boiled in a cloth with seasonal berries in the middle was a family favourite. It magically appeared and was eaten with custard but Rose discovered there was skill involved in the making of it. There were so many things to learn about making a house in the rows into a home. Her mam was a conjuror who could make a meal out of very little and she was her cack-handed apprentice.

30

Rose worked hard at school and at home. She gave up after-school clubs but still spent a half hour with Frank. She had told him about her mother's illness and it was the part of the day that kept her sane because she could talk about Mam and her fears for the family.

'How long do you think someone can continue with secondary cancer, Frank? The books in the library are vague but they do say there is no cure.' It was a chilly November day and Rose could see her breath as she talked.

'I only know from animals and you can't predict. Some cancers are slow and others race along. Your mam's idea of operations speeding up cancer isn't right, I asked Dad, but after what seems like a successful operation it can come back. It's a terrible disease, Rose.' Sometimes they linked arms and sometimes Frank held her hand. He squeezed her hand and said, 'So the answer is, I don't know.'

'It's not contagious but it can be hereditary. I suppose I've got those genes too.'

Frank pulled her to him and put his arm around her. 'God, I hope not. Don't talk that way, Rose.'

She got on the bus to go home and waved at Frank. He was a good friend. Was he a boyfriend? They held hands but they hadn't hugged until today. She liked him… a lot.

As she replayed their conversation, a cold fear seeped

through Rose. Why hadn't she thought of it before? She wasn't Mam's only daughter, what about Joy? Joy was unaware of what her birth mother might have passed on.

As Christmas approached, Rose and her mam became caught up in the excitement of Miss Wakenshaw's wedding. Rose was to be a Christmas Eve bridesmaid and Mam seemed more excited than her. At last the day arrived and their little chapel, decorated with holly and Christmas roses was packed with well-wishers. There was a crowd standing outside to see Miss Wakenshaw and her groom arrive.

Miss Wakenshaw looked beautiful in a simple long white gown and veil and her sister and Rose carried her train. They both wore long midnight blue dresses that could be worn to parties afterwards and carried fur-trimmed muffs instead of bouquets. A Christmas rose pinned in their hair was the only other adornment.

Dad and Mary-from-next-door helped Mam, who hadn't been out in weeks, to the chapel. She had her powder blue coat and felt hat on, although the coat hung loosely on her now. Rose remembered that happy day when she had worn the same outfit and it had just been her and her mam at the Morpeth interview. How young her mam had looked then. Four and a half years later, she looked older and tired but, today, her smile had made it right to her eyes, how they shone as Rose walked down the aisle.

After the photos outside the chapel, Mam whispered, 'You looked like the smartest carrot, our Rose. I could just imagine the day when you walk down that same aisle in your wedding dress.' Her eyes were glassy.

Rose's chin trembled as she gripped both of Mam's hands. 'Don't cry, or I will too.'

'They are happy tears, hinny. I'm happy just to be here to see this Christmas and come to chapel.'

Mam sat by the range and gave a few instructions but it was Rose, with her recipe book to hand, who made the Christmas dinner. 'You're getting better, our Rose, but it's still not exactly like Mam's,' Stanley said as he sat back looking stuffed.

'You didn't leave any,' Dad said. 'I thought it was a triumph, hinny.' He winked at her and Rose felt that was praise enough.

'Mam, you haven't eaten much. Is that all you're having?'

'It was the best Christmas dinner I've had because I didn't have to make it. Thank you, pet.'

On Boxing Day, Rose found Dad sobbing in his shed. She'd popped over for some carrots and a leek to make soup with the chicken carcass. 'I canna imagine a world without her. What'll we do?' All Rose could do was hug him. She couldn't imagine home without Mam either.

Two days later, she was gone.

Ginnie Kelly left them in the middle of the night while John was down the pit and her bairns were sleeping.

John took her a cup of tea up while Rose made his breakfast and, when he didn't come down, Rose went upstairs quietly so she didn't wake Stanley or Terry. She found him on his knees weeping and Mam was still... too still.

Rose froze. Mam wouldn't see Terry start school or Stanley start work. A flare of anger coursed through Rose's body. She was at war with God again. Why couldn't he have let her mam have just a few more months?

It was Stanley who gave her some comfort. 'She's with David. I know she is and I'll miss Mam but it's David's turn to have her. Remember what you said to me about David? They are only in the next room. I still talk to David all the time, Rose. I talk to him more than I pray.'

There was no way she could stay on until the end of the year to take her school certificate exams. Mary-from-next-door had offered to look after Terry during the week but she was in her seventies and it wasn't fair on her or Terry. He missed Mam so much. They all did but, for Terry, the idea of never seeing his mammy again had him wailing and wetting the bed every night.

Then there was the washing, cooking and cleaning to do and she couldn't fit that around a full school day and homework. She wanted to stay so much but she would *have* to leave. The school leaving age was fifteen now and she had celebrated her fifteenth birthday in August so she could leave at any time. She hadn't discussed it with Dad. He was in a daze of grief and, after his shift, he disappeared to his shed, even though it was freezing during the winter months. 'I need to paint and be by myself, hinny.'

31

1950

Big Ben chimed in the New Year then Rose stood up and turned off the radio. She was on her own; Dad and the boys had already gone to bed. A new decade to face, one without Mam. They were burying her tomorrow beside David. Was she really reunited with her little brother? Rose wished she had a stronger belief. She shivered even though the fire was still glowing in the grate. Her resolution for the year was to look after Dad and her brothers just like her mam had done. She could never take Mam's place but she'd try anyway.

The funeral passed in a blur of tears and traditions. Two days afterwards, Rose walked to the phone box. She pulled her coat around her and shivered as she entered the chilly kiosk that smelled of damp paper and cigarette smoke. She told the school secretary about her mother's death and asked for an appointment with her form teacher to discuss her education. 'I think the headmistress will want to see you. Can you come in at ten on Monday morning?'

'That'll be fine.'

'I'm so sorry for your loss, Rose.' The secretary, usually fierce, either had a heavy cold or she was upset by Rose's news.

While she was at the phone box, she phoned Frank. She

got Vera, Mr. Maxwell's receptionist, who told her that Frank was out for the day with the family.

'Can you tell Frank I won't be back at school this term because there has been a death in my family?'

'Oh Rose, I'm so sorry.' People were very kind but all the kindness in the world wasn't going to bring her mam back. Tears that had been held back for so long flowed as she put the phone back on its cradle. She stayed in the box for a while until there was a knocking on the door. Flaming hell, Lottie of all people.

'Sorry, it's all yours.' Rose forced a smile and slipped out of the box.

Lottie caught her and hugged her. 'I don't need the phone. I saw you in there for ages and realised you were upset. I'm so, so sorry, Rose. Sorry about your mam and about everything.'

Rose relaxed into Lottie's embrace. 'I've missed you.'

'I've missed you too. I was an idiot. I should've been around before now. Rose, let's go for a walk.'

'I don't have time, Lottie. I have Terry to pick up from Mary's and a dinner to prepare.'

'Oh… I see. Okay.' Lottie's crestfallen face pulled at Rose's heart.

'You can come around for a cuppa and watch me make corned beef hash, though.' Lottie linked her arm and they headed for First Row.

Some friendships wax and wane but they don't break completely. Rose was glad to have Lottie back.

'I can't stress enough that this is a disastrous choice for your future, Rose.' The headmistress had given her condolences and then her face had dropped in horror when Rose explained that she would be leaving. 'You have less than two terms until you take your school certificate and we expect you to get distinctions in every subject. You wanted to do your highers after that.'

'There is nobody else to look after my father and two brothers, Miss. I need to be at home for them.' Rose studied her hands on her lap, she'd bitten her nail right down in the past week.

'Can't they help you out and look after themselves just a little? This is your life you're throwing away, Rose. Your chance for a bright future.'

How could she explain to someone who didn't understand her world? 'My little brother hasn't started school yet and he's missing his mother. My father works long hours and has the right to a clean house and a hot meal when he comes home and Stanley won't leave school until next year.'

'You have had such a successful time here, Rose. I was certain you would stay on for your higher certificate and go to a good university. Isn't that what you want?'

Rose lifted her eyes to meet the headmistress's piercing stare. 'I would love to stay on and go to university, of course I would… but not at the expense of my family, their happiness. If I stayed on, the boys would be left to God and good neighbours and I would hang my head in shame. My mind is set. I *want* to stay on at school but I *need* to stay at home. I couldn't live with the consequences.'

'I hope you can live with the consequences of what you're doing, Rose. I wish you luck.' The headmistress rang her bell and the receptionist opened the door. She was dismissed.

Rose walked over to Bon Accord, the old house was part of the school and it was where she had taken art lessons up in the rafters. Dad had braved coming along several times to talk about painting to the higher certificate pupils. She'd taken French lessons on the floor below. She passed the beautiful oak room in the main building, she'd learnt about music there, and walked through the gardens to leave by the back gate. She found herself going uphill along Cottingwood Lane. She reached the boys' school gates. This was where she'd cut her leg – she still had a crescent-shaped scar – and met Frank.

She would miss all this but her decision was final. This wasn't the hardest choice she'd had to make. Nothing compared to keeping quiet about her little sister. Her heart was telling her she was right to do this but she was sore with sadness at so many things. No school, no David, no Mam and this might be the end of her friendship with Frank.

That weekend, Dad came in from a day at the allotment with a portrait. 'Ginnie didn't like too many paintings up but I want her in here, in the kitchen, with us. Is that alright with you, hinny?'

Rose looked at the portrait of her mam. Dad had used pastels to capture her with her head back laughing in that way of hers. 'You've caught her perfectly, Dad.'

'Aye, well I've looked at her often enough. It's the best I can do but it's still not as bonny as my Ginnie.'

'We'll put it on the wall over here. I think it'll be good for the boys to see her laughing again, Dad.'

'We need to talk about your school as well our Rose. It's time you were back, pet. You have exams at the end of the year.'

Rose stiffened. This wasn't going to be easy. 'I'm not going back Dad so don't mention it again. I want to look after the lads and you. Little Terry needs me here.'

Her dad stood up his fists clenched in anger. 'You will not leave that school, Rose Kelly. You had no right to do anything without asking me. Your mam would turn in her grave to think that you'd leave without your certificate.'

'No Dad. Mam always said I was educated enough and she'd want me to watch out for Terry.'

'She told me different. She was proud to have a lassie who could choose her own life. She didn't want you hampered because she was ill.'

'It's different now she is not here. I've chosen, Dad. I've chosen staying at home for you and my brothers. I'm old enough to leave and I have.'

Dad grabbed his coat and left the house again. Flaming hell, what did he think they could do with Terry all day? Did he have any idea of how hard Mam had worked to keep this household going?

She sat all evening waiting for her dad to come back. He hadn't come back for his tea and she had made a bacon and egg pie that he was fond of. The radio was turned low and the boys were in bed. Mary-from-next-door popped in for a cup of tea and sided with her dad. 'I can help out and there are others who would help too. I wouldn't want to see you throw away your chances, hinny.'

The portrait was propped against the wall. 'Have I done the right thing Mam?' she asked.

'No you flaming well haven't.' Dad was standing by the open back door looking bleary eyed.

'Where have you been until this time?' She sounded like her mam.

'I needed to go to the 'tute. Just for tonight. Now get yourself off to bed and we'll talk properly when I've had time to think.'

Rose went upstairs. She hadn't prayed since her mam's death. She was going through a spell of being bleeding angry with God again. She hadn't asked him or anybody else what to do about school. She was feeling a bit lost and buried herself under her blankets welcoming the relief of being able to shed tears in private and curse the illness that had stolen her mam and her plans for the future.

JOHN KELLY

John Kelly stood in front of his likeness of Ginnie. It captured her spirit more than their wedding portrait that stood on the dresser in the bedroom. Her head thrown back in laughter and mischief dancing in those brown eyes, that's the image he always carried of the woman he married.

He understood Ginnie's fear of doctors. After she'd seen her own mother and sister suffer, she had more faith in the passed down remedies of the local women, but he wished she had confided in him earlier. Ginnie had always been private about what she considered to be women's business and so he'd never heard her complain during pregnancies or this awful illness.

Losing David and that last pregnancy with Terry had taken it out of her. She just hadn't been the same Ginnie, since David's death.

'Oh Ginnie I miss you.' Sinking onto a fireside chair, he gave way to the tears that racked through him until, at last, his grief seemed spent.

Now, he had to keep going because he had his living children to consider. Terry worried him most but Stanley needed a steady hand to guide him and Rose... Rose couldn't give up her chances to look after all of them, he couldn't live with that burden. Terry's little heart would heal and, once he was up and independent, Rose would regret leaving school, he was sure of that.

He knew the headmistress through the art sessions he had held during the years so maybe she could give him some advice about Rose's decision.

'What should I do, Ginnie?' he asked the laughing woman on the canvas whose eyes danced in the firelight. 'What are we going to do without you?'

32

Rose's days sorted themselves into a routine but she didn't get pleasure out of the daily round of tasks in the same way as Mam had. Was it her age or would she never find pride in having the whitest sheets on the line and a well scrubbed, 'red cardinal' polished doorstep? She hated black leading the range every week but the tasks got easier; on a good day, her Yorkshire puds rose, her rice pudding had a nice nutmegged brown topping that Stanley loved and she could get Terry bathed, storied and in bed by seven.

By bedtime she was tired but felt restless. She read until her eyes refused to stay open. She missed her schoolfriends and lessons. She missed chapel too but she just hadn't the heart to go along and sing God's praises when he'd left the Kellys in this state.

It had been three weeks since the night Dad stormed out, he'd come out of the awful despair he'd been in and had been more hands on with Terry. Terry followed him everywhere when he came in from work just as he had followed Mam. Dad had started taking Terry with him to the allotment at the weekend to let him dig and play with his paints. Rose could remember doing the same thing herself a lifetime ago. Dad hadn't brought up school again so she left that particular dog slumbering.

Last week, Dad came in from first shift and, instead of going to bed after his breakfast, he got changed into his going out clothes. He'd explained he had some business to attend to but didn't expand on that. Rose couldn't help worrying in case he was going to the doctors. She couldn't bear another illness. To her, relief he'd come back looking cheerful.

Today, the postman brought him an official looking letter in a long cream envelope and, from the postmark, Rose was sure it was from her old school. She'd propped it up by the clock on the mantelpiece where it taunted her. She dreaded bringing the subject up with him again but she wouldn't hide or read his mail. Maybe they wanted him to talk about art to the sixth form again? Whatever it was, it would remind him of how she was missing her exams. Hell's Bells, there was always something to worry about.

Dad came in from the allotment with Terry. He was on the back shift and that meant starting late afternoon.

'We've dug you taties 'n' a turnip, Rose.' Terry's cheeks were rosy with battling the January wind and he stamped in muddy wellies into the scullery.

'Wipe your feet, Terry Kelly!' She sounded more and more like Mam but she'd just mopped the lino and put a clean mat down. There was a boot scraper and coco matting at the back door but did Stanley or him use them? Never.

'He's just a bairn.' Dad ruffled his hair. 'Something smells good, our Rose.'

'I've made shepherd's pie, Dad.'

'You look peaky, hinny. Have you had a bad day?' Dad took off his boots and placed them by the back door with Terry's wellies. She'd have to clean them later.

'No, Dad I'm fine... There's a letter for you.' She turned and filled the kettle. She'd stay in the scullery and give him time to read it.' The hairs of her neck prickled as she heard the envelope being torn open. Silence. She stood at the sink waiting. She'd put the kettle on the range when he'd finished. Best not to disturb his reading.

'Rose! Come in here. I have some news.'

It turned out that Dad had been to Morpeth to see the headmistress. That's where he'd been in his going out clothes. He discussed Rose's situation with the head and they had come up with a solution. Rose could repeat the fifth form year. She was one of the youngest because of her August birthday and, in July 1951, she could be one of the first to take individual GCEs instead of the leaving certificate. The headmistress thought she was an ideal candidate for them.

'Terry will be at school in September. I'll be home for him on two shifts and Mary will watch him after school when I can't.'

'There's the whole house to run, Dad.' Rose objected.

'You learnt quickly enough so me and Stanley will learn too and we'll all do our bit. You know I'm all for equality our Rose.'

What could she say? 'Well you can start by learning to clean your own boots and showing Terry how to clean his wellies.'

'That's the spirit. By September, we'll be a well-oiled Kelly machine that operates more smoothly than the pit wheel.'

Frank sent a letter of condolence and asked to meet her at Carlisle Park one Saturday. Luckily, Newcastle United weren't playing on the eleventh so she asked the Norrises for the day off. Before leaving, she made sure there was a pan of soup on the range and some scufflers to have with the soup. Little Terry loved those rolls; baked on the oven bottom they had a chewy texture.

She only had her school mac or a Sunday coat that was a year too small so it had to be the bottle green mac. It looked silly with her best shoes so she wore flat shoes. She added a knitted red beret and scarf and took Lucky along with her.

Frank was waiting at the bus station. He looked different in jeans and a duffel coat. He seemed older too. At first, it felt strange and Rose wasn't sure whether to shake hands or give him a hug but Lucky broke the ice by wagging his tail and sitting smartly for a head rub.

He stood up, after obliging Lucky with a brisk rub behind his ears, and caught her looking at his coat. 'Ruth told me they've started wearing navy surplus coats at uni so I'm trying to make it look a bit worn before I go.' Frank reached out for her hand and they set off through the park.

'I thought we'd walk through the park and then take Lucky for a run on Morpeth common. What do you think?' He looked down at her and Rose noticed the golden flecks lighting his hazel eyes. She had missed him.

'Lucky would like that.'

It was a squally day with flurries of rain but they were wrapped up and enjoyed the walk. Rose talked over what her dad and headmistress wanted to do. 'I'm not sure about repeating the year when most of my friends will have left and the rest who are my age will be sixth formers and I'm not sure Dad and Stanley will be much use in the house.'

'Men are just as capable as women, Rose. You shouldn't underestimate us. As for repeating a year, it didn't do Ruth any harm at uni. Mind you, it didn't improve her final results much either.'

'Did she get a degree in the end?' Rose asked.

'Scraped a third. She still doesn't have a clue about what she wants to do next. She wants a husband and a life like Mum's, she says.'

Rose didn't reply. If you can't say something nice, say nothing, was always her mam's advice.

They had a cup of tea and scone in the Clock Tower Tea Rooms but Lucky had to stay tied outside. They could see him but he looked forlorn so they didn't stay long and Frank kept him a piece of scone.

Later, as they stood at the bus stop, Frank asked, 'Could we do this on the middle of every month, Rose? Could you get away?'

Could she? Why not? 'I'd love to do that, Frank. Could we make it a Sunday next time? I work Saturdays at the corner shop. Maybe we could see a film at the Coliseum?'

'Perfect.' He grinned and thrust a small package into her hands just as the bus pulled in to the station. 'Open that on Tuesday.' He gave a wave and was off to his own bus stand.

Why Tuesday? That was the fourteenth. Rose flushed and couldn't stop smiling... Valentine's day, did he think of her as more than a friend, as a girlfriend?

33

The first thing on Rose's mind on Tuesday morning was the package pushed to the back of her underwear drawer. She slipped across to the chest of drawers to retrieve it and huddled back under the covers. It was dark and chilly but Rose had a torch by her bedside, her 'reading lamp'. She buried under the covers, switched on the torch and carefully unwrapped the pink wrapping paper thinking she could re-use it. Inside, she found three pretty handkerchiefs with an embroidered rose in one corner. A note said, 'All Yours x

She smiled, he meant the hankies were all hers, didn't he? Of course he did. Or did he mean that *he* was all hers?

The postman delivered a card that morning as she was cleaning the grate. It had an ornate red heart on the front and inside it said, 'The rose is thought of love divine, Oh be thou my Valentine.' Underneath there was a single kiss.

Rose didn't think the card was Frank's style and it wasn't his writing on the envelope. The only other suspect was Danny Dodd. Would Danny send a card?

She may be a girl with an admirer, maybe two, but she still had to finish cleaning the range and lighting the fire then tackle a pile of ironing from Monday's wash. After that she had a pie to bake.

When she opened the front door later that morning, there was a posy of flowers left on her step for all to see. She quickly scooped them up and read the note. 'DD x'

'It was written in the same pen as the card. What had she done to attract Danny's attention? Nothing but he definitely had a soft spot for her.

Now they were friendly again, Lottie came around a couple of nights during the week after Terry was in bed. She was good company for Rose and they never referred to the gap in their friendship. Rose was glad to have her back but was careful not to talk about Frank or Brenda and her Morpeth friends when she was with her. She'd learnt that some friends just don't mix well.

After turning sixteen in April, Lottie started courting. Dennis, the friend of Danny Dodd who had been new to the rows in the summer that Lucky was rescued. He'd turned out to be a nice-natured lad who was a calming influence on Danny. They were always together at weekends and Lottie tried to persuade Rose to make up a foursome.

'Don't ask me again, Lottie. I'm just fifteen and I haven't time for boys. I have three here who need looking after and that's enough. Anyway, Danny is not for me.'

'Who is then? Have you got your eye on Robbie?' Lottie put down her progger and scrutinised Rose. She was helping Rose to finish a proggy mat her mam had started but they weren't getting far.

Rose laughed. 'No! He's worse than Danny. Now look at what we've done to this pattern Lottie, we're not concentrating and I can just hear my mam saying. 'You two are making a pig's ear of my mat.'

'I miss her, your mam. She was the best cook, wasn't she?' Lottie looked teary eyed.

'She was, and I don't take after her for cooking or crafts but at least I'm trying.' Rose pursed her lips as she looked at the mat; the pattern had gone awry and would need unpicking. 'Shall we leave this for now and I'll ask Mary-from-next-door to give me a hand with it?'

'Yes! Let's have a cuppa and leave this to an expert.'

As they drank their tea and ate one of the rock buns that Rose had made, Lottie returned to the wonders of courting. 'It's lovely to go to the cinema and hold hands, Rose. Dennis buys me chocolate or we get an ice cream at the interval and talk about the picture afterwards.'

It was on the tip of Rose's tongue to say she knew. Hadn't she sat with Frank and eaten ice cream when they went to see 'The Blue Lamp' together? Her friendship with Frank, it was something special that she didn't want to share yet, so she said nothing.

Rose still turned to Mary-from-next-door, the expert, when the boys' shirts needed the collars turning so the worn side was hidden underneath or when an invisible patch was needed on their trousers. She could sew on buttons and do a bit of darning if their jumpers got holes in the elbows but she was no seamstress.

'What would I do without you, Mary?' she asked one day as Mary sat at her mam's treadle machine and ran up a pair of shorts for Terry using some old trousers that Stanley had outgrown.

'These old skills won't be needed soon. The rationing of clothes won't go on forever, hinny. But while they are, come over here and I'll show you what I've done. You're a quick learner.'

Rose sighed, she could see what Mary had done but making new shorts out of old was right up there on her hate list along with washing the net curtains, making jam and the dozens of domestic jobs that ate up all the hours in a day. Housekeeping was a never ending line up of task after task.

One event she did enjoy preparing for was Terry's fourth birthday. March was too chilly for an outdoor party so she had five of his little pals round for tea and games. Lottie offered to help with the games and Mary-from-next-door was helping with the food.

When the day dawned, she couldn't help thinking about young Joy; it would be her birthday too and she was bound to have a wonderful party. Rose swiftly wiped away a tear. You were wrong, Mam. I could have managed two little 'uns and they would have had each other. It was no use thinking what if, she knew that, but on days like this she couldn't help it. Twins might bring double trouble but they'd bring double the love into their family too.

The next Sunday, Rose took Terry along to Sunday school for the first time. His blonde curls were cut off by the barber so he looked like a big boy and his green eyes, like her own, were the double of their dad's. Rose tried not to think of his twin but she popped into her mind. Was Joy as clever as Terry? Was she still like him in looks? Was she a left hander like her, Terry and Dad? Did she go to Sunday school? Douglas had attended so she probably would be starting somewhere just like Terence.

Miss Wakenshaw was waiting to see her as she collected Terry. 'He enjoyed his morning, Rose. I could stop by next week and collect him and bring him back with the Sunday school crocodile if you want?'

'I was thinking I could bring him and take a class of the little ones again… if you and Eddie don't mind?'

'We'd love to have you.' Miss Wakenshaw beamed. 'Actually, Rose I'm expecting a baby and I'll be leaving Linwood elementary and the Sunday school after the summer. Eddie will welcome another Sunday school helper with open arms.

'Congratulations, Miss. You'll be a wonderful mother!'

'Thanks, and please just call me Bella. You're a young woman yourself, now.'

34

It was a cool spring night and Lottie and Rose were going into Ashington to see *Annie Get Your Gun* at the Hippo.

'Why aren't you going with Dennis?' Rose had asked earlier in the week.

'Musicals aren't his thing and I *love* them. Please say you'll come.'

Rose agreed to go. Dad would be home to look after the boys and she liked a musical herself.

As they reached the entrance to the Hippo, Rose spied Danny and Dennis. She tugged at Lottie's sleeve. 'Have you set me up, Lottie Simpson?'

'What?' Lottie saw the boys too. 'Eeeh, no! I wouldn't do that. It's that Dennis, he knew we were coming.'

Lottie went straight up to Dennis. 'What a flaming nerve. You're going to get me into trouble with Rose here.' She sounded cross but she was laughing and clearly pleased to see Dennis.

The frown on Danny's face showed that he wasn't sure what was going on. As the trick Dennis had pulled dawned on him, his neck turned blotchy and he studied a film poster intently. Until then, Rose had been about to turn on her heel and go home but she could tell that Danny was as embarrassed as she was. Danny, who was usually so sure of himself, couldn't meet her eyes.

She gave him a nudge. 'Hi Danny, from your face I can tell we have both been stitched up by Dennis the Menace.'

'I could punch him, I could! He told me you wanted to go to the pictures with me and I don't even like flaming musicals.'

Rose linked his arm. 'We can either leave these two to go to the film on their own or join them. What do you think?'

Danny recovered his composure. 'Seeing as we're here, we might as well go in. No holding hands though, Rose Kelly.' He grinned and the blotches had faded slightly.

'No holding hands,' she agreed.

Danny insisted on paying for her ticket so she got the ice creams at the interval. Danny rolled his eyes towards Lottie and Dennis when they cuddled up together after the interval and pulled a silly face. She was glad that he didn't try to do the same. They shared a bag of chips from Charlie's afterwards and he walked her right to the door.

'How's work going, Danny?'

'It's grand. Old Mr Williams is that pleased with me that he's got me working in the back and learning the trade when deliveries are slack.'

'Baking?'

'No. Choosing the best suppliers, ordering the ingredients and making sure the equipment is running properly, shop management and the like.'

'That'll put a hole in your bookie's running. What happens to your side line then?'

'How do you know about my running?' he asked.

'I just do. Does Mr Williams know, though?'

'He misses nothing. He turns a blind eye because I'm the quickest delivery lad he's ever had and I'm honest, no missing loaves or stotties and the takings are always correct on my rounds.'

'Honest except for a few extra house calls for the book-maker in work time?'

'I don't take a tea break, Rose, and I work later than I need to finish my deliveries. I'm not a cheat to my employer and he knows what I do, he just doesn't mention it. He has his eye on me to manage a shop one day, he told me.' Danny scrumpled the chip paper and threw it into a bin. 'I'm not the scallywag I was when I was a bairn, Rose. I want to make something of myself. Running for the bookies gives me a few extra bob to save and it's rare I have a bet because I see with my own eyes that the Shepherds, the bookmakers I work for, are always the winners.'

'I'd love to see the horses race. A day at the races must be fun.'

'The only day I go to the track and the only day I bet for fun is every July for the pitman's derby. When you're older, maybe you'll let me take you.'

They reached her door. 'I've had a lovely night, Danny. Thank you.'

He took both of her hands. 'Aye, it's been grand. We could always do it again Rose... if you fancy.'

Rose looked into his eyes, they were dark blue in this light and seemed to be trying to read her mind. He bent forward and kissed her cheek.

Stepping back, she said, 'Sorry, Danny. I'm not ready for courting or anything like that. Find another lass to fancy. I'm going back to school next year and my mind is on learning not lads or romance.'

He grinned as he dropped her hands. 'You always say what you mean and I like that about you Rose. You might have your sights set on learning now but maybe one day you'll change your mind and if you do I'll be waiting.'

He turned and walked off. She wanted to call out don't wait for me but Dad opened the front door.

'Who's that you're talking to Rose?' Her dad looked along the row. 'Danny Dodd! I'll kick his hintend if he thinks he can come courting here. You're not sixteen yet and he's got to ask me first.'

'Come inside, Dad. It's not what you think, I'll explain.'

35

On the Tuesday of Rose's sixteenth birthday, she met up with Brenda in Morpeth. Brenda had gained her school certificate and was starting work for a solicitor in Rothbury the next week. 'I'll still be able to meet up at the weekends when you have some free time, Rose. When I'm earning, I'll treat you to a night at the Coliseum.'

They linked arms and headed for the tennis courts. Rose won the game, but only just, she was fit but out of practice. Afterwards, they headed to their favourite tea room near the Clock Tower for tea and cake. That's where they heard that Princess Elizabeth had given birth to a little girl that morning.

'You share your birthday with a princess! You could share your name. Do you think they'll call her Rose after her aunt? Brenda asked, her eyes wide with excitement. 'Princess Margaret's middle name is Rose.'

Rose shrugged. 'We'll have to wait and see. You never know, they might choose Brenda, or your middle name, Anne.'

Brenda swallowed a chunk of Victoria sponge and picked up her teacup. 'Ha! There's no chance of that. Neither of my sturdy names are princess-like at all.'

Two weeks later, Rose heard that the baby was to be named Princess Anne. Brenda would be delighted.

September came around and Terry started at Linwood school. The same week, Rose returned to Morpeth Girl's High for the year. Her uniform still fit her, thank goodness. She had decided she would take the new GCE exams at ordinary level and then leave to find a good job. She didn't want an office job like Brenda. A job working with animals or something active was what she was after, one with no cooking or cleaning involved.

After her spell away, school seemed different. Brenda along with most of their circle of friends had left. Only a handful of her year group were taking the higher exams and not many of them would carry on to university. It was strange being in the year below but she buckled down to work.

Frank Maxwell met her from school on her first Friday. It was lovely to take their old walk to the bus stop on the outskirts of town. 'I'll write when I get a moment Rose and you must write to me. I'll miss you.' With a long hug, she was on her bus and he was waving until he was a speck in the distance.

Frank was off to Cambridge to study veterinary medicine. What an adventure! She couldn't wait to hear what it was like.

She didn't hear from him straight away but she imagined it must be a busy life. Her own life was hectic with schoolwork and housework. The house ticked along but sometimes they got behind with the ironing or they just had egg and chips for tea. Rose felt like a juggler and tried her best not to drop anything important.

Christmas and its run up was a hard time. Mam had been ill but she had been here a year ago and bringing out the decorations brought it all back. Her dad went to the allotment more frequently, Stanley was unusually quiet and only Terry stayed his cheery self.

'D'ya think he's forgotten our Mam?' Stanley watched as Terry ran around with a paper chain and laughed at Lucky chasing him and pouncing on it.

'Not in his heart but little lads live more in the present. I wouldn't want him feeling sad at Christmas and neither would Mam so we have to make it as magical as it was for us.' Rose was struggling to stir the Christmas plum duff and was not feeling magical about it at all. Christmas was hard work in the kitchen. 'Here you stir that our Stanley. My arm is breaking.'

Stanley took over. He had tried to do more this past year and would make somebody a helpful husband. 'Remember the year we got the radio as well as our stockings. We cuddled up to Mam until Dad had the range going and then we found an annual under the tree. That was a good Christmas.'

'We got the radio *before* Christmas so Mam and Dad could listen to news about the war,' Rose corrected him. 'But, yes I do remember that being a special year.'

'What have you asked Dad for, this year?' Stanley's stirring had slowed down but he was persevering.

'Not a thing. What about you?'

'A gramophone!' He laughed and handed her the well-stirred bowl. 'But pigs might fly.'

'No chance of that, Stanley. Dad's got money saved but he likes keeping some for rainy days.'

On Christmas Eve, Terry had been asleep for hours and Stanley had just gone up to bed when Dad put down his sketch pad and whispered, 'It's time for Father Christmas, hinny... you'll have to help me.'

Rose sat up, a wide-awake excitement shook off her drowsiness. 'What Dad? What do I have to do?' You stand by the back door and keep it open and don't let Stanley back down the stairs.

Dad left and went to Mary's back door. After a while, he came back with a few beautifully wrapped presents. Mary-from-next-door had been Dad's wrapping elf. 'Put them under the tree but leave the door open, I'll be back.'

Rose placed a large box for Terry, a flat square present for Stanley and a soft, squashy present for herself under the tree. She opened the sideboard and added the new brushes she'd bought for Dad to the pile and got out Terry's little striped sock filled with chocolate coins, a tangerine and a tiny toy car.

Dad came back with Mr Simpson, both were huffing and puffing, struggling with a heavy box. 'What on Earth have you got there, Dad?'

'Shush and I'll show you.' He opened the box; it wasn't a flying pig but it was a sleek radiogram.

'This is for the whole family to enjoy. I know Stanley likes his popular music so this should give him something useful to save his pocket money for.'

Mr Simpson had a tot of whisky then left and Dad spent a while setting the radiogram up. At last, he was satisfied it was ready to play. 'I hope I've got Stanley the right records to start off his collection.'

'What did you choose?'

'I bought something by Frank Sinatra and another one by Perry Como. The lad in the shop said they were popular.'

'He'll love them, Dad.' Rose kissed her dad goodnight and went upstairs.

She placed Terry's stocking at the bottom of his bed. His cheeks were rosy and his hand was curled around Cubby, David's old teddy was still loved. Rose felt tears welling and threatening to fall. She swallowed the lump of emotion down, tears could wait until she was under the covers.

This little lad hadn't a mother but he had a family who loved him and he would have a happy Christmas. She couldn't help thinking of the sister who could have been cuddled up beside him and hoped that Joy was sleeping as peacefully as her twin.

Terry opened up his train set and Stanley was as excited to set it up as Terry was. Rose loved the pale pink cardigan that Mary-from-next-door must have chosen and wrapped for Dad and she was touched to be given her mam's silver brooch with a picture of Mam's own parents inside it. 'This is lovely, Dad. Thank you.'

Bella Wakenshaw called to add Terry to her crocodile going to chapel. Rose had to give the morning a miss because Christmas dinner was a full morning's work.

Frank and Perry crooned all day except for when King George's Christmas message was due on the radio. The new radio message was as clear as a bell.

'It's much better than the old radio. That's progress isn't it? We didn't know what we were missing until we got this,' Frank said as he smoothed his hand over the polished top.

Rose had an idea. 'Mary's radio is on its way out and she doesn't want to buy a new one. Could she have our old one, Dad?'

'I'll take it over tomorrow, hinny.'

Nothing was ever wasted in the rows.

'I'm going to chapel at six, do either of you want to come?' Rose asked.

'I'll watch our Terry, sweetheart,' Dad said.

'No, Dad. I'll play with him and his train. You go with our Rose.' Stanley insisted.

Rose smiled. 'You two are a pair of heathens. I'll go myself but mind you I want a plate of sandwiches made and the kettle on so we can have supper when I get back.'

After the evening service, she said goodbye to Bella and Eddie and chatted to a few of Mam's friends. As she walked past the 'tute, Danny appeared and fell into step with her. 'Been to church, have you?' he asked.

'I have.' He knew fine well where she'd been. Had he been waiting for her? 'What've you been up to?'

'The usual. Christmas dinner then a walk and an hour at the 'tute with Dennis. He's off to see Lottie, now.'

'Ah, so you're at a loose end?'

'No, I wanted to catch up with you. I was remembering that year you had diphtheria, Rose. I prayed then, you know. After I delivered your cards, I went into the back of your chapel and prayed you'd come home.'

Rose stopped and turned to face him. 'Thanks Danny. I remember your kindness that Christmas.' His eyes were alight with warmth and her words brought a grin to his face. Realisation swept through her, Danny loved her, thought the world of her, and she mustn't hurt him.

'I wrapped these for you... Rose's chocolates. Merry Christmas.' He handed her the box, linked her arm in his and said, 'I'll walk you to your row.'

When they got to her door, he said, 'I'll scarper. Don't want your dad coming out to chase me again. See you, Rose.'

She almost called out, *Don't go.* Standing there, she felt flat... disappointed even. Some of the fizz had gone out of the day. It was nice to be admired and Danny hadn't forgotten her at Christmas. Not like Frank flaming Maxwell. He hadn't written once or sent his Cambridge address like he'd promised. She had posted a letter and card to his home address last week, he'd be back there now for Christmas, and she'd had no reply.

36

1951

Rose was going to the New Year's Eve dance at Burnside Village Hall. All the young folk from around and about had bought tickets weeks ago but Rose hadn't bothered. Lottie was going with Dennis and she didn't like to invite herself along with Betty and the other lasses from the rows because she didn't see much of them and didn't feel comfortable tagging on. Her invitation to the dance was a surprise.

On Boxing day, Danny Dodd sought out her dad at his allotment and asked his permission to invite her. He was taking his baker's van, he had been given a van in place of his bicycle when he turned eighteen. They would be with Lottie and Dennis, he wasn't going to drink except to toast the New Year at midnight and he would bring the girls home straight after the New Year was chimed in. Dad had agreed as long as Rose wanted to go.

Oh how she wanted to go! She had heard lots about the fun of the village dances but this would be her first. What on earth could she wear? She'd have to consult with Lottie.

'I knew Danny was going to ask your dad but I didn't dare breathe a word in case it went wrong. Your dad is quite strict.' Lottie confessed.

'He just finds it hard to believe I'm sixteen and ready for dances.'

'And *romances*.' Lottie giggled.

'Stop it Lottie!' Rose couldn't help herself laughing at the dreamy face Lottie was pulling. 'I'm dancing not romancing on New Year's Eve.'

'*We'll* see! Now let's look through your wardrobe. You need something fancy for the dance. What'll you do with your hair?'

The contents of her drawers were scattered over the floor but they settled on an outfit. Rose's best short-sleeved cream blouse was teamed with a flared red skirt patterned with cream flowers and her black T-bar shoes with a bit of a heel. She borrowed an extra petticoat from Lottie to make her skirt stick out and added the new red patent belt that she'd chosen for Christmas. It was the most dressed up that Rose had been since Bella Wakenshaw's wedding.

Their plan was for Rose to go to Lottie's once she was dressed, to add powder and lipstick, but her dad insisted that Danny pick her up at her own door so she slipped her brand new coral lipstick into her bag and she'd have to wait to borrow Lottie's powder compact at the dance.

Danny arrived wearing an open necked shirt with a sleeveless pullover and jacket. He was polite to her dad, brought Terry a bar of chocolate and gave her a wink that said she looked okay. She sat in the front seat with Danny because Lottie and Dennis were already propped on cushions in the back of his van.

The hall was decked with streamers and balloons and a trestle table laden with pies and sandwiches stood at one side. Next to it, a table selling soft drinks and bottles of beer was manned by the warden's wife and her friends. The hall warden was busy with the gramophone that played through a large speaker.

First of all, there was a waltz, followed by the military two step and the Bradford barn dance. Rose had learned those dances on wet lunch breaks at school so she could lead a clumsy-footed Danny around the hall.

'Rose you're the best dancer here. You're good at everything you try.' Danny led her by the hand to buy a lemonade.

Rose laughed. 'I think you'll find I know three or four dances and that's it.'

'Can you Lindy Hop?'

'Sort of. I've tried at school but I'm no great shakes.'

There was a short interval for food and then the swing records came on. Danny was a natural at the Lindy Hop and she had fun learning new moves. The time flew by until the warden stopped a record and checked his watch. He turned on the radio so they could hear the chimes of Big Ben ringing out over the hall. After that the hall was filled with cries of 'Happy New Year' followed by kissing and hugging everywhere.

Danny seemed unsure, he took both of Rose's hands and looked into her eyes. His dark blue eyes expressed happiness and something else. Rose took a breath, closed her eyes and raised her face to his. She smelt the sharp tang of lemons and felt sharp stubble brush her skin as he softly kissed her cheek. A delicious tingle of excitement ran through her body; he was so close. Opening her eyes, the inviting full lips that were always verging on a smile drew her to him and she draped her arms around Danny's neck. *Kiss me, Danny.* They locked eyes as their lips touched. Rose felt hot or was she cold? For a moment, she was a swirl of emotions, lost in the sensation of his soft mouth over hers. Eventually, Danny pulled away leaving her breathless but wanting the kissing to go on.

'I told you Rose Kelly, you're good at everything you do.'

She blushed. The kiss had seemed so natural. Far too short. He squeezed her hand. 'Come on Rose. I'm having one beer to see in the New Year and then I'm getting you home or else the pitman painter will have my skin for a canvas.'

On the way back to Linwood, she sat in the front of the van with Danny and she could guess from the silence in the back that Lottie and Dennis were kissing. 'Necking on' Lottie called it. She watched Danny's strong hands at the wheel and looked at his handsome profile. She had fallen for him with one kiss and wished she could try another but there was no chance. Her dad would be waiting behind that door.

After that, Danny and Rose were an item; courting it was called in the rows. Sometimes, if he was delivering in the neighbourhood, he collected her from the bus stop after school, on Saturdays, he collected her from Norris's shop. He always had a box of leftover cream cakes or fruit tarts, baker's perks, that she could serve to her dad and the lads after their dinner. An hour or so later, he collected her to take her to the pictures or dancing. He insisted on paying because she was still at school so she used her Saturday job money to buy a few 'going out' outfits.

Danny was handsome, good fun and took good care of her. She couldn't wait for his kisses at the end of a night out but it was always Danny who pulled away. He didn't try the 'heavy petting' that Lottie talked about and Rose was partly glad yet partly disappointed.

She got the book about relationships out of the library again and looked at the section on intercourse with new eyes. This would actually be a pleasurable thing. What a pity she was sixteen and had years to wait before she was married. Rose knew what Lottie and Dennis got up to and decided she would be happy to allow Danny to put his hand up her blouse and touch her breasts, she would like that and it didn't lead to babies. The thing was, Danny avoided her attempts to go further. She always left him aching for more. She even imagined becoming Mrs Rose Dodd and lying in his arms.

37

Terry's first Sunday school anniversary was coming up and he had to learn a 'piece', a few lines to say to the congregation. Rose helped him and he was word perfect on the morning of the anniversary. They had an early lunch and a whole pew of people set off to hear Terry's words of wisdom.

Dad and Stanley were spruced up, Mary-from-next-door wasn't so good on her feet anymore so Danny was taking her to the chapel door in his van. 'Seeing as I'm on the chapel's doorstep, I'll pop in too, Rose. I want to hear the bairn.'

Rose didn't have to tell Danny to dress up, he always wore lovely clothes when he called for a walk or a talk on a Sunday night before going to the 'tute for an hour.

The chapel was filled to capacity; it was always standing room only and the doors open when the bairns had their anniversary. Rose's heart pounded as little Terence stood up and stepped to the podium. *Oh, Mam I wish you were here to see this day*, she thought as she brushed a tear from her eye and Danny squeezed her hand. She couldn't push her second thought way; he should be holding hands and sharing this moment with his twin sister. He looked so forlorn up there on his own.

Silence. His teacher gave him an encouraging nod but Terry's eyes were roaming the congregation... for her? Rose sat tall and gave a little wave as his eyes alighted on her. 'Rose,' he pleaded and beckoned her to come to the front. Rose slipped past Danny, walked up the aisle and knelt beside Danny. Behind his hand he whispered, 'I've lost my start!'

There was a ripple of laughter through one or two benches of older ones and Rose cast them a frown before whispering. '*I am...*' That was it. Terry was off with a loud clear voice and gestures. 'I am just a little boy. I've never spoke before but, when I get a bigger boy, I'll tell you something more.' He ended with a smart bow and a grin.

Rose and Terry were both relieved that was over and they could go back to their seats. Next week, he would get his Sunday School bible for his first public speech.

Danny's eyes glistened as she took her place beside him. 'I wish I'd done that when I was younger. Just wait until I have kids, they'll go to chapel.'

Danny's mam was lovely but she was an older mam with a houseful of all ages when she had him. She was very easy on discipline with her boys and, from being a little'un, he'd done pretty much as he pleased. Rose said a prayer of thanks for having a mother and father who had loved them all but kept them in line. It seemed to her that Dad was keeping Danny in line too nowadays because Danny was always checking what John Kelly thought about things and liked to discuss politics and world events with him.

How could a perfect Sunday like that one be followed by such horror? Rose heard of the tragedy when she came home from school to see her dad making a frame for one of his canvases. Nothing unusual there but his look as he said. 'Hello, pet,' was empty.

'What's happened? Where's Terry?' Her first thought was of her little brother. 'He's down at the burn with Stanley. I wanted a bit of peace afore work. Thinking time... There's been an explosion in Durham. Firedamp in the Duckbill seam at Easington, hinny.'

Rose put the kettle on and placed a mug of tea in front of her dad. 'What do you know?'

'A blunt pick generated sparks. Firedamp ignited and cause an explosion. Over a hundred yards of roof was brought down as thirty-eight were ending their shift and forty-three were going in. There's a hell of a lot of rescue work going on and we'll be on standby if they need more.'

Now Rose understood how people say could say they were speechless. A loss of words seldom happened to Rose but what can you say to eighty-one men being trapped? Not all of them grown men, either. Young sons, brothers, new earners, grandads nearly retired, lads just starting out along with the fit pitmen of Easington.

The disaster at Easington on Tuesday 29th May was in all the papers. It brought grief and despair to every mining community not just the folk of Easington in their neighbouring county.

Later in the week, Rose read that two rescuers, whilst wearing full breathing apparatus, had somehow been overcome by noxious gas and died, bringing the total number of deaths to eighty-three. That could have been Dad's rescue team. How she wished her dad didn't have to hew coal. It would be Stanley next, never-ending worry.

Next Sunday, before Dad carved the Sunday roast, he asked Stanley and Rose to sit at the table. 'What I have to say is something I've thought long and hard about. I know it might upset you, Stanley, but I've decided that no son of mine, not you or our Terry, will work down the mine. I will be the last Kelly to go into the bowels of the Earth and hew coal. Our luck will run out and I canna face losing a son like that. You'll have to find yourself a different job this summer or go back to school and do your exams.'

Stanley pushed his chair back roughly and stood up. 'But

Dad! I want to drive the horses. You said I could. I'm leaving as soon as I'm fifteen. I'm no good at exams. I'm not like Rose.' His fists were clenched and his face flushed.

Dad stood up too so they were toe to toe and he still had a couple of inches of height over Stanley. 'You'll get a different job by September or I'll send you back to school, laddie. I tell you, my mind is made up.'

Stanley left the kitchen banging the back door. 'Put his dinner in the oven, pet. He'll be back and, one day, he'll thank me for it. His pit wages are not worth his life.'

Rose had to agree with her dad but she felt sorry for Stanley. He hated sticking his head in a book and, like her, he loved animals. The colliery blacksmith had a son Stanley's age who would become his apprentice so that wasn't an option. Who could help?

Rose brooded over what Stanley could do all evening but couldn't come up with an answer. It finally came to her as she travelled to school on the Morpeth bus. After school, she made a detour and her germ of an idea started to take root.

Two weeks later, she arranged a Sunday out for the Kellys. Her dad was in the know and approved, Terry would love the adventure of a day out and she had fingers and toes crossed that Stanley would enjoy the day.

They dressed in sturdy shoes and warm coats and walked to the main road where they got the bus to Morpeth and changed for Rothbury. Just before Rothbury, they got off at a deserted bus stop.

'Where is this adventure taking us Rose? Stanley asked. 'I'm starving.'

Before she could answer, Mr Charlton, Brenda's dad, pulled up in his truck. 'Hop in! You're just in time for a scone and a cup of tea before we do the rounds.'

Stanley and Dad helped Mr Charlton to check on his

sheep and his fences while Brenda, Mrs Charlton and Rose enjoyed a good catch up and made a roast lamb dinner. Terry played amongst the hens in the yard and helped feed the pet lambs.

When Stanley returned, he was full of the wonders of Mr Charlton's dogs, Bess and Blue. 'They are amazing at rounding up the sheep and understanding Mr Charlton's commands; even cleverer than Lucky!'

After dinner, Brenda took Stanley to the field where her horse and his little Shetland pal were out to grass. When they were out of sight, Mr Charlton said, 'I'll not muck about. I need a good strong lad who likes the farm and he'll do nicely. The wages aren't as good as mining but we'll feed him well and, if he shapes up, there'll be opportunities.'

'Thank you, Alf.' Her dad looked relieved.

Rose just hoped that the farm had sold itself to Stanley. He came back with Brenda, shiny-eyed. 'I've just ridden Blaze bareback around the field, Dad.'

'Would you like a job here, son? Working with the sheep and pitching in with everything else? It's hard work but you seem to have a feel for the animals.' Stanley gulped and looked at Rose then his dad. 'Can I, Dad? Can I work for Mr Charlton as soon as I'm fifteen?'

Dad nodded and Stanley grabbed Mr Charlton's big gnarled hand and nearly shook it off. 'Yes, sir. Yes, Mr Charlton. I'd love to!'

Rose would miss his company at home but was relieved that Stanley was sorted. She knew that the Charltons would treat him well. All she had to do now was knuckle down to her GCEs. The exams loomed and this extra year at school had to be worthwhile. What job would she find for herself when her studying was over?

38

When the summer term ended, Terry was delighted to join his friends for a summer of freedom and Stanley left for his new farming life at Rothbury. Rose put away her books and picked up her pinny to give the house a good clean. Exams were over so she had no excuses and the house was crying out for attention.

The evenings came later as the summer sky brought spectacular sunsets of coral and pink and seemed reluctant to give way to darkness. Rose sat by the window to save turning on the light and scanned the jobs section of the evening paper. She had a pen ready to circle anything of interest but, so far, there was nothing. There were office and shop vacancies but nothing resembling a circus or working with animals. Where were those jobs advertised? Certainly not the *Evening Chronicle*.

She'd have loved the farm job that Stanley started a few weeks ago but she knew that Mr Charlton wouldn't consider a girl for the farm work he had in mind. Lucky Stanley. When he came home last week laden with butter and eggs and preserves from Mrs Charlton, he seemed to be filling out already.

Stanley had talked an awful lot about Brenda; how funny she was, how she was teaching him to ride. Rose thought he had a bit of a crush on her friend but she didn't tease him. She was happy that he had settled and a weight of worry had been lifted from Dad's shoulders.

Dad was only in his late forties, a handsome man, but since losing Mam and then the explosion at Easington, he had worry lines etched on his brow and he had become even more reclusive. He still went to his Ashington art group, he retreated to his allotment for hours and he read a lot. His paintings had gone dark again; palettes of inky blues and steely greys merged with pitch black. The colours he mixed told Rose he was putting his emotions into his paintings. That had to be better than bottling them up.

Rose could have taken a full time job with the Norrises in July but her dad was determined she should do something with her GCEs. When the letter announcing her grades arrived, they were delighted she'd passed the nine subjects that she had taken. For Rose, getting top grades for all but French, which she still passed, was a real surprise.

'I knew you'd do well, pet. Now you have to find a job that'll make use of that good brain of yours.'

'I keep looking, Dad. There's nothing but stuffy shops and offices.'

'You could stop on you know, take the advanced certificate, hinny. We'll manage.'

'No Dad. I felt daft enough going to school at sixteen, nearly seventeen, with everybody around here working and I'm ready to take my turn and work. Besides, Terence is getting to the age where I want to keep an eye on him and his studies. Something will catch my eye or I'll apply for an office job like Brenda's.'

Once the Norrises knew Rose was looking elsewhere for permanent work, they took on Lottie Simpson. Lottie had been an apprentice dressmaker but she didn't like her boss so she persuaded the Norrises to give her a try out in the shop.

'Your friend Lottie is grand at serving and putting up orders but she can't help with the books like you did, Rose.' Mrs Norris admitted.

'I'll look over them once a month, if you like.' Rose knew Mr Norris struggled and got frustrated if they didn't balance.

'That's champion, lassie! We'll pay you mind.' She hugged Rose.

'Put me up a few groceries and that'll be fine, Mrs Norris.'

Cinders falling through the grate brought her back to the present, the fire was getting low and needed more coal. As she was folding the paper neatly back into order, Dad hated a rumpled paper, she caught sight of an ad in the 'pets for sale' section.

Maxwell's Veterinary Surgery
requires an assistant for office work who is capable of handling domestic animals. Apply in writing…

It must have been placed in the wrong section, not many would have seen it. Working at Maxwell's would be perfect but… No.

Rose couldn't apply for the job even though she liked Mr Maxwell. She hadn't heard from Frank for almost a year and it would be too humiliating to meet up after he'd dumped their friendship as soon as he reached Cambridge. She didn't want regular encounters with Ruth either.

It gave her an idea though. Next morning, she set off for the library and researched every vet's practice in the vicinity. There were four more nearby besides Maxwell's; another in Ashington, one in Gosforth and two in Morpeth. Her plan was to visit each one and hand in her CV.

Next day, Gosforth was first on Rose's list. 'Just a moment, Miss. I'll pass this to Mr James and see if he would like to take your offer any further.'

Rose looked around the well-furnished waiting room of the Gosforth practice and perched on a seat. She waited there for a few minutes before being joined by an elderly lady. She sat upright with a wicker basket on her knee and the mewling told Rose there was a cat desperate to escape.

Mr James came out. He wore a white coat and looked more doctor than vet but he seemed cheery. 'Good morning Miss Willis. Trouble with Topsy? I'll be with you in a moment.'

The lady nodded. 'She seems to have a hairball stuck in her throat again.'

'We'll soon deal with that,' he assured her before turning his attention to Rose. 'Miss Kelly,' he held out his hand, 'I'm Mr James, pleased to meet you.'

Rose stood up and shook his hand. 'I'm glad you've taken the time to look at my CV.'

'It is very impressive. Good GCE results, well done. Those new exams look tricky but Morpeth is a good school. So you're after a job working with animals?'

'Yes, Mr James. I'll try my hand at anything and I think a vet's practice would be an interesting position.'

He scratched his chin. 'I think you may be in luck, I don't need staff at the moment but a very good friend of mine does. Don't know if he's advertised yet or a bright young lady like you would have seen it in the paper.'

Rose's heart flipped. Oh heck! He was going to say Mr Maxwell. 'Oh, where is that, sir?'

'It's on your school stamping ground, Morpeth.'

'Morpeth?' Rose couldn't think of anything else to say. She was so sure he'd been going to mention Maxwell's.

'Campbell's of Morpeth. His receptionist is going off whelping herself. He's a one man set up and needs someone who is willing to do everything from typing to sterilising operating tools.'

'That's me!' Rose found her voice. 'Thank you for letting me know, Mr James. I intended on taking my CV there tomorrow morning. I'm trying everywhere.'

'Are you now?' Mr James was scrutinising her. 'Tell you

what, young lady, I'll give Roger a call tonight and tell him to look out for you.'

'Can you tell him I'll be there first thing?'

Rose was at the door of Campbell's at eight thirty. Mr Campbell arrived at nine. 'Come in, come in lassie and take your coat off.' He bellowed in a broad Scottish accent. He removed his tartan cap and scarf, his dour look making her feel nervous. 'I've had a good report from Gerald James so I'll not bother with your CV. You might as well stay the morning and see if you like the work and I like you. I canna stand a lot of chatter I'm warning ye.'

Rose discovered that Wednesday was half day opening and his assistant's day off. Mr Campbell was in his consulting room all morning so Rose was left to greet clients, answer the phone and find out the filing system for herself. She loved it.

At twelve o'clock a big shaggy dog came in panting and looking petrified. 'Bruno doesn't like the vets,' his red faced owner explained as he tugged Bruno into the consulting room.

Rose heard scuffles then a large dog's paws scrabbling at the door. Mr Campbell, looking as florid as the owner, opened the door a fraction. 'Miss Kelly, we'll be needing your assistance.'

Bruno was friendly but he was big and frightened. He had backed himself into a corner and both men couldn't budge him. Rose's strength wasn't going to shift him. She remembered how the pit lads handled frightened gallowas. She took off her scarf and gently covered his eyes then started singing 'You are my sunshine,' quietly in Bruno's ear. As he stopped his struggling to listen, Mr Campbell gave him his jab. He didn't even flinch. Rose gently took the scarf away and tickled Bruno under the chin. 'Good boy, Bruno.' He rewarded her with a drooly smile.

'Thank you,' the owner and Bruno left delighted.

Mr Campbell took off his glasses and rubbed them. 'Can ye make a decent cup of tea lassie?'

She grinned. 'I certainly can.'

'You've got yourself a job, then.'

39

On a mild mid-August evening, Danny was waiting outside for Rose when she finished work at Campbell's. He was taking her to the Coliseum to see *The Six Men*. She loved being with Danny, he always made her feel special.

'Happy Birthday. Roses for a Rose.' He'd brought a box of Roses for her, by now she knew that he would. He always bought some before going to watch a film, he always said "Roses for a rose" and he always ate more than half. He kept the nutty caramel one for her though. He handed the chocolates over and kissed her cheek.

She smiled and linked his arm. After the film, a thriller that Danny wanted to see, they were getting the bus back to Linwood and stopping for Charlie's fish and chips to share with Dad when they got in. A perfect seventeenth birthday.

It was on their way out of the cinema that Rose felt the back of her neck prickle as though eyes were boring into her. She turned to meet the cold stare of Ruth Maxwell. Ruth's hair was peroxide, all fluffed out, and she looked overdressed in a bright pink suit and very high heels. She could stare but she couldn't spoil her day. Rose raised her eyebrows as if to say who are you looking at and was about to turn away without saying a word when Ruth was joined by Frank.

Frank! Her heart did a triple flip.

His blonde hair was cut shorter and he was using a stick.

What had he done? She must ask. Their eyes met and Rose saw pleasure then a guarded look. Was he as embarrassed as she felt? *He* was the one who didn't write.

Her Morpeth Girls' etiquette kicked in and she strode forward. 'Frank, Ruth what a lovely surprise! Did you enjoy the film?'

Ruth sniffed and looked away. She never did have manners, that one.

'It was a real melodrama, wasn't it? Not that long, but long enough, eh?' He echoed her thoughts on the film. She'd always enjoyed pulling apart films with him. 'Happy birthday, Rose.' Frank stuttered. Frank Maxwell, usually so confident, seemed ill at ease.

'Thanks, Frank. I'm surprised you remembered.' Rose replied as he glanced past her at Danny.

'Frank may I introduce you to Danny Dodd, a friend of mine. Danny this is Frank Maxwell. He went to school at King Edward's and is now at Cambridge.'

'Pleased to meet you, Frank.' Danny held out his hand.

Frank shook hands as Ruth tugged at his sleeve. 'We must go now, Frank. I'm starving. Please excuse us.' She practically dragged Frank off.

'What a strange couple,' Danny said as they watched them disappear into the street.

'*She* is his sister and an unhappy girl, a bit of a bully. *He...* well I used to think of him as a friend but I haven't seen him in ages.'

'Nobody for me to be jealous about then?' Danny linked her arm.

'No.' She laughed and pulled Danny towards her to kiss his cheek. 'Not at all!'

'Has he always had that limp? He's walking quite badly.'

'No, he hasn't. I didn't get a chance to ask, probably a sporting injury.'

Rose's cheeks felt flushed. Facing Frank had taken some

doing. Seeing him like that made her realise, even though he had behaved badly and ignored her, she missed their talks. She missed his easy going outlook on life. She missed him.

'What did you think of the plot of *The Six Men*, Danny?' They were cuddled up together on the bus home.

'Great, but I like a colour film better.' Rose put her head on his shoulder and rested her eyes. Danny didn't go in for dissecting films but he had a comfy shoulder and he didn't let her down.

Rose had another uncomfortable meeting later in the month. She was catching up with some filing and making sure she was free at two o'clock to help Mr Campbell with two wily Siamese cats who'd been in every day for a week because they wouldn't let their owner use eye drops, when the door from the street chimed. Rose popped out from behind the filing cabinets and came face to face with Mr Fletcher struggling with a lively looking box. He looked more portly and his hair had receded but he looked well.

'Why, it's Rose Kelly! Fancy meeting you here. You can't be working already?'

Rose let out a sigh of relief when she saw he wasn't followed by Mrs Fletcher or... or Joy. 'I'm past seventeen now, Mr Fletcher.'

'Of course, time flies.'

Oh no, he'd be thinking of Douglas, Rose searched for something else to say. 'What's in the box? May I look?'

He placed the box on the counter. 'A present for Joy, our lassie. She's been asking for a pup and we think she's just old enough to enjoy looking after this little 'un.'

Rose took out a brown and white wriggling scrap with floppy ears. Checking the pup's undercarriage, she said, 'She is a little sweetie. Joy will love her.'

'She can't be put on the floor until she's had injections and Mrs Fletcher is insistent on every vaccination going.'

Another awkward pause; after losing Douglas to diphtheria, who could blame her? 'How is your wife and your little girl?'

'Just grand. She's been at a lovely little primary school in Morpeth for a year. We're nearby so it's easy to drive her here.' Rose's stomach churned, her sister was so close by. 'How about those brothers of yours? Did Stanley get to work with the pit ponies?'

'No, Mr Fletcher. Dad put his foot down after Easington. He's working with animals though… a farm Rothbury way.'

'Good for him!' Mr Fletcher looked delighted. 'Pit work wouldn't be my choice for a son of mine, either.'

She had to say it. 'I often think of Douglas; that day… the test. Life's unfair isn't it?'

Mr Fletcher patted her hand. 'It is lassie, it is but it can produce miracles too. You should see our little Joy, she is a true joy to us and she makes life worth living.'

Rose gulped back a huge lump. 'Shall we take this little pup in to see the vet now?'

Mam had made the wrong choice, she was sure of it; yet Joy was happy and she had given the Fletchers a new life even if it was all on a web of lies.

Mr Fletcher's visit was a warning. From now, she would be ready to see Mrs Fletcher and Joy at some time in the vets. When she did, she would be professional and not cause Mrs Fletcher another moment of panic. What good could come of digging up the past?

Next lunch-time, she found herself taking a walk past the primary school. She couldn't help it. And there she was! Joy. It didn't harm anybody if she walked that way to see her little sister looking lively and happy. At six, she was still like Terence.

Later in the week, Mr Campbell took Rose to one side. 'Here's a strange do, Rose! We've lost a new client to Maxwell's in Ashington. Remember the fella who brought the spaniel pup for her jabs? I canna think why. Can you send Mr Maxwell the file we started?'

Rose could guess why. Mrs Fletcher must have heard from Mr Fletcher that she was here and didn't want any chance encounters. She was sorry to cause her worry but this is what happened when lies were spun around lives. She posted off the file to Frank Maxwell senior and couldn't help wondering how his son was faring. He'd have returned to Cambridge for his second year by now.

40

Rose answered the phone a few days later, 'Campbell's animal practice, how may I help you?'

'Is that you, Rose Kelly?' She recognised Mr Maxwell's cheery voice and her heart started racing.

'It is.'

'It's Frank Maxwell here. I saw your name on the file you sent from Campbell's and couldn't believe you'd leave school and work for a vet without trying here first.'

What could she say? 'I just feel lucky to have a job working with animals anywhere, Mr Maxwell.'

'Remember Vera? She's retiring and I've tried a couple of assistants to take her place but they aren't like her.'

'I remember her, she'll be hard to replace.'

'One applicant was good at office duties but too squeamish with the animals and one loved the animals but couldn't speak on the phone. If you ever want a change, I'd love to have you at the practice, Rose. I'll say that to Roger's face too. He's landed on his feet, getting you.'

'Thanks for the compliment, Mr Maxwell but I'm new and inexperienced so I'm still learning the ropes.'

'A bright spark like you could have been a vet. Put Rog on the phone and I'll tell him what he can trust you with.'

Rose put the phone on the counter. How embarrassing,

should she pretend Mr Campbell was out? Just then, Mr Campbell poked his head around the door. 'Who's that, Rose?'

'It's Maxwell's. Mr Maxwell wants a word.' She handed him the receiver and slipped around the corner to busy herself with some filing.

Mr Campbell found where she was hiding. 'You certainly got a glowing report from Frank Maxwell, Rose. Thinks you should be hands on with the animals… reckons you know your animal biology.'

'I do, a bit. I have a GCE in biology and I get books from the library. I really liked *Hobday's Surgical Diseases of the Dog and Cat.'*

'Never read it. If it's good, buy a copy for the bookshelf.'

'I will. It includes a chapter on veterinary nursing that says there is scope for a registration system in the future. A certificate of registration could be used as a sign of competence. I'd love to have that qualification, one day.'

'I canna see that day coming lassie but, if you're as quick to learn as Frank thinks you are, I'm happy to put you to the test.'

Rose and Roger were on first name terms after they both spent an exhausting day delivering twin foals. By the end of the month, she knew that Roger and herself made a good team; he had the strength and experience and she could soothe animals, farmers and fretting pet owners. Farms were mucky work so she ordered a couple of sets of brown overalls for helping with the farm animals and kept her white aprons for work with the domestics in the surgery.

As they were having a brief rest and a cuppa one day, Roger admitted, 'This practice has thrived since you came here with your calm manner and your way with sick bleeding rabbits and cats. Gi' me a horse or cow any day.'

Rose smiled. Roger could be volatile but he was skilled at surgery and knew his animal medicines. She loved to watch and learn. 'I love helping out with the animals but I think I need to spend a day or two on the files and accounts, Roger.'

'Is that so?' He puffed on his pipe.

'I've kept on top of the mail but there is other office work and not enough hours to do it.'

'You work hard, lassie. I'll see what I can do. My old receptionist, Audrey, she wants to work a couple of days, you know. I don't really hold with mothers working but she's good at the office work.'

'Roger! You are so old-fashioned at times. Women had children and kept England going during the war. We can do so much more than you give us credit for.'

'M'be you're right. If I give Audrey two days a week in the office and reception, you can be my right hand man.'

'You mean right hand woman,' Rose corrected.

'You'll need to learn to drive mind you,' he said, his eyes glinting with mischief. 'I could do wi' a chauffeur, so I'll pay for your test when you're ready.'

Her? Driving? Rose couldn't wait.

Danny took Rose out in his van. She loved being behind the wheel. 'You're not bad, for a girl,' he admitted.

'Danny Dodd, you know how that sort of talk vexes me.'

'I'm only joking. You look so pretty when you're mad.'

'Danny! That's even worse.'

He pulled a face and she couldn't help laughing. The best bit about having Danny as her instructor was the kissing at the end of the lesson.

She practiced all through the ice and snow of winter and Danny was sure she would pass first time.

41

1952

Rose returned to work after the Christmas break and, after wishing Roger Happy New Year and asking about Hogmanay with his family in Edinburgh, she sprung her news. 'I'm ready to sit my driving test, now. Shall I book it and take a few practice drives in the Land Rover?'

'Already, lassie? Are ye sure?' Roger raised bushy eyebrows.

'Yes. I don't dither about when I want to do something.' She took the application form from her bag.

'You certainly don't.' As Roger laughed, she caught a glint in his eye. 'Come on then, show me how to go on at these blasted new zebra crossings. They are cropping up all over the place! We'll get some L plates onto the Land Rover and you can drive me over to Otterburn. That should test your skills.'

In February, King George's death was in all the papers. It took them by surprise even though he had been poorly with his chest. Who would have thought he'd go before his mother? It meant they would have a young queen on the throne and that was exciting, although Rose felt sorry for Elizabeth. Imagine losing your father and having such a responsibility so young.

The new queen would make a good job of it, Rose was

sure of that. Women tended to get on and make the best of things out of duty and love, whether it was in a palace or a colliery row. She worked long hours and then had Dad and Terry to wash and prepare meals for so her days flew by but she managed and, most days, she enjoyed it.

This year, Terry had taken over walking Lucky after school and took his part in helping out very seriously. He was a good-natured little lad – more independent than he'd be if he had a mammy at home – who tagged along with his dad, played footie in the street or found something to entertain himself when his dad and sister were busy, but Rose made sure she was home to read him his bedtime story and give him a cuddle every night.

Terry loved football but their dad didn't go to the matches. She mentioned it to Mr Norris and he offered to take him for a birthday treat. On the nearest Saturday to Terry's sixth birthday that March, Rose presented him with a black and white club scarf and hat and off he went to watch Portsmouth play Newcastle. When she tried to pay for the ticket, Mr Norris insisted it was his pleasure.

Rose was waiting with Mrs Norris when they returned from the game.

'I saw six goals, Rose! We drew three goals to three. Jackie Milburn, George Robledo and Bobby Mitchell all scored.'

'Did they now? That must have been all your cheering.' Rose hugged him.

'He's been as good as gold, Rose. Sat at the front with the other little'uns and had a grand time.'

'You've been as good as gold too,' Mrs Norris replied. 'This is the first time you've come home and not looked the worse for wear. You should take the bairn again.'

'I will. I'll do that.' He ruffled Terry's hair.

When Terry was snuggling down to sleep, he said, 'We're going to win the cup again, this year, Rose. Mr Norris says so. He says it'll be the *fifth* time. *He's* getting a ticket for Wembley.'

'What cup is that then, Terry?' Rose asked him.

'That very big shiny one for champions,' he yawned. 'I'm going to be a footballer like Wor Jackie when I'm bigger.'

Rose stroked his brow and remembered her dreams of working in a circus and looking after animals. 'Dreams change shape but they can happen, Terry,' she whispered before kissing him goodnight.

Rose was more delighted for Terence than the team when the Magpies did bring home the FA cup for the fifth time that May. The little 'uns from the rows had a street party with black and white bunting and their dads drank black and white Guinness. Rose contributed the sandwiches that Mam had always made for her parties, two plates of good old corned beef mixed with a big dollop of sauce to make it go further and cut into party triangles. She didn't make a cake; baking still wasn't her forte. She could make a very good poultice for a horse when it was needed though.

Above Campbell's surgery was a bedsit, bathroom and kitchen. Roger, Audrey and Rose used the kitchen and bathroom for their breaks and, on odd occasions when there was a domestic animal who needed watching overnight, Rose offered to stay in the little bedsitting room. She could only do the overnights if her dad's shift fell in with the stay, because of Terry, but she loved being in charge of the premises and helping a cat or dog to make it through another night.

If Dad happened to be working nights and the pet could travel, Danny was only too happy to pick them up and she nursed her patient at home by the kitchen fire. A vet's assistant couldn't stick to regular hours but she loved the variety and the responsibility. It was the next best thing to being a vet.

On the hot sultry evening of her eighteenth birthday, Rose turned the door sign of Campbell's to 'closed' at five o'clock prompt. It was hard to believe she'd been there for over a year; she loved it. The things she'd learned! She could fix broken legs and wings, she could sew up after Roger had operated, she could deliver calves, lambs and foals and she could drive in any weather.

Earlier, Roger pulled her to one side saying, 'I'm giving you a pay rise because you'll be eighteen this month and you've become a great asset to the practice. You could have been a vet yourself, lassie.' Great praise indeed from Roger!

'I'm closing up now, Roger. I'm going dancing… for my birthday,' she called.

He came out of his consulting room and handed her the keys to the practice's Land Rover. 'You take it home, lassie. You work long hours and I'm just a walk away. If we're called out at night, you can always come and pick me up.'

'Roger, it's a kind thought and I appreciate your trust in me but we don't have a phone at home. You couldn't reach me. Besides, I look after my little brother and he's only six; I can't leave him at night when Dad's at work.' Reluctantly, she handed the keys back.

'Sorry, I didn't realise you had so much on your plate, Rose. You do so much here and never grumble.'

'I don't have time.' She smiled and added, 'I love work and our little Terry is a treasure. Why would I complain?'

Roger nodded as he walked her to the door. 'Enjoy your night, Rose.'

'I will!' She laughed at the thought of a phone at number one First Row and a Land Rover outside. Rose could imagine what some folk in the row would say to that.

What a wonderful night she had. The Friday dance in Burnside village hall was packed with couples they knew and they Lindy Hopped and jived all night.

Before going in, Danny had given her a card with

sweetheart on the front and a box of Cadbury's Roses. 'Roses for a Rose,' he whispered before sweeping her off her feet into a birthday kiss. She was eighteen and felt so grown up. She had even left the house with powder and lipstick on and Dad hadn't said a word.

At eleven, Danny drove her home, parking the car just before he got to First Row so they could kiss goodnight. Her dad listened for his van and would open the door as soon as the engine stopped so there was no kissing on her doorstep.

As Danny's mouth found hers, a flame of desire whipped through her. Long, deep kisses and Danny's caresses stirred sensations within her that urged her to demand more and to grasp him closer. As always, it was Danny who pulled away. 'We can't go further Rose, I worry I won't be able to stop.'

Rose took steady breaths and felt the excitement and need that threatened to envelope her slowly ebb away to a frustrating ache. 'I feel the same.' She lay her head on his shoulder. 'I know Lottie and Dennis go further. They touch… everywhere.'

'Did she *tell* you that?' Danny stroked her hair but it was more kissing and petting that she craved.

'Lottie was asking what *we* did. We sometimes talk about that sort of thing, you know.'

'I don't want you talking about us, it's private.' Danny lit a cigarette and rolled the window down. He didn't smoke much nowadays and never around her.

'Not details, silly. Just about feelings and how you can… relieve them without having intercourse. They do it.'

Danny shook his head. 'You come out with some things, Rose Kelly. Are you knowledgeable about everything?'

Rose laughed. 'I work with animals and they aren't shy. I know the basics but I'm as inexperienced as you, Danny.'

'Who says I'm inexperienced?' Danny threw the end of his cigarette out of the window and turned to face her.

'Aren't you?' she asked. Had he been with other girls?

He hung his head. 'I am short of experience. Even though

I'm twenty-one in a couple of months. The thing is I fell for you, I love you and I don't want us to do anything we'll regret.'

'I love you too, Danny.' She kissed him gently. 'Our feelings can't be wrong.'

'Maybe we should marry, when I'm twenty-one? Would you… would you marry me, Rose?'

She didn't have to think. 'One day I will, but not when you're twenty-one. We'll both have to wait a bit longer.'

She wanted Danny, but she had to care for little Terry and Dad for a little longer and she loved working at Campbell's. From what she'd seen, marriage meant sacrificing a career and becoming a homemaker. If their love was true, it would wait, and she would have to resist the insistent demands of her body.

42

1953

A chilly March day with grey skies hinted that winter wasn't quite ready to leave the rows. Terry, running to meet her without a coat and rosy-cheeked, panted, 'Dad is just putting his paints away but he said I could meet you off the bus. It was the best afternoon ever, Rose.'

'Was it now? You'll have to tell me all about it while I'm making dinner.' She would heat up the pie she'd made last night and serve it with potatoes and peas.

'Can we have chips with the pie to make it an even better best day ever?'

How could she refuse those wide eyes looking up at her? She squeezed his hand. 'Just this once, Terence Kelly.'

As she peeled large potatoes for chips, Terry told her every detail of his dad's school visit. Dad arranged the treat before Terry's seventh birthday and the teacher was only too glad to have a painter coming to teach art. Rose remembered Miss Tweddle wasn't keen on paint or mess.

'Dad showed everyone how to mix primary colours to get a full palette of colours. I knew them all but lots of the class didn't and thought mixing blue and yellow to get green was... brilliant!'

'Brilliant was it?' Rose loved the way Terry's face lit up with pleasure at finding the right word.

'Then Dad had a plan, a brilliant plan. We all put a hand in our favourite colour and made a handprint. You should've seen Miss Tweddle's face.' He laughed and pulled a shocked face to demonstrate. 'Then, all the handprints went on the wall to make a huge tree and Dad painted the best tree trunk ever with a squirrel hiding in it.'

'That sounds wonderful. You've had quite an afternoon and I can see you chose blue for your print. You need to scrub that left hand clean before dinner.'

'It was brilliant, Rose.'

Now, can you go and take Lucky to the allotment and tell Dad his dinner is almost ready?'

'Come on Lucky, let's run.'

The dog was middle aged but bounded after Terry like a pup.

Rose was about to close the scullery door, Terry always left it open, when Lottie slipped through the back gate looking upset. 'I saw Terry go towards the allotments, are you by yourself?'

One look at Lottie's puffy eyes and she knew something was amiss. 'Yes, I'll put the kettle on and you can tell me what's troubling you. Is it you and Dennis?'

'No. Well, yes… sort of.' Lottie blew her nose and pulled her cardigan tightly around her. 'I haven't told another soul, yet but I'm in big trouble, Rose.'

Sacked or expecting? It had to be something major for Lottie to be in tears. 'Do you want to tell me?'

Lottie nodded. 'I'm expecting… I've missed twice and I was sick this morning. They'll kill me, Rose!' She sank onto a chair by the range in the kitchen and gave in to a fresh bout of sobbing.

Crikey Moses! Rose knew Lottie's parents well enough and Dennis would certainly get it in the neck. 'They won't be pleased but they'll stand by you, Lottie and so will Dennis. It's not like you two have just met.'

'I still have to tell Dennis.'

'He will marry you, won't he?' Rose heart lurched. Being single and having a baby didn't bear thinking about.

'We've talked about it but he wants to wait until he's out of his apprenticeship. He'll be on decent money then.'

Dennis was an apprentice electrician at the pit for another year and wouldn't bring home much. Rose racked her brains for something supportive to say. 'Do you think Mrs Norris might keep you on part-time?'

'I hope so!' Lottie sipped the tea that Rose handed her.

'I thought you and Dennis were being careful. What went wrong?' Rose asked in a low voice even though there was nobody to hear them.

'We just got careless, I suppose. We're both Catholic so we don't use… you know.'

'You don't use condoms?' Rose's eyes widened.

'It's not allowed in our church so we just… well he got off at Manors, if you know what I mean?'

Manors was the train station before Newcastle, where the heck did that come into things? It took Rose a minute to work out what Lottie was on about. 'Ah! You mean you used the early withdrawal method? That's far too risky.'

'Don't I know it now! I'll have to tell Dennis tonight and then just hope he'll ask Dad if he can marry me. They'll guess why straight off and there'll be ructions on.'

Rose hugged Lottie. What could she say? Thank goodness Danny Dodd had shown more willpower than her and had always resisted going any further. She'd hate to be wearing Lottie's shoes.

Rose broke the news about the wedding and being Lottie's bridesmaid and was surprised that her dad had very little to say about it. 'Next month? I take it they have to? There's a bairn on the way?' he asked.

Rose nodded. 'They're marrying in a rush before the baby shows but the women in the rows will be counting the months on their fingers, won't they Dad?'

'Some will and some will feel sorry for the lass. They're not the first and they won't be the last but it's not the best start to married life. Dennis's mother won't be easy to share a kitchen with.' Lottie was moving in to Fifth Row with Dennis's family after the wedding.

Later in the week, Dad got on his high horse about a piece of national news. 'He's getting a bleedin' knighthood now! I would knight a hundred other folk before him!' He showed Mr Dodd the paper.

'The strings he has yanked to get where he is. It's bad enough having him as Prime Minister again... Sir! Bloody disgrace.' Danny's dad was standing at the scullery door with a bowl of eggs fresh from his allotment.

Rose had read quite a lot of Winston Churchill's writing over the years and could see touches of brilliance and great leadership as well as his failings. Wasn't everyone flawed to some extent? He upheld strong opinions but he wasn't all bad and probably deserved his knighthood for getting them through the war. She knew better than to share that view right now.

'Thanks for the eggs, Mr Dodd.' She took the bowl into the scullery.

The eggs were for baking because the rows were getting ready to celebrate the coronation in June and she was making fruit cakes with Lottie. With sugar still being rationed, everyone in the row made a small contribution of either sugar or dried fruit.

They made two rich fruit cakes, one for Lottie's wedding

and one for Queen Elizabeth's coronation. Rose was the chief weigher and stirrer and Lottie was in charge of the baking and decorating. The two cakes looked perfect. Lottie glazed them and covered the top in cherries and nuts. They made a small tester cake and shared it, cutting it into slices for Sunday tea.

On Sunday afternoon, Rose flushed when Dad teased her. 'What's this lassie? *You've* made a cake, at last? What's the occasion?' He took a slice and handed the plate to Terry.

'It's to celebrate Sir Winston getting his knighthood, of course.' She could tease too. Dad choked on his tea and she had to pat him on the back. 'Sorry, poor humour,' she laughed.

'That old beggar? You've put me right off, our Rose.'

He soon recovered and every crumb of Winston's cake got eaten.

Lottie walked down the aisle in an ivory dress and long veil; a beautiful bride. Rose followed her; the bridesmaid's dress she wore for Bella Wakenshaw's wedding still fit her so she'd shortened it to calf length, adding an ivory sash over the deep blue dress to match Lottie, and pinned her hair back with a spray of cream blossom. Danny was Dennis's best man and they all posed for photographs in the beautiful gardens behind St John the Baptist Church.

A ham salad and trifle in the church hall finished the cele-bration before Lottie and Dennis left for an overnight stay at The Rosemount, a B&B in Whitley Bay. Danny's cleaned up van was taking them to the coast. Before leaving, Lottie threw her bouquet of spring flowers backwards into the crowd and it flew towards Rose. She couldn't help but catch it.

Danny clasped her hand. 'That was a lucky catch, Rose. It's supposed to mean that you're next.'

'Do you want to tell my dad that?' She reached up and kissed his cheek.

'One day, but not yet.' He drew her to him in a hug and

kissed her before she helped the bride to gather her wedding dress and arrange it neatly in the front seat of the baker's van.

Dennis climbed in the back and they were off. Lottie waved, her face radiant and, just for a moment, Rose envied her. Tonight and every night Lottie would be snuggled up to the man she loved; what bliss.

43

It was coronation fever that did it; they bought their first television. A new transmitter at Pontop Pike meant that reception would be as good in the North as it was down South and one or two other families in the rows were splashing out.

'Dad, I know you're not that bothered about having a television but I'd *love* to watch Elizabeth being crowned. So... I'm thinking of using some of my savings to put a deposit on a set. I can afford to pay it off weekly; you would have to be a guarantor, though.'

'You'll do no such thing, my bonny lass. I don't hold with this hire purchase tricking folk into buying what they can't afford to pay up front. If and when we get a television in this house, *I'll* buy it and pay cash.'

Dad could be forward thinking about a lot of things but, at times, he was Neanderthal, he really was!

After a week of drip feeding the notion, Dad was wavering, she could tell. 'There are children's programmes that Terry would love and I hear that the BBC television news is *really* good... live footage of events.' She was trying to sew a patch over a rip in Terry's trousers and was making a real pig's ear of it.

Dad, listening to music on their radio, gazed into the fire. 'It's sounds to me like we canna do without one.'

His dry tone wasn't lost on Rose. 'Remember how we

got our first radio so we could hear news about the war? We couldn't imagine being without one now and it'll be the same with a television.'

'Let me think about it a bit longer, pet.'

She let it rest but he was coming around to the idea, she knew it.

Sure enough, their Bush television was installed at the end of May, just in time for the coronation.

June the second brought typical English weather! The street parties in the rows got such a drenching but the lads and lassies didn't mind and the grown-ups kept their umbrellas handy. Rose was glad she could nip indoors and watch the whole proceedings with Dennis and Lottie and a few others who had found their way into her kitchen.

Dad did a bit of sketching in their row then left. He'd treated himself to new oil paints so he took Terry and they made themselves scarce down the allotment with a plateful of food each. He was more excited about painting the street party doused with rain than actually being there and Terry was happy to be his paint mixer for the afternoon.

Throughout June and the following months, rainy days were followed by sunny spells and, though the weather was mixed, it was a perfect summer. Rose enjoyed being outdoors all weathers and loved driving out into the wilds of Northumberland to tend the farm animals with Roger. She spent Saturdays and Sundays out and about with Danny and, most of the time, Terry and Lucky tagged along. In Danny's van, it took five minutes to reach beach or countryside and they made the most of the longer days.

During the week, Rose enjoyed going for a late evening stroll or dancing the light summer evenings away with Danny. She spent evenings with Lottie who was happier to call at Rose's than sit in with Dennis's mam but she didn't attempt to knit anything for Lottie's baby. She just wasn't domesticated and the last time she knitted… she brushed the thought aside. She hated the way those memories kept popping up. Mum's deceit plagued her, still hurt. She should have knitted two pairs of bootees. There was a bigger gap in her family than there should be.

Time sped by and, before Rose knew it, they were well into 1954 and the start of another school year. Terry had new shorts and shirts hanging in his wardrobe for returning to school. With her wages, Stanley sending home money each month, Dad's housekeeping and the end of rationing, they didn't have to turn collars, let down trousers, or rely on hand-me-downs, and thank the lord for that. Rose didn't have the skills of Mam or Mary-from-next-door; a darn or a patch was her limit. Not that Mary sewed now; she had become frail and was staying with Larry in Burnside. She still kept on her home at number two though, in the hope of getting stronger.

As she bathed Terry and tried to scrub a summer's worth of muck from his nails, Rose remembered the excitement of a new school term.

'Ouch, you're too rough our Rose.' Terry flinched as she got to work on his knees that were more scab than skin.

'When I was little, our Mam scrubbed me even harder and put my hair into tight rag curlers so think yourself lucky my lad.'

'I bet Lottie doesn't scrub her baby this hard. Isn't he ugly?'

Rose laughed. 'He is not! All babies start out looking a bit crumpled but he'll fill out.'

'Paul is a daft name for a baby.' Terry splashed at Lucky who loved this game of running from the soap suds.

'Paul will grow into his name too. Now stop splashing or there will be no water in the bath.'

'I wish I had our mam here. Everybody else has one but me.'

She grabbed the towel warming by the range, lifted Terry out and hugged him. 'Mam would love to be here, dumpling. She didn't want to get sick and leave us.'

'Her picture watches us doesn't it Rose?'

'It does.' Above the mantlepiece, Dad's painting of Mam, forever young and joyous, laughed down at them.

When Terence had gone to bed, Dad, who still held a session or two every year at her old school, prepared his school toolkit for a demonstration later in the month.

'What are you planning to do, Dad?' Rose took Dad's bottle of glycerine and rosewater and rubbed some into her hands. He always used it after work and after painting to keep his hands soft and supple and her own hands, forever in water, needed some attention too. This potion was cheap and worked better than fancy creams.

'I'm talking about Monet and demonstrating impressionism to the advanced level art class.' He retrieved the bottle from her and rubbed a few drops into his own hands. 'It's a nice fee to donate to the Ashington group's coffers.'

'You would've made a great teacher. You have the patience and you give encouragement.'

'I really enjoyed that session with the young'uns, our Terry's class. They're free… uninhibited.'

'I'm sure you'd be welcome back, Dad. Specially if the primary teacher hates painting afternoons.'

At the end of the month, autumn gusts blew coal dust along the row and into the yard as Rose held her scarf to her mouth and shut the back door quickly behind her. It was a battle to keep a fine film from settling on the sills and furniture and trying its damndest to coat her lungs. She shivered as she filled the kettle. A fire burned in the range, Dad had added coals, but the house, it had that feel to it… emptiness. She used to feel that way when she came home and Mam had gone out somewhere unexpectedly.

Before taking off her coat, she added a few more coals and took a step back. What? Where the heck? Mam's picture wasn't on the wall above the mantelpiece. The darker colour of the wall where it should be hanging taunted her with questions.

The portrait's whereabouts continued to puzzle her as she heated the ham and pea soup she'd made at the weekend. The frame had been fine, she had dusted it on Saturday. They hadn't been burgled; nobody got burgled in the rows. Maybe the cord attaching it to the wall needed fixing? Dad must've taken it to his shed.

'Hi Rose, I'm starving.' Terry and Lucky bounded into the scullery leaving the door open and a cold blast entered the room.

'Where's Dad?' Rose hugged Terry and crouched to receive wet kisses from Lucky.

'He isn't coming for his dinner. He says he's working down there until late. He's made a brilliant bonfire and he's going to light it when it gets dark. I was too hungry to stay.'

They ate their soup with bread from a bought loaf. Mam's scufflers always went well with soup but Rose didn't have time to bake bread. Her attempts were always on the stodgy and yeasty side anyway. Thank goodness for Hovis. Rose half listened to Terry's chatter but an uneasy feeling pervaded. Was Dad okay? That missing painting had her worried.

44

Rose watched the evening news but her mind wouldn't rest. Darkness was about to fall and Dad still wasn't home. She'd never sleep for wondering what was wrong. Action would be better than sitting here fretting. She'd heat him some soup and slip along for a few minutes… see if he was okay.

She put the soup in a billy can, took a torch and left Lucky at the foot of the stairs to watch over Terry.

As she approached their allotment, her heart leapt. There was Dad's silhouette hunched on a low stool by the bonfire; he was okay.

His head lifted as she opened the gate. 'Dad, You're out late. I've brought you some warm soup.'

'You're a canny lassie.' His smile was half-hearted.

'There's something wrong isn't there? I can feel it.' Rose wrapped her scarf around her neck more tightly. The wind was cutting; they should be indoors.

'Pull up yonder cracket and get a warm at the fire, hinny.'

Rose took the small stool he was pointing at and moved closer to the flames. 'It's a funny hour to have a garden fire, Dad.'

'I wanted to burn a few canvases and bits of art without folk nebbin'.'

Not Mam's portrait? A spike of heat surged through her. 'Not the one from the kitchen? You couldn't!'

'No I couldn't. I nearly did… couldn't do it… need to be really sure first.' Dad's elbows were propped on his knees and his head was in his hands.

'Tell me what's wrong. You're don't sound like yourself, Dad.'

'You're right there, hinny. I canna tell you what's wrong because I'm not sure I believe it and I'm hoping it's me that's wrong.'

'You're… You're talking in riddles.'

'I'm trying to solve a riddle Rose. It's all a bleedin' riddle to me.'

'What is? Tell me then you can have some soup and I can go home to little Terry. I can only leave him a short while.'

'Little Terry? He's part of the riddle, too. I don't know how to say this, it's not something a lassie of mine should hear but…'

'But *what?*'

'Promise you won't breathe a word? I could be making a mistake. I damn well hope I am.'

Rose nodded as icy shivers ran through her. Let it be anything but…

'This may sound daft but I think I met his sister today. I'm damned well sure of it but, I mean, how could that be?'

No! Heart pounding, she forced herself to look at her dad. His eyes were searching her face, looking for… for what? A reaction, an answer or reassurance he was wrong? What can she say? Her head swam, darkness swooped and she gripped the edge of the cracket to stop herself falling into the fire. From a distance she heard Dad's plea.

'Say something, Rose. Tell me I'm goin' doolally.'

'What gives you that idea?' Her voice sounded hoarse but the darkness receded and she was back there with him. Play for time. Delay giving an answer.

From the safety of the fire's leaping shadows, she watched Dad struggle to make sense of his discovery.

'I visited a primary class in Morpeth today. Repeating that paint mixing activity that I'd done with Terry's class. A lovely little class, they were.'

Joy's class? She'd thought… assumed… he was going back to the high school, today. Why didn't she know? Maybe she could have stopped it, called Mrs Fletcher and warned her to keep Joy off? Her mind raced as he continued.

'I talked about the session I'd taken at Linwood with the art teacher of the high school a couple of weeks ago and she asked me to do it at a Morpeth primary school as a favour for a friend of hers. Anyway, I went along this afternoon and we got started and there was this little lassie…' He shook his head.

'Go on, Dad, you were saying,'

'A bright button she was, put me in the mind of you at first, she showed me her own sketches. For eight years old, she was gifted, I tell you. She was a chatty little thing and she felt… familiar. I know that sounds funny, but she did.

I started the session and she kept catching my eye; she was a left hander like me and then she threw her head back and laughed at something and it hit me, our Terry's exact laugh and stance and his colouring.

I felt funny for the rest of the session. Was I imagining things? At the end, I asked her name and found she was a Fletcher. I dreaded asking her birthday but I had to. I had to know, and Rose… you'll never believe…' He shook his head and looked into the flames.

Silence.

'Same as Terry's.' Rose's voice trembled.

'Aye! What can it mean? I mean I know what it *looks* like but how could that be? I'll have to go to the Fletcher's and find out if there's been some sort of… of jiggery-pokery going on.'

'You can't do that, Dad!' Her fists clenched and she tucked them under her elbows. She want to tug at him and keep him there.

'And why not? I think I'll go to Larry's and speak to Mary-from-next-door first; she delivered Terry, did she deliver two?

Mary and Ginnie were as thick as thieves. I'll find out what she knows before I visit the Fletcher's. Mr Fletcher is at the Gloria colliery near Morpeth so he'll have a manager's house there.

'Don't do that, Dad.' Her mouth was dry but she managed to spit that out.

'Don't you want to know whether you've got a sister or not and what on God's earth has gone on? Has somebody broken the law? I certainly need answers.'

'You don't need to go and upset Mary. You don't need to ask, Dad. I... I can tell you.'

It was a whisper but he heard because he grabbed her arm. 'What? You mean you know something about this lassie?'

'Yes, Dad, I know the whole sorry tale and you're right, she *is* Terry's twin. Mam gave birth to both of them.' Her eyes flooded with tears as she witnessed the pain her words were causing.

He jumped up. 'How long have you known this? How long have you kept this from me? Did your mother tell you about it?' He paced from the shed to the fire and back.

'Yes, she had to because I found out... a bit like you. Sit back down and I'll tell you all I know.'

Rose was relieved to unload the burden she had carried for years. It had put a distance between her and her dad and, now he had discovered the truth, there would be no secrets. She made sure that Dad knew Mam's reasoning, her fear of falling ill and leaving two little ones. There was a long silence after she finished her telling of events but she felt lighter... cleansed... no secrets.

'You never said? You kept all this from me, your own father?' He stood up and poked at the orange embers of the bonfire.

'It wasn't my secret to tell, Dad. It was Mam's. For what it's worth, even though you're hurt, I'm so glad that I don't have to keep it a secret from you anymore.'

'Go home. Get out of my sight. I canna look at you…
or her a minute longer!' He picked up the portrait that had
watched over them since they'd lost Mam and flung it onto
the bonfire. Flames licked over her laughing face. 'You lassie…
You've deceived me just like her. You can keep out of my way
and pack your bags as soon as you like because I don't want
you under my roof. I have no time for either of you.'

JOHN KELLY

John Kelly watched the flames lick around the laughing eyes that seemed to mock him. The canvas turned to ash. *Ginnie how could you? Such a secret? From me?*

It was like she'd died all over again. Had he ever known Ginnie? Or his Rose? His first born had betrayed him too.

A hard lump formed in his chest. His heart hadn't broken but hardened into coal, black, heavy, full of supressed fire and rage.

He had watched Rose grow and flourish. How he'd worshipped that young lass. How could he have missed the secrets she kept from him? To side with her mother over something like this? He'd never have believed it.

Today, he'd not only been robbed of the little lass, Joy, he had lost his good memories of his wife. They were both gone and, hardest of all, he couldn't find space in the coal blackness of his heavy heart to forgive Rose.

45

From her bedroom window, Rose watched the first rays of morning lighten the strip of sky that sat above the neatly lined slate roofs of the rows. Like one of Dad's palettes, streaks of navy and indigo merged into cobalt and sapphire. Soon they'd give way to silver and steel and the house sparrows would start their chirping.

She hadn't slept, hadn't even undressed. An hour ago, she'd nipped to the outside toilet then darted back indoors to light the fire in the kitchen before making a brew and preparing Dad's work bait, a slice of bread and dripping wrapped in paper. The tea was masting in the teapot, keeping warm by the range for Dad. She'd brought herself a cup upstairs because she didn't want to bump into him before work yet she couldn't let him go down the pit on an empty stomach.

Had he meant all he said to her, last night? His words had scalded her heart. He'd been so upset and angry and hadn't come home until well after midnight, his footsteps slow and weary as he trod upstairs. Had *he* slept? He would be up and leaving for his shift soon.

From the window, in the murky morning light, she saw the first outlines of miners trudging to work. Whatever their troubles at home, the cage dropped them underground and they put their lives to one side. To do their job in the bowels of the earth, pitmen needed their wits about them and all their senses fully functioning.

Every creak and sound alerted Rose to what her dad was doing, getting dressed, drinking a mug of strong tea and then opening the door to go to the pit. Her fingertips touched the hard barrier of glass as he appeared on the street below. She wanted to reach out as he merged into the work pool with the others. As he disappeared into a stream of miners heading towards the big pit wheel, tears ran down her cheeks. Fancy her dad thinking she had betrayed him. Was there nothing she could do or say to take that hollow look out of his eyes?

He'd been deceived by her as well as Mam. At times, she'd hated her mam for forcing this secret on her but never so much as now. How could you ever think you'd get away with such a plan, Mam? Yes, she hated her all right but she missed her and loved her too.

She dried her tears and forced a smile when Terry woke up. 'Terry, I won't be here tonight after school. I have to stay at work for a few nights. You can go over to Third Row to see Mrs Dodd or Gracie after school or if you need anything. I'll let them know.'

'Aye.' Terry wasn't taking any notice, he had Lucky dancing and doing side rolls for crumbs of his toast.

Rose crouched and turned him to face her, a giant lump in her throat. 'Terry, I'll be back as soon as I can and remember I love you, my little dumpling.'

'Stop being soppy, our Rose! I'm eight and a big lad now.' He laughed and squirmed from her arms. 'I'm taking Lucky for a trot around the rows before I call on Spike for school.'

Rose packed enough clothes for a few days into two shopping bags; she didn't want anyone in the rows to see her with a suitcase. Dad might have calmed down by the weekend. If not… if not? Her stomach clenched and she felt sick. Her dad and brothers were her life so he had to find it in his heart to forgive her. *'You can keep out of my way and pack your bags as soon as you like because I don't want you under my roof.'* Dad's words… she couldn't shake them out of her head.

She called at Norris's, Lottie wasn't there yet so that was a relief; it would be hard to evade Lottie's questions.

'Are you all right Rose? You look… you look a bit under the weather, pet.'

'I'm fine… a bit of a cold, I think.' She told Mrs Norris that she was away for a few days, staying at the vet's surgery, and asked her to keep an eye on Terry.

'I will, hinny. I'll send your usual order over tomorrow, shall I?'

'Yes please.' She opened her purse.

'It can wait until the weekend, no rush.'

'Thanks Mrs Norris.' She had better go carefully with her money until she got her next wages. The housekeeping was in a tea caddy at home so there was money to pay the grocery bill.

Next stop was Danny's house. He was already off to work and Mrs Dodd opened the door. 'Eeh, Rose lass, is something the matter? You look like a ghost.'

'A bit of a cold, that's all and there's an emergency at work Mrs Dodd so I have to stay over at the surgery for a night or two.'

Gracie came in from the scullery. 'Have you time for a cup of tea to warm you through, pet?'

'No Gracie, I'm late as it is. I called to ask if you'll keep an eye on Terry… after school you know. He's just…' Tears fell and she brushed them away.

'Don't go getting upset.' Ample arms encircled Rose and she rested against Gracie soaking up the warmth and love. 'Of course I'll watch out for him. That job is asking too much if you have to leave the bairn. You can always say no.'

Rose was tempted to spill out part of the story but where

would she be able to stop? Dad would be even more angry if any folk in the rows knew their business. He was a private man. 'I have to go, it's just a few days, Gracie.'

Gracie scrutinised her face, 'Rose… Is this anything to do with our Danny? I mean… he hasn't got you into trouble has he?'

Rose stepped back. 'No, Gracie. Danny's not like that… he would *never*. I can't lie… It's more than work but I really can't say. It's not Danny; it's between me and Dad.'

Mrs Dodd stood up and placed both hands firmly on the kitchen table. 'Gracie, why don't you go over to First Row when it's time for the bairn to come home from school for the rest of the week and give him his tea? You can leave something on the range for Mr Kelly as well. I can manage here without you and it'll put Rose's mind at rest.'

'Would you? Just until the weekend?' The hard knot in Rose's chest loosened and she could breathe more easily.

Gracie nodded. 'You get off to that job of yours, lassie and, when he gets home from work, we'll tell Danny to call in and see you're all right.'

Rose arrived at work an hour late and knocked on Roger's surgery door. 'Come in, come in,' he bellowed. 'Ah, you're here. I thought you must be sick, Rose.' He looked at her more closely. 'You don't look too good, m'lass. Should you be here?'

'I've nowhere else to go, Roger. My dad's thrown me out.'

Roger didn't ask awkward questions and he was only too happy to let Rose stay in the bedsit above the surgery. 'I'll pay you rent, Roger.'

'You'll do no such thing. The room is sitting there empty and it means I have an assistant on hand if I need one.'

'I hope I can sort things out with Dad at the weekend.'

'If not, you're welcome to make that place your own. Now take your stuff up, get settled and make us a brew, I'm parched.'

Rose's head pounded, the tension in her neck and the knot in her chest weren't as bad but she felt on edge, waiting for the repercussions. Would Dad still go to Mary's or the Fletcher's? How much could she tell Danny? What if Dad meant what he said?

A cup of tea then she'd get stuck into her work, she'd do that and leave her worries about Dad and Terry and the whole tangled web until she was safely tucked away upstairs tonight.

46

At closing time, Miss Alexander, red faced and out of breath, burst into the surgery. 'I'm sure Monty has swallowed something! He keeps vomiting and he's very weak. I came in from school and he didn't even raise his head. Am I in time for Mr Campbell to look at him?'

Rose knew Miss Alexander from her schooldays and had never seen her so distressed. 'Of course, he will. Just sit down here and I'll pop into his surgery with Monty and tell him it's an emergency.'

Roger took the large cream cat out of the carrier and was silent as he checked him over. 'He doesn't look good, Rose. I can't feel an obvious obstruction but it is possible he's swallowed something. Did you know that cats can't spit something out? If they get something in their throat they have to keep swallowing.'

'I've read that. They usually pass it in a bowel movement though, don't they?' She stroked the limp cat who was purring loudly. A loud purr was the way they coped with pain; it didn't always mean they were happy.

'Yes, you're right. He may well shit the blighter out.' Roger frowned and gently prodded the cat's belly.

Rose smiled. You could rely on Roger to call a spade a bleeding shovel. 'If we keep him here, I'll monitor him, Rog. Miss Alexander has school tomorrow.'

'In that case, we'll put him straight on a drip. He's vomited a lot so he'll be dehydrated and fluids will perk him up. You prepare the equipment and I'll have a word with Miss Alexander and send her on her way.'

When Roger came back he said, 'Miss Alexander has gone but your young man is waiting by the door for you.'

Danny! How she'd love his arms around her right now but she had a very sick animal on her hands. 'Oh blast! I've just scrubbed up to help you. Would you mind telling him I'm dealing with this emergency? He'll understand. Tell him, I'll see him tomorrow, any time.'

'Aye, I'll be your messenger boy and send him on his way.' Roger saluted and Rose turned her attention to her patient.

Roger left after Monty was comfortably settled for the night. Rose locked the surgery door after him and, as she turned she saw a package on the reception desk. She smiled at the familiar shape. Scribbled on the paper bag was 'Roses for a Rose.' She loved Danny Dodd. He was the best.

Rose hadn't slept at all the night before so she took a mug of Ovaltine and a book to bed but couldn't read for thinking about Dad. What was he going to do? Would he have calmed down by the weekend? She wished Danny was here to talk it over with. He hadn't a phone or she could have least called from the kitchen phone to say goodnight and thank him for her chocolates.

She turned off the light expecting to toss and turn but exhaustion won and sleep came straight away. She woke in the black of night in the strange room and the whirl of thoughts started again. Would Dad have calmed down by the weekend? How was Monty doing? She may as well go down and check on him seeing as she was awake. Pushing her feet into slippers and buttoning up her dressing gown, she yawned. Her alarm clock showed it was almost three o'clock.

Monty's third eyelid was over his eyes and he was panting. Even on the drip, he was very dehydrated, poor soul. He had vomited; the dark liquid matted his beautiful fur. It was foul, metallic, was it blood? She bit her lip, this was not good. Taking a breath, she decided to make a call and wake Roger.

'Monty is fading and won't make it unless you have a solution, Rog.'

'I was thinking it over before bed and, if there is an obstruction it would be possible to operate and take it out of his bowel but I canna do that with a small animal. I've just not got the skill or equipment to do it, Rose. If he was no better in the morning, I was going to scoot him along to Frank Maxwell in Ashington because he's a fine surgeon in the domestic sector and would at least have a go. Give the lad a chance.'

'He won't last that long, I'm sure. I don't think he'll last a car journey.' Rose rubbed the back of her neck with her free hand. Losing someone's beloved pet was the very worst part of this job. Surely, there was something they could do.

'Prepare the surgery for an op, lassie. Scrub up. I'll call Frank Maxwell and ask if he'll be heroic and drive out to you to try to save the moggy. He's daft enough to.'

Rose smiled. Rog was his most brusque when he was upset. 'Thanks Rog.'

'Rose, if he's not available. I'm coming in to put the poor lad to sleep, okay?'

Roger called to say help was coming and to unlock the door. She'd unlocked the front door, pulled on an apron and tied her hair under a cap. The surgery was ready. Monty was hanging on. Where the heck was Mr Maxwell? At last, the doorbell jangled to announce he had arrived.

'Hello there!'

'In through here, Mr Maxwell.'

The surgery door opened and in came Frank. Young Frank.

'Rose!'

'Frank… I was expecting your father.'

'A lecture in Edinburgh. I've watched and assisted him in this sort of operation lots of times so he agreed I should have a go. I'm still in training but Mr Campbell thinks that it's this lad's only chance.'

Miss Alexander's gut feeling had been right. A one inch diameter ring attached to a short piece of string had caused the blockage, part of a cat toy. Rose put it in a jar after it was removed to show Roger and Miss Alexander the offender. Once the cat was stitched up, Frank inserted a temporary line in his neck for fluids, meds and nutrition. 'This will give his bowel time to heal and make it easy for his owner to give him pain relief and some liquid food,' he explained.

Rose fashioned a little wraparound vest out of muslin to keep the tube out of the cat's way. She was quite proud of her effort. She *could* be handy with a needle when she needed to be.

It was still dark when they carried the sedated cat up to Rose's bedsit. 'I'll keep watch over him. We can't lose him after all this. If you send your bill to us, we'll pass it on to Miss Alexander.'

Frank limped over to a dining chair and sat down. 'Sorry, I still get stiffness and pain in this leg when I stand in one place for too long. Not great for surgery. About the bill, I'm not Dad… not fully qualified, Rose. It was life or death. What could I do? Tell Monty's owner my part is free because it was for experience.'

'Thanks for taking the risk, Frank. Do you want a cuppa before you go?' Now the emergency was over, she felt a bit awkward but it would be bad manners to push him out of the door.

'Anything stronger?' His hazel eyes looked bloodshot and weary.

'Medicinal brandy in a cup of tea. That's what we'll have. I know where Roger keeps the bottle and I'm sure he won't mind.'

They chatted about anaesthesia for domestic animals over their laced tea and it was almost like the old times when they walked home from school except for the giant question mark squeezed between them. Why didn't you write? she wanted to ask.

The question was so dominant in her thoughts that she was shocked when Frank said, 'I have to ask you, Rose. Why didn't you write? You never answered my letters.'

'*Me*? I didn't hear from you all term but I still sent you a Christmas card… and a letter.' Her cheeks flushed. The nerve of him blaming this on her.

Frank sat up and clasped her hand, his gaze searching hers. 'I did write. I wrote as soon as I was able to. I wrote about my accident… Having to defer Cambridge and I… I thought you didn't reply because I was likely to be disabled. Mightn't walk, you know. I thought—'

'You wrote? I didn't get a letter or a postcard, nothing. I thought you'd met lots of clever Cambridge friends and forgotten me.'

'Rose! Would I? I didn't receive your card or letter at Christmas either. I waited all holiday to see if you would reply to mine and meet up.'

'If I didn't get your letters and you didn't get mine, what happened? I even hand delivered your Christmas card to Vera to pass on to you.'

'You did?'

Rose nodded. She could tell he believed her and, sitting here with Frank, she didn't doubt him either. 'It can't just be coincidence.'

'It can't and I have a nasty feeling about it. About it being done deliberately by someone callous, mean spirited.'

'Ruth?' Even Ruth couldn't be so evil, could she?

Frank nodded. 'If it was, I'll never forgive her. She was so attentive and kind after my accident and went to the post office for me, collected my mail, posted it.'

'Crikey, Frank! She must hate me.'

'She's jealous. Jealous of me... everyone. She seemed kind for a while but then I realised she was keeping friends away and wanted me to be dependent on her. Remember that day at the cinema when we met?'

'Yes, of course. I felt awkward because we'd dropped contact.'

'I was about to ask you to meet and talk to find out why but she whisked us away and... and you had a boyfriend with you so... well, I thought it was best to let it go.'

'Tell me what happened to your leg, Frank.'

'I took a tumble from my bike in my first week at Cambridge. A careless driver knocked me into a wall and I had multiple injuries. I'm lucky I wasn't killed but my left leg was badly damaged. Dad found a surgeon here at the Royal Victoria Infirmary who saved it from amputation but I needed several operations and I had to defer my course for a full year.'

'Oh Frank, to think I didn't know and you could have died!'

'I'm still here but it was a hellish few months. I'm here now, for a couple of days, for a check-up with the surgeon; hope he doesn't want to put more pins in it.' Frank managed a grin, wiping his hand across his eyes and through his hair as if it would disperse the memories. 'Ruth, who wasn't working, offered to be my companion and assistant while I was convalescing. At the time, I felt grateful but she seemed to resent my recovery and need to return to a normal life.'

'She's a strange girl. It looks like Vera passed the Christmas card to Ruth to give to you and you didn't get it.'

'I'll ask Vera, when I get the chance. I can't understand why Ruth has tried to ruin our friendship.'

The birds were chirping and a pale blue sky welcomed them as Rose opened the door to let Frank out. 'Let me know how Monty is getting on. It's lovely to be friends again, Rose.' He bent and kissed her on the cheek and she smiled. She had missed Frank and their discussions.

The smile froze on her face as she spotted Danny's van parked over the road. Danny was looking right at them. She raised her hand to wave him over. She must introduce him to Frank and explain why he was here. He saw her wave but turned his face and drove off.

'Who's that in the van?' Frank asked.

'That's Danny, my boyfriend. He's just watched you kiss my cheek at the door of my bedsit at seven in the morning, Frank. No wonder he's driven off. I'll have some explaining to do.'

47

Miss Alexander answered her phone after the first ring. 'How's Monty? I've worried all night.'

'He's holding up, Miss Alexander. We had to operate to remove an obstruction last night or we would've lost him but now he has a good chance of recovering.'

'Can I call in before school?'

'You certainly can and I'll tell you about his op and aftercare.'

Rose hurried to wash and dress before Monty's visitor arrived and, after that brief visit, her day was hectic. Personal worries – Dad wanting nothing to do with her and Danny driving off – were placed firmly at the back of her mind as she gave her attention to pets and their anxious owners for the rest of the day.

'You look off colour, lassie. I know you're tired but your fallout with your Dad must be worrying you too.'

She must look a sight if Roger had noticed. 'Monty kept me up last night but I'm sure he'll be a better patient tonight. As for Dad... it'll have to wait until the weekend.'

'No, you're wrong there, I don't think it can wait. You can keep an eye on Monty tonight and then we'll put him under Audrey's watch in the morning and ask the school mistress to collect him at teatime. Tomorrow, you're having a day off to rest and see your family and that's an order.'

'You're a good boss, Roger.' Rose managed a smile.

'You put in extra hours all the time so no need to praise me. You've earned some time off and I hope you and your father can sort out your differences.'

Rose and Monty had a good night's rest. 'We both look better this morning, Monty.' she told him as she checked his line and gave him fluids and medication. Monty's eyes were back to a bright green and, checking her own in the mirror, she saw that the dark smudges under them had all but disappeared.

Audrey came into the shop at nine and, after handing her charge over with a page of instructions, Rose caught the bus to Linwood. First of all she'd visit Mrs Dodd and Gracie to find out how Danny and Terry were doing and then she'd try to talk to Dad.

The bus left the suburbs of Morpeth and they passed green rows of potatoes almost ready for picking, corn stubbled fields of gold and herds of grazing cows. She looked out for Batey's rust and white Ayrshire herd to see if they were in good shape. Rose had helped Roger to deliver a couple of their calves.

After admiring the Ayrshires, Rose tried out a few openers for the talk with Dad. In her head they had a calm and reasoned conversation and made up; the trouble was, things might not go the way she wanted them to. The fields gave way to terraced housing and Rose got ready to jump off near Burnside and take the short walk into Linwood.

All too soon, she reached the rows. Her heart was thudding in her chest as she knocked on the Dodd's door then walked into the kitchen. 'Well look who the cat dragged in!' Mrs Dodd's tone sent out a warning that this wasn't going to be the friendly visit she hoped for.

'Hello Mrs Dodd. I've got an extra day off so I've come to see how Terry and Danny are.' She hovered in the middle of the room. She didn't like to take a seat until she was asked.

Mrs Dodd rose from her fireside chair and, hands on hips, asked, 'Have you now? Your Terry is fine. He's being looked after and fed by our Gracie and she's just popped over there making a batch of bread for him and his father for the weekend.'

'Oh, that's a relief. I'm so grateful to Gracie for stepping in like this.'

'Are you sure? It doesn't look like you're grateful to me when you go and upset our lad!'

Rose hadn't experienced Mrs Dodd's angry side before and it took all of her nerve to stand there and look her in the eye. 'Danny? What's Danny said?' Her throat felt dry and she hoped he hadn't told any of them about Frank's overnight visit. They'd have a field day along the row with that bit of gossip.

'He didn't need to say much. He came home yesterday with a face like a slapped arse and then went to the 'tute and got drunk. That's not like our Danny. When he came in, he was in a sorry state. That's when he told me.'

'Told you what?'

'That he's thinking of moving. Leaving Linwood and moving all the way to Alnwick to work in the Williams branch there. Wants to make a fresh start, he reckons.'

'And you think he's leaving here because of me, Mrs Dodd?'

'I'd bet a pound to a penny that you've either egged him on to move and better himself or you've knocked him back when he's proposed and that's the reason he's moving away. Nobody else could upset our Danny. Nobody but you.'

Mrs Dodd had always been pleasant towards her until now. She wasn't a woman to cross but Rose couldn't let this accusation go. 'You'd lose your pound then. I'd never ever give Danny ultimatums and… and we have an agreement. Danny knows I love him and we'll marry when the time is right.'

Mrs Dodd's frown showed she was unconvinced. 'He didn't look like he knew it last night. Something must've happened.'

'We had a misunderstanding. I need to talk to him. I'll put it right Mrs Dodd.'

'I hope you do or you'll have me to answer to. It's just not on, giving my lad the run around.'

Rose was glad to leave Mrs Dodd and her accusations. She walked to the miners' welfare playground and sat on a bench. She had to gather her thoughts before she went to First Row. Why was everything going wrong? Danny had never ever mentioned moving to Williams' shop in Alnwick before. He knew that she needed to be near Terry and Dad and he wanted to be near her.

Maybe, now that Dad had thrown her out, he'd thought it was a chance to make changes? No… that wasn't the reason. He'd have talked it over first.

He was thinking of moving because he'd seen her with Frank and thought the worst. Could he really think that she'd let another man stay overnight when she hadn't even done such a thing with him? How could he think like that? Where was his trust? Tears threatened to fall and Rose didn't know whether her insides churned with anger or disappointment. Danny couldn't think so badly of her, but why didn't he stop to hear her out yesterday?

The situation with Danny was bad enough without her fall-out with Dad on top of it all. She had to go home and smooth things over. She couldn't bear not speaking to Dad but she felt the same about him as she did about Danny. Angry. Disappointed. For years she'd kept a secret that she hadn't wanted to keep. It hadn't been her secret to tell and, if she had spoken to Dad, the fall-out would've split the family asunder just like it threatened to do now. Dad was placing the blame for what Mam had done onto her shoulders. She was bearing the brunt of his anger because he couldn't direct it towards Mam. Would he see that if she talked about it?

'Lovely day isn't it Rose? Mind if I sit here a minute? I've walked the rows and just got this teething bairn to sleep.'Tilly Johnson sat beside her and she pushed her anguish to one side, managing to smile and chat for a minute or two before making her excuses and heading towards First Row.

48

The aroma of bread warm from the oven met Rose as she opened the back door bringing with it a reminder of her mother at the range. What she would give to see her mam turn around, face flushed from the oven and hands floury from her baking.

Gracie, stouter, plainer but with a smile just as welcoming turned around instead. 'There you are, Rose! Come in, lass.' Rose took off her coat and hung it on the back of the door as Gracie went on, 'I was hoping you'd come around to see young Terry and put us in the picture with what's got into our Danny. Mam's in a right state.'

Rose sat on the nearest chair. 'Don't I know it. I called there first and she blames me for Danny acting funny.'

'You don't know what up with him then?' Gracie wiped her hands on her apron and pulled up the dining chair next to Rose. She perched on the edge.

Rose met her anxious look. 'Ah... I do, I suppose... nothing I want to talk about, though. I'd rather see Danny first. Clear a few things up.'

Gracie stood up. 'I've put in two loaves and made the left-over dough into a stottie and a few scufflers to use the bottom of the oven. I'm parched now, do you fancy a cup of tea?'

'Thanks Gracie, I do but you sit back down and I'll make the tea. I'm more than grateful for you looking after these two.'

Rose walked into the scullery. She reached automatically for the caddy and had to stop herself tutting when it wasn't in its usual place.

'Between you and me, Rose I love coming here. It gets me away from my mother; she can be hard work to listen to all day and I get to do the baking as well as the clearing up. I've been meeting the bairn on the corner after school and then we have a good talk while we walk to Mam's. He has a slice then he's out of the door until his dinner. He's as good as gold.' Gracie beamed and Rose felt shocked at the flash of jealousy searing through her. She was glad things had gone well but she wanted to be back and running the Kelly home. She wanted to be caring for Terry and Dad.

'It's just been a couple of days!' She caught Gracie's crestfallen look and added, 'You've been a great help, Gracie but I need to sort things out with my dad before he goes on first shift. He'll *have* to come round because he won't want Terry left overnight on his own.'

Gracie got up to reach for the poker. She prodded at the coals on the range. 'He seems pretty set on managing without you, Rose.' She put the poker down and turned to Rose, her expression apologetic. 'John's asked me to stop over with Terry when he's on nights. He's offered me your room. Hope you don't mind, pet. I'd hate to fall out over it but the bairn does need somebody here.'

Rose clashed the tea caddy onto the table. 'Do you think he means to go on with this… this daftness?'

'If I were you I'd let him stew over it all for a while… he's still that vexed.'

Rose shook her head. 'No, I want to go over to the allotment and talk to him this afternoon.'

'I'd… I'd leave it a bit, if it was me.'

Gracie Dodd was enjoying being here. Was that it? Immediately Rose felt mean. No Gracie was just saying things as she saw them. 'It's complicated with me and Dad. You wouldn't understand and I can't tell you.'

'I know, pet.' Gracie squeezed Rose's shoulder.

'You know? *What* do you know?' Rose sank to a chair certain that Gracie didn't know the whole story.

'The whole sorry tale. Aye… your dad… he talked… he had to talk to somebody and I was here.'

'H-he couldn't. He wouldn't betray M- us.' Rose shook the thought from her head.

'Don't worry. I'd never repeat a word, not even to my mother. Your dad understands that I don't tittle-tattle. I know enough about gossip and putting two and two together without knowing the full story along these rows.'

Rose shook her head. 'I can't believe he's told *you* about our family.'

'Have a heart, Rose. He's that worked up about the bairn and being deceived it's nearly driven him to… well to give up on things. Thank Christ for young Terry; he's been his salvation. That bairn is all he's caring for now.'

Rose shivered. Her teeth chattered even though she the kitchen was warmed by a roaring coal fire. 'What exactly did he tell you?'

'Your mam's dealings with Mrs Fletcher, Mary-from-number-two's part and you finding out too. The whole sorry tale, I think.'

'Did he ask your advice?'

'Me? No hinny. I've just listened… said that things happen for a reason and we don't always know why.'

'Do you believe that?'

'Aye, I do. I believe he's found out now for a reason too. All this upset, some good has got to come out of it one day.'

'I admire your optimism Gracie but I can't sit still and let this resolve itself in its own good time.' She sounded hoity toity to her own ears but she was angry, damn it, and what did Gracie Dodd know about anything? Why on earth had Dad confided in *her*?

'I think you'll have to be patient pet, 'cause your dad isn't in a state to give you a fair hearing just now.'

Rose sat with her elbows on the table and her face cupped in her hands. She just couldn't think straight anymore and couldn't bear to hear another word about Dad.

'What you can do is try to make things right with our Danny. Is it a little tiff or something more?' Gracie asked.

'A silly misunderstanding I'd say. Danny being hot-headed. Now he's going to move and he hasn't even talked it over with me.' Rose started crying with the frustration. 'Oh Gracie everything is such a bleeding mess!'

'I'll just make us that cuppa, pet and you can tell me what happened. I might be able to help.' Gracie took the caddy from Rose.

'You couldn't help with Dad,' Rose flung back.

'Okay, maybe a cup of tea won't help.' Gracie put the caddy back on the table then went towards the back door. 'I'll just get my coat and be off to leave you in peace. Do you want to meet Terry from school?'

Rose took a deep breath and let out a sigh. 'Sorry, Gracie I didn't mean to shun you. I'm just so bleeding angry and taking it out on you. I'm sick of worrying about Danny and Dad. Stay a while and tell me what Terry's been up to. It'll take my mind off things.'

Rose met Terry from school and took him along to the miners' welfare park to play on the swings and have a chat.

'Dad says you're too busy with work to be at home but Gracie will help us out. I miss you, Rose.'

She grabbed his hand. 'I miss you too, dumpling.'

'Stop it, Rose! I've told you I'm not your bloody dumpling! I'm a big lad now.' He shook her off his hand and ran off grinning.

She caught up with him at the teapot lid. 'I don't want to

hear that word from you or I'll be putting mustard on your tongue, okay?'

'Mustard?'

'Yes, that's what Mam would tell you.'

He climbed to the top and shouted, 'Anyway, Gracie makes proper bread and brilliant cakes!'

Was she replaced so easily? She wiped a tear from her cheek before shouting, 'Does she buy you gobstoppers and sherbet dips, though?'

'Have you? He slid down the lid and dropped at her feet.

'I have.' She smiled and produced his favourites.

They chatted on a bench as he devoured the dip. 'I'll keep the gobstopper for later.'

Just on five, she dropped him off at the Dodd's back door. She didn't stay. She didn't want any more questions about Danny and, though she was grateful to her, she didn't want to see Gracie fussing around her little brother.

Rose was surprised to find herself heading towards the chapel. She had no reason to rush back to Morpeth but she hadn't planned on stopping off here. She tried the door, it wasn't locked so she walked right to the front and sank onto the pew she had first sat in as a three-year-old. So much had changed since then.

No prayer came. She was out of sorts with Jesus and his lot and was tired. She'd just rest and put her troubles down for a while. She wished her chattering inner voice would fall silent. She sat until her hands and feet were frozen but, thankfully, the nagging voice in her head finally stopped and she could examine her own behaviour without it declaring everything was her fault.

If she *could* turn back time to when she found out about Joy, would she behave any differently? No, she'd still keep Mam's secret. It would've split two families to reveal the truth and who would be happy then?

Suppose she turned back time even further so she hadn't

ever met Joy? She'd have found out about her eventually from Dad. They wouldn't have argued but then neither of them would have had the chance to hear Mam's side of the story. She was glad that she couldn't turn back time because everything had happened for a reason. Gracie had told her that but she had been too agitated to listen.

Look at last week, if she had a choice she wouldn't upset Danny. But, if she hadn't chatted all night to Frank, she'd never know that their friendship was ruined by someone else. Even if seeing Frank and her together upset Danny, she was glad to learn the truth. She had done nothing wrong that night and if Danny had stayed to ask, he'd know that.

Two problems threatened to ruin her life but she wouldn't want do anything differently. What she wanted to do was make Dad and Danny see things her way. That was her trouble. She had to accept that Dad and Danny would make their own choices too even if their choices didn't suit her.

She was frozen stiff but felt calm as she walked back to the door. She stopped, the stained glass above it grabbed her attention. Jesus, as a shepherd looking with love at his flock. She was one of them. Hadn't she come running here and found some answers? It was a funny old flock in Linwood.

49

Rose had one last stop to make before going back to Morpeth. She was starving, she'd had nothing since arriving in Linwood and the smell of chips wafting her way from Charlie's was irresistible. She popped in and ate a bag of piping hot chips that filled her and warmed her hands as she walked the winding road to Burnside. She had to see Mary.

'It's late to call around. Mary is very poorly you know.' Kate, her arms folded, sniffed as though she could smell the chips and vinegar on Rose and left her standing on the step.

'I know it's after seven, but I wouldn't stay long especially if she's tired. I haven't seen Mary for weeks.' Kate Elliot liked to be awkward at the best of times so Rose wasn't surprised at the lack of a welcome.

'Come in then,' Kate sighed. 'I'll see if she's up to a visitor.'

As Rose stepped inside, she heard Mary calling, 'Who's that you've kept at the door? Is it Rose Kelly?'

'There's nothing wrong with her hearing.' Kate rolled her eyes.

Rose smiled at Kate and ignored the remark. 'Shall I pop up?'

'Seeing as she's awake you can go on up but don't stay too long.'

Rose slipped past her and made her way upstairs. One door was ajar and there she found Mary, propped up in bed. She looked frail but her smile was welcoming and Rose rushed over to hug her. 'Oh Mary, it's so good to see you.'

Mary put her finger to her lips and pointed to the door. Rose nodded. She'd been an excellent earwigger all of her life so she was well aware that Kate might be listening at the bottom of the stairs.

'Ask her to put the kettle on and then close the door,' Mary whispered.

Rose walked back to the top of the stairs and looked down at Katie hovering at the foot of them. 'Ah there you are Kate. Mary was just asking for a cup of strong sweet tea. Would you be a real darling and make her one? I'll come down for it in a minute or two, save your legs.' She firmly closed the bedroom door and went back to sit on the bed.

'I bet her face was tripping her. She's such a miserable beggar. How our Larry got lumbered with that one I don't know.'

'Never mind her, Mary. How are you?'

'I've been better but more important… how are you? I've had your dad here. I was glad Kate was out and didn't even know. By he was vexed. Would he listen to reason? No. And when he told me he'd sent you away, I was foaming!' Mary sank back on her pillows breathless.

'I came here to check he hadn't upset you. You were a good friend to Mam and we both know she was determined to do things her way.' Mary nodded and squeezed her hand as she added, 'Don't fret about me, Mary. I've a nice little room above the surgery in Morpeth. I'll wait till Dad calms down.'

'How are you and young Danny getting on?' Mary's eyes held a twinkle. 'I'd like to hear news of an engagement before I'm laid to rest.'

'Don't get your hopes up there. We're not speaking at the moment but nothing to worry you about. His sister though, Gracie Dodd, she's looking after Dad and Terry. Mary, I'm ashamed to admit I'm right jealous! Dad's even spilled the beans, told her… you know, everything!'

Mary shuffled up. 'Plump up these pillows, pet.' When she was more upright she beckoned Rose closer. 'This is between you and me and the bedpost, hinny. There's whispers around the rows and there's the truth and I know the truth.'

Rose wasn't sure if she wanted to know more truths as Mary held both her hands 'Gracie Dodd is a fine woman and would never let your family secret slip. Gracie will be good for your dad. She's been at the end of rumours for years so she won't go spreading gossip.'

'If you're sure. It's just Mrs Dodd, her mam, doesn't seem keen on me at the moment,' Rose confessed.

Mary patted her hand and sank back on her pillows. 'She's protective of Danny and of Gracie is Mrs Dodd. You see, those whispers I mentioned, they are partly true. Folks say that Gracie is young Danny's mother, had him at seventeen, and I know that is true. They say she had him to a married chap but that's not true. She had him to a young lad but she didn't want to name him or trap him you see.'

'Gracie is Danny's Mam?' Rose's mind whirred with this revelation. 'Does he know?'

'I wouldn't know, pet. He'll have heard the rumours and guessed as much, no doubt.'

'Well I haven't heard them.'

'You've always been a bit sheltered, hinny. Rumours are just spread by gossips and your mam didn't mix with that sort.'

'Why didn't Gracie marry, if she was expecting?'

'The lad didn't want to and afterwards she was... well others don't want spoiled goods around here.'

'But you said that nobody knew for sure.'

'Not for sure but there were rumours, as I say. Mrs Dodd was in her forties and Gracie went to stay with an aunt for a bit. Folk soon try to put two and two together.'

That was the phrase Gracie had used earlier. It all made sense why she wouldn't spread gossip. 'How do you know so much? And about the lad... Danny's father?'

'Because, to my shame, he was my own lad, Larry. He fathered Danny when he was sixteen. He confessed to me once she was sent off and, by then, it seemed best to do nothing about it. I wish to God he'd married Gracie then instead of getting tangled with that miserable beggar downstairs.'

Rose sat speechless for a moment.

'I feel better for you knowing that, hinny. It's a weight off my mind to know that you can explain to Danny that I've always been proud of him, if this all ever comes to light. I wish I'd intervened and persuaded Larry to make a go of it with Gracie but he was our only lad by then and we spoilt him.' She wiped a tear from her eye. 'Now you'd better get that tea from Kate, pet. You look like you need it more than me.'

Rose found Kate in the scullery; she had set out just the one cup for Mary.

'She's not long for this world is she?' Kate said as she poured tea into the cup. Rose was parched but she couldn't bring herself to ask for a cup.

'Don't speak about Mary like that. I hope she'll pull through and be up and about soon, Kate.' She took the tea from the bench, her mind still reeling with all that Mary had revealed.

When she returned to the bedroom, Mary had dropped off to sleep. Sinking onto the bed, she noticed she had a long brown envelope in her hand. Her frail hand had written 'For Rose, for Danny' in shaky lettering and the pen was on the covers. She put the pen on the bedside table and the envelope in her bag. Mary wanted her to deliver this to Danny but when would she get the chance? She watched the old lady at rest and drank the hot liquid herself. The sweetness made her shudder but it was meant to be good for shock.

Mary's health seemed feeble but she was still as bright as a brass button. So Danny was Larry's boy? Mary's grandson? Mary always had a soft spot for Rose so it was no wonder she was keen on her and Danny getting together.

50

Rose sat up in bed and wrote a letter to Dad before falling into an exhausted sleep.

Next morning, she addressed the envelope and slipped along to the post office before opening the surgery and before she could change her mind about making her feelings clear.

She could fret and try her best to change Dad's view but it wouldn't happen. He couldn't hurt Mam but he could hurt her and place some blame on her even though it might mean hurting himself too.

The rift with Danny was just as hard to live with. She wanted to solve it but decided to let the situation ride for a while. He knew where she was and could call her. She was so tempted to find him and explain things but, last night in the chapel, she'd decided that her actions sat comfortably with her. What if she was to run after Danny to explain about Frank and herself? No, it wasn't the answer. Danny should think over all they were to each other and realise he was too hasty because how could she ever be with Danny if he didn't have faith in her?

Saturday opening was strictly ten until twelve. Because she was sleeping over, she opened up for Roger and stayed for half an hour until his client list was organised and then she had the day to herself. It would be a long day without the flurry of housework, shopping, Terry to care for, cooking and then a night out with Danny. She tried to settle with a book, that always helped her to escape her troubles, but Agatha Christie was no help today. Maybe a walk? She usually had Lucky for company but she couldn't bring herself to part him from Terry, it wouldn't be as much fun on her own.

The phone rang in the kitchen next to her room and she jumped up to answer it. Could it be Danny? Please let it be him. She tried her best to sound cheery. 'Hello Campbell's veterinary practice.'

'Hi Rose, Frank here. Do you fancy a walk by the Wansbeck this afternoon?'

Her heart sank. It was Frank not Danny and, lovely as he was, she didn't feel up to meeting him. Not today when she needed to be home in case Danny called. 'Thanks for ringing, Frank but I already have plans.'

'I travel back to Cambridge tomorrow so it would have been lovely to see you again before I go.'

Another time, when you're back at Christmas, maybe?'

'I hope so. Did you sort out the misunderstanding with your boyfriend, Rose?'

'I haven't Frank. Not yet, but I hope I will. How was your hospital check-up?'

'I might need a tweak at a later date but I'm okay for now. No need to stop my studies again.'

'Good.'

'Yes, it's all good… I'll write, if I may?'

'Yes, Frank. Keep in touch.'

At school, she'd had a crush on Frank and she thought she was over all that but she wasn't sure. Could she stay friendly with Frank or would it cause more problems for her with Danny?

Rose left the kitchen door open and returned to her chair by the window. Picking up *A Murder is Announced*, she read the same page for the fourth time. Even Miss Marple couldn't grab her attention today.

The phone startled her awake. She must've dozed off curled up in the armchair. Blast, she had pins and needles in her legs and had to limp towards the phone in the kitchen. It could be Danny, *please don't hang up.*

'Hello Campell's Veterinary s—'

'It's me, Gracie.'

Rose held the phone away from Gracie's shouting. 'Oh, Gracie! Hello. Is everything okay?'

'No. No it's not, Rose. I've sad news.'

A spear of fear shot through Rose. 'Who? What?'

Gracie was putting more coins in the phone box. 'It's your old neighbour, Mary. She didn't wake up this morning. Larry says you were the last to speak to her.'

JOHN KELLY

John Kelly read his letter again.

Dear Dad

I'm sorry that we have fallen out. I can't change the past just as I can't change Mam's decision and neither can you. I did what I thought was right at the time and obeyed Mam. I'd do the same again.

I don't want to lose touch with Terry. I'd like to pick him up every Friday and drop him back home on Saturday teatime.

I'm happy to see you whenever you find it in your heart to see me. I will miss you so much but I'm not sorry for anything I have done, Dad.

Love to you always,
Your daughter, Rose.

He crumpled the paper in his fist before throwing it on the fire. How could Rose, his pride and joy, have kept such a secret? He couldn't understand her or her mother. Everything he held dear about them had been turned to dust. He didn't know them at all.

He couldn't stop loving either of them, even as rage ran through him, but he couldn't forgive them. He didn't want Rose back in the house.

He wouldn't stop the lass from seeing her brother because Terry had suffered enough. That little lad had lost a sister at birth, a mother at four and John wouldn't keep his big sister away from him.

He'd called to see Mary-from-next-door for some answers about the birth but she'd told him nothing more than he already knew and now he'd heard she'd slipped away. Mary Elliot, his neighbour all those years and keeping a secret like that! He'd stay away from her funeral and that would set a few tongues wagging but he couldn't trust himself to be civil.

51

Rose whiled away the lengthy hours of the weekend sorting out the surgery's stock room and walking by the river. The Wansbeck was swift flowing and swollen due to heavy October rains and, as Rose threw sticks and pebbles into it, she watched them disappear into its grasp. She felt as though life was sucking her in and carrying her along like in its current; in a flash, she could disappear under its harsh twists and turns. If she could just vanish, she'd leave her troubles behind and who would miss her?

Mary, so close to her mam, had gone. Rose couldn't chat about Mam with anyone else like she had with Mary. She chided herself, she should be glad her departure had been peaceful even though she'd miss her. Why, oh why had Mary managed to leave her with another secret and a blasted message to deliver? She didn't want to be burdened with it.

One thing was certain, if they ever got back together, she didn't want any secrets from Danny; look at what had happened between her and Dad.

Almost a week dragged by and Danny hadn't called. Lottie came by bus to see her and told her the arrangements for Mary's funeral. It would be at St John the Baptist's and refreshments would be served at Linwood 'tute.

Lottie couldn't contain her excitement at 'being in with a chance' of Mary's house in First Row. 'Dennis is just out of his time and, as a pit electrician, he could get the keys to number two. Imagine! Our own place away from his mam. I'll be able to bring up our Paul exactly as *I* want.' Lottie's eyes glowed with excitement.

Young Paul seemed a contented little boy and Lottie had a willing babysitter for nights like tonight but the two women in Dennis's life just didn't see eye to eye. 'Steady on, Lottie. I know you're keen to move out but Mary's not even buried yet.'

'She'd love me to have it, I bet, and it's in such good order. Kate'll not be wanting Mary's furniture either so we might get some of that.'

She had a point. Mary would love to see her house go to someone she liked and Rose wouldn't have to listen to weekly bulletins about Dennis's mam's interfering ways. 'Is Danny going to the funeral?' she finally dared to ask. If anyone knew, it would be Lottie.

'I'm not sure. He's started as manager of the Alnwick branch this week so it'll depend on whether he can get cover. I'd think he would try because... well... you know.'

'No, I don't. What do you mean?' Rose went onto high alert; she knew Lottie so well and could see that Lottie was ready to say something.

Lottie leaned forward. 'There are some rumours. Folk say things... not me mind, but some.'

'What are you on about. Lottie? Who says what?' Now Rose was aware of Danny's connection with Mary, she wanted to know who else might have an inkling.

'Some say that Danny could be related to the Elliots...'

'Lottie! Where did you hear that?' This fresh news to Rose was clearly nothing new to the Linwood gossips, whatever Mary had thought.

'There's quite a bit of tittle-tattling goes on around Dennis's mam's kitchen, believe you me; her and her cronies. I knew the rumour that Danny was Gracie's lad years ago but just heard the connection to the Elliots when I moved there.'

'I hope there's not gossip about us Kellys.' The thought sent a shudder down Rose.

'Why would there be? There aren't any hidden pregnancies in your family are there.' Lottie nudged her and laughed.

Mary's funeral car set off from Larry's on an overcast November day. Sombre clouds seemed to meet the streets and envelope everyone in a wet mist that wasn't quite rain but soaked them just the same. Larry had invited Rose to travel in the funeral car with him and Kate and she accepted.

When she dropped Terry off on Saturday, Gracie was at the house and told her that her dad wasn't going and neither was she. She hadn't mentioned Danny or his new job and Rose hadn't asked. Would he be there?

Rose shivered as they left for the church, even though she was wearing a thick navy coat and had tied a navy and gold silk scarf around her head to protect her hair.

'You were the last to speak to her, Rose,' Kate whispered once they were settled in the car. 'Did she say owt we should know? Did she seem to know she was on her way?'

'Her last words were about getting her cup of tea from you and she said I looked like I needed it more than her.' Kate wouldn't be hearing about the weight Mary offloaded first of all. 'She was sound asleep when I took it up so I drank it then brought the cup down and left.'

'Mam was always thinking of others,' Larry said. 'Did without her last cuppa.'

'There was plenty in the pot,' Kate hissed.

'Why didn't you give Rose two to take up, then?'

Rose looked out of the car window and suppressed a smile. Mary had told her they bickered all the time.

They stopped close to the church and Rose was waylaid by

Lottie at the entrance. 'Sit with us, Rose. We're slipping into a pew at the back.'

Rose hesitated and nodded. She was grateful to escape prying eyes and join Lottie and Dennis in the last pew. As she knelt, saying a prayer for Mary, she felt someone move in to sit right next to her. A squeeze of her shoulder and a hint of lime aftershave confirmed who it was. Danny had come to the funeral.

During the service, she dared to look at him out of the corner of her eye. Her heart thudded, a marching drum within her chest, as she met his eyes glinting with unshed tears. 'This is a funny way to meet up Rose Kelly,' he whispered.

She nodded. 'How are you, Danny?'

'I've been better... but I'm glad to see you today. Glad you came to give Mary a good send off.' He reached for her hand and held it tightly.

Sharing a hymn book and singing Psalm 23 together, Rose prayed that they could be together again. 'Are... are you going to the 'tute after the burial?' Rose managed to ask. They were the last row to leave the church.

'I'm giving Lottie and Dennis a lift there but I'm not staying. Could we go somewhere after? Somewhere to talk?'

Rose couldn't find her voice. Danny wanted to talk to her, maybe there was a chance for them? She nodded.

He hooked her arm with his. 'Right then, we'll do that.'

Danny gave Larry a friendly nod as they stood back from the grave and Rose watched Kate's theatrical tears as Larry threw down the first clods of earth. Now that she knew the connection, Rose couldn't get over how alike Danny and Larry were in stature and stance. Did Danny not realise what some in Linwood had guessed?

52

Rose looked for Danny's van. He pointed to a black car parked opposite the 'tute. 'I've got a Hillman Minx instead of the van now that Mr William's has made me a manager.'

'It's lovely Danny!'

'It's Mr William's old 'un and it's been well looked after. He's treated himself to a new Rover and he's taking a bit out of my wages every week for this 'un.'

They headed towards Morpeth and Danny talked about his new job and the rooms he had above William's shop. 'I've got a bedroom – no more sharing with Joe – and a kitchen, bathroom and living room to rattle about in but, you know me, I can just about boil the kettle.'

He turned into a lane just before the bridge that would take them into the town centre. 'Where are we going?' she asked.

'I thought we'd have a drink and a chat in the snug of The Joiners Arms,' Danny answered as he parked the car.

'I've never been in a pub before.' She felt excited and nervous.

'It's about time you did, then.' He laughed as he put a finger under her chin and scrutinised her face. 'You're twenty, you'll get served.' His eyes lingered on her mouth and his voice sounded husky as he added. 'Did I ever tell you you're the bonniest lass I've ever seen?'

She couldn't answer because his lips gently touched hers and she responded to their touch. The kiss became firmer and they clung to one another as their mouths revealed their ardour, their need for one another.

It's going to be alright. In Danny's arms, Rose believed that they'd be able to make up and move on. Together, they could face anything.

Rose sat in the back room of the Joiners absorbing the mix of smoke and beer and the noise from the bar. A group of men and women played dominoes, a couple held hands and talked in a corner and she took off her coat and tried to relax. Danny was buying a pint and bringing her a port and lemonade. He'd offered her a lemonade but seeing as she was here in a pub, she decided to try something new.

Danny sat beside her and whispered, 'Sip it. I don't want to get into bother with John Kelly for getting you drunk.'

Rose raised her eyes. 'That won't happen now seeing as he's refusing to speak to me.'

'Things sort themselves out. Like us… we can sort out our tiff can't we Rose?'

Rose nodded fervently, 'I want to… Dan—'

'Ro—'

'You first,' Rose insisted.

'Okay… Rose, you can't know how sorry I am and how much I've tortured myself for being a doylem and driving off that morning.'

'I don't blame you for that. You got a shock, but I did think you'd call to find out what was going on.'

'I was angry for a day or two then too ashamed to call and dreaded you putting the phone down on me.'

'You don't know me well, if you think I'd do that.'

'That was it Rose I thought I knew you very well, a good

person inside and out and someone I adored, then I had words with your Dad and he… well I was confused.'

'What do you mean, you had words with Dad?

'When you were too busy in the surgery to see me, I went round to your dad to talk him into letting you back home. I thought I'd help. He wasn't having it. "You don't know what I know," he said. You don't know that that girl is as capable of deceit as her mother." I tell you Rose I stood up and I almost punched him… your dad talking about you and Ginnie Kelly in that way.' Danny took a sip of his pint and shook his head as if he still couldn't believe it.

'He squared up to me. "Danny," he says, "one day, you'll learn that Rose can harbour secrets and make a fool of a man. Mark my words.". I left and I didn't believe him of course. Then I came to see you next morning and there you were letting a man out of the door and being kissed.'

'On the cheek,' Rose said.

'On the cheek, I grant you, but Rose I was that shocked and your dad's words whizzed in my head for a day or two. Was he trying to tell me you were two timing me? I thought for a while that he was.'

'What changed your mind?' Rose played with the edges of a beer mat and tried to put herself in Danny's position.

'I just couldn't imagine you doing it. I kept remembering our walks and talks and the way our kisses are just… just magic. Gracie told me you were asking after me and said I should get in touch but I was ashamed by then. When I saw you at the funeral, I swear I almost stopped breathing, I wanted to make things right and didn't know if I could.'

'You can and you have.' Love for this vulnerable man flooded Rose's heart. 'You saw me letting the Ashington vet out of the house after we had been up all night operating on a dying cat.'

'The kiss?'

'He… he was a schoolfriend from Morpeth, an old friend and it was nothing.'

'Was it that posh fella we bumped into at the pictures? The one with the limp?'

'It was. Frank Maxwell, he's called.'

Danny studied her closely. 'I believe you.' He managed a smile. 'But don't make a habit of kissing all of the boys you met at that school.'

'I wouldn't! Frank is the son of the vet that saved our Lucky.'

'That makes it alright then.'

Rose took a long sip of her port and coughed. 'Danny could they add more lemonade?'

After he returned with her drink, he asked, 'Do you want to tell me about your dad and this secret you've upset him with?'

'Yes, I don't want to keep secrets from you but can we leave it for another night?'

'We've got all the time in the world. After this, I'll take you home and we can talk it all over at the weekend.'

Rose drank her port and lemon. Now it was weaker, she liked the flavour and it was a warming drink for a November night. She wouldn't mind coming to the pub and ordering this again.

Danny met her on Sunday and telling him the whole story of her mam and how she'd made the discovery about the twins was surprisingly easy. Danny, always a good listener, didn't interrupt and she found herself telling him about going to Mary's.

'So that's how you were there the night before Mary died and you were the last person she spoke to. Did she say anything to make you think she might go quickly?'

'Not at the time. But now… maybe.'

'What do you mean?'

They walked slowly by the banks of the Wansbeck. Rose's

hands tingled with cold even through her gloves and her nose and ears felt numb. 'Shall we go back to my kitchen and I'll make some cocoa and we can talk about it there?'

'Your cocoa? Do we have to?' Danny's eyes held laughter and brimmed with love.

'My cocoa making is getting better Danny Dodd, and we can't all be wonderful cooks like Gracie or your mam.'

Danny slipped his arms around her. 'I'd rather have your burnt offerings than the Dodd's Sunday dinner. Marry me, Rose.'

'What did you say?' Rose's frozen ears began to burn and she felt a rush of blood shoot to her head as her cheeks flushed.

Danny went onto his knees on the muddy bank. 'Marry me, Rose. I love you.'

'Yes!'

'Soon?'

'Yes!'

'I'd better get used to your cocoa then.' Danny took her hand and they headed back to the town centre.

As they walked back, they discussed her dad's reaction to meeting Joy and whether he would stay away from their wedding. 'I think your dad is shocked but he's blaming you for something a bairn couldn't do, and that's go against their mother. I'll tell him that one day but, for now, we'll let him lick his wounds and enjoy being fussed over by our Gracie.'

At the mention of Gracie, Rose swallowed hard. If she was to be free of secrets, she had to talk to Danny about Gracie and Larry and what Mary had told her. How would that go down?

53

It was chilly as they climbed up the stairs above Campbell's. Rose bent to light the gas fire that warmed her room.

'It's not as posh as I imagined, Rose.' Danny stood in the middle of the small room with his hands in his pockets.

'It's really just here for when we have animals overnight and it's not that often. We all use the kitchen and toilet and this didn't get used much at all until I needed it.'

Danny took her in his arms, 'It must be lonely after living with Terry and your dad.'

'It's far too quiet. I used to long for some peace so I could read but now I've got it…'

'Let's make that cocoa and you can tell me what's on your mind because, even after that tale of your mam, I can see you've got something else to say.'

They were in the middle of a hug to keep each other warm until the room thawed out when Rose sniffed and shrieked, 'Damn it!' She'd let the milk boil over and it had flooded all over the hob.

'I'll make the cocoa, you just sit by the fire and get warmed.' Danny planted a kiss on her cold nose.

She pulled the two comfy chairs up to the fire and swallowed hard. How would Danny take what she had to say?

'Come on, out with it. You've got me all jittery,' Danny said as he passed her a frothy creamy cocoa like she couldn't make.

'It's about Mary. About what she said when I went to see her.' She sipped her cocoa and caught the worried look in Danny's eyes.

'Go on.'

'She talked about you, Danny. After we discussed Mam and the way she had behaved, she said that a few bairns in the row didn't know everything about their parentage.'

'What did she mean? Danny brushed his hands through his hair. He did it when he was nervous.

'They didn't know about their birth and their parents.'

'I know that! I meant what did she mean bringing me into it?'

'She thought you might be... might be...'

'I might be one of them.'

'Yes. That's what she said.'

Danny stood and walked towards the window. He looked out onto the yard below. 'Rose, it's been rumoured since I was a nipper, that my mam was my sister; that Gracie went away and had me. As far as I'm concerned Mam and Gracie both love me and I love them and I'd never dream of asking or upsetting either of them.

'They know I must know and I know they know I know. It's there but it's not a big white elephant in the room eating away at me. Your trouble is, Rose, that everything has to be talked about and spelt out in big letters.'

Rose drew a breath, 'That's not fair Danny. I got into trouble with Dad for not sharing a secret about this very thing so I don't want to keep any secrets from you, the man who wants to marry me.'

'Okay. Sorry, it *was* unfair but I've heard those rumours and dodged that conversation for so long.'

'Don't you want to know more?'

'I do know. I know enough.' Danny turned from the window and sat at her feet.

'What about your dad?' Rose stroked his hair back from his eyes.

'I'm never gonna find who he was but I know he was a good-for-nothing. He must have been to leave Gracie high and dry at seventeen. I've heard whispers he was a married man but who knows, eh?'

Rose wasn't sure whether to go on or not. Her heart thudded in the silence. Did she want this to be between her and Danny, a great barrier of knowledge between them? 'Danny, Mary wanted to tell me about your dad and she wanted me to pass it on when the time was right.'

'Mary? How the hell did she know? It wasn't… it wasn't old Tom Elliot? He wasn't the married man was he?' Danny stood up and paced back to the window.

'No. She told me it was her son, just sixteen and he couldn't face it.'

Danny wheeled around, his face red with anger. 'Her… Larry? Larry bleedin' Elliot? Are you sure?'

'Mary seemed sure.' What else could she say?

'He couldn't face it, having me, the scally. Well, Gracie had to didn't she?'

'That's why her mam and dad stepped in, helped her. It was all done for the best at the time.'

'Aye maybe, but Gracie, she didn't get anybody courting her after that. He has got off scot-free and then married when he was finally ready for a bairn or two.'

'You don't know that he hasn't had regrets. You haven't walked in his shoes, Danny.'

Danny knelt in front of her and grasped her hands. 'Don't speak well of him, Rose. You've got to be on my side in this. He's a loser, a damned loser!' Danny buried his head in her lap and sobbed.

Rose was glad she had told him for their sakes but she wished he didn't hurt like this. 'It was years ago, Danny. You've had the love of all the Dodd family and, in the background,

Mary loved you too but couldn't ever say. She told me. She said it was a weight off her mind to know that I could explain this to you, if this all ever came to light, and that she'd always been proud of you.'

'It needn't have come to light.'

'After my row with Dad, I couldn't keep another secret like that. I couldn't have married you and kept that secret.'

'Rose, from today, I don't want to talk about it. I love my family whatever they're called and it's nobody's business. I don't know how I'll look at that excuse for a father though.'

'One more thing, I almost forgot, Mary wanted me to give you an envelope.'

'A letter? Keep it. I don't want to read it yet. Maybe, one day but it's too raw.'

Rose reached down to kiss his head, still resting in her lap. He looked up, there was still that spark in his eyes. 'We come from a right set of folk, don't we? Let's do the right thing and get married and have bairns to each other, it canna be that hard.'

Rose smiled. 'You're right. Danny, let's get wed soon.'

'Next week?'

'Give me time to sort a dress out. How about December? No fuss, no family, just us.'

54

Danny called into the surgery during Rose's lunch-time. He had half an hour to spare before he drove to the shop in Alnwick. 'I've had a meeting with Mr Williams and told him we're getting married. I had to tell him because of the flat. He told me I'm getting a bonus at Christmas so that's the wedding paid for. He's pleased with how things are going and that I'm settling down.'

'I'm glad for you.' Rose managed a smile even though talk of their wedding reminded her of how much she wanted to see her dad. She hadn't heard a thing from him.

'Come on, Rose. Cheer up!' Danny could always tell when she was feeling low. 'Let's take a walk by the river.'

'I'll come out for a bit but I want to take you somewhere else.' Rose had an urge to visit the schoolyard to see how Joy was doing.

'Where are we going?'

Rose took his hand. 'You'll see.'

They sat on a bench opposite the school but Joy didn't appear. When the school bell rang to signal the end of lunch, Danny jumped up and went to the fence. 'Hoi there, come here a minute,' he asked a lad picking up a football. The lad ran over to him.

'I'm looking for a lassie called Joy, Joy Fletcher… Do you know her?'

'Aye but she's not here.'

'I can see that. Where would she be?'

'I mean she's not here 'cause she's moved.'

'Where to?'

The lad shrugged. 'How would I know?' he asked before running to the school entrance.

Danny turned and shrugged his shoulders. 'You heard that?'

Rose bit her lip and nodded. Mrs Fletcher wasn't taking any chances. Could she blame her? Mrs Fletcher loved Joy and didn't want to risk losing another child. They'd moved again.

Rose wrote to Frank and told him that she would be busy over the Christmas holidays because she was arranging her wedding to Danny. She explained that, as it was a quiet one, she wasn't sending invitations to friends and she hoped he understood.

His reply came back by return of post. It had a more formal tone than usual but it congratulated her. It ended with, 'I'm sorry that I can't be there on your happy day but I wish you well. Kind regards, Frank.'

Roger was getting used to Rose being on the premises. Now Rose was sleeping there, she was 'on call' during the night for emergencies and he thought she was much better at consoling clients who had a howling pooch on heat or a sickly cat. A farm vet at heart, he was still always ready for a call-out involving cattle or horses.

Because of this extra responsibility, he was only too pleased to agree to Rose leaving early on Fridays to pick up Terry. Terry stayed over at the flat and, after her breakfast with him, she popped downstairs to open up at ten for the Saturday surgery. Clients were sitting in a neat row when Roger arrived at ten thirty. He liked that extra half hour and the organised start to the day. 'Yes, this flexible arrangement suits us both, Rose. We make a good team.'

Lottie came back to Morpeth with Rose one Friday night when Rose picked Terry up from school. 'I'd rather have fish and chips with you two and then get the bus to meet Dennis when he leaves the 'tute than sit in with his mam all night.'

'Are you no further forward with the move?' Rose asked.

Dennis has been told that we've got number two as soon as the Elliots hand in Mary's keys but, beggar me, Larry's paid another week's rent and they've been there turning the place upside down.'

'I didn't think Kate would want much of Mary's stuff.' Rose kept her eyes on the road. These roads were getting busier and everybody seemed to have somewhere to go on a Friday teatime.

'Dennis's mam and her cronies say they're looking for Mary's savings. They thought she had a bit put away and canna find it. Kate's furious and blaming Larry for not asking his mam about it.'

'Mary and Tom weren't rich. They lived quite frugally.'

'Frugally?'

'Make do and mend sort of thing.'

'Say that then, clever britches.' Lottie gave her a nudge. ' Aye, if they were frugalling they'd be saving too, wouldn't they? Anyway, they'll be ripping the floorboards up before we can get the keys, and we wanted to be in for Christmas.'

When Terry was tucked up at the tail end of her bed – they slept head to toe in the tiny bed and Terry kicked like crazy but she loved having him to stay – Rose made her announcement.

'Danny and I are getting married on New Year's Eve and we want you and Dennis to be our witnesses.'

Lottie's eyes widened. 'Really? Where? What'll we wear? What does your dad say?'

'I'm not speaking to him remember. There'll be nobody to give me away just the two of us and you two as witnesses, so keep New Year's Eve free and don't breathe a word!'

55

They would be living in Alnwick, above Williams the Bakers, and Rose loved the rooms. She had a big airy living room, a galley kitchen, an inside toilet and bathroom and a little box room that would be suitable for Terry.

'That's the nursery, one day,' Danny told her as he showed her around.

'Danny, about that, a family—'

'Yes? You do want bairns don't you, Rose? Danny's brow furrowed as he hugged her to him.

'I do, just not straight away. I enjoy work and we're young. Let's wait a while, eh? I've read up on the latest contraception.'

'Leave that to me. We'll wait but not too long. A bairn running around will be grand. We'll get your twenty-first birthday over with first.' He kissed her.

Her twenty-first was just nine months away, she meant longer than that. Rose loved her work at Campbell's and housework and nappies didn't have the same appeal. Danny had better sort out some contraception or she would. He was nuzzling her neck and sparked that longing within her that had never been satisfied.

She knew all of the facts and practicalities about making love but she hadn't a clue about what it would be like. Her body told her she wanted, needed, to be closer to Danny and she melted to his touch but they'd never gone too far because Danny was afraid they'd never stop.

'We'll keep the rest for our wedding night,' he'd murmur as a sweet ache racked her body and she was on the point of not caring about waiting.

It doesn't take long to arrange a wedding, if you're determined. Rose visited Bella Temperley who she always thought of as Miss Wakenshaw. 'We're at home and the children will be staying with my parents so Andrew can marry you here, in the Gosforth chapel if you don't want to use Linwood but what a shame, Rose. Linwood chapel holds such happy memories.'

'Dad and I are not on good terms and I'd rather it be as small as possible.'

'That's such a shame, but I insist that you return here afterwards for drinks and a buffet before you go off. That will be our present to you both.'

'Thank you so much, Bella.'

A dark crimson dress with a matching swing jacket hung in the window of Hannah's on Gosforth High Street. The price tag shocked her but she went in to try it on. It was a perfect fit. She could hear her mam remarking, 'You look as smart as a carrot in that.'

She turned this way and that but her stomach was churning at the weeks of wages she would have to hand over. As she took the jacket off to study the dress again, she noticed one of the ornate buttons missing from the sleeve. An assistant came over, 'Is something wrong, Madam?'

'I love this outfit but there's a button missing. Is this the only one you've got?'

'Hannah's only carries one of each garment, madam. You wouldn't want anyone else in the area to be wearing what you're wearing.'

Rose tried to keep her grin inside. So that's what folk paid for, to be the only one with that particular outfit. 'The buttons are so unusual that I'll never get a match. I suppose I could put two plain ones on the sleeves.'

'Would you be wanting discount for the garment being faulty? You can't bring it back if you do?'

'Discount?'

'I'll go into the back and talk to our manager.'

Rose went back into the changing room and took off the dress. It was a lovely outfit but could she really spend that? It was way over her budget and there were shoes to buy too, maybe a hat.

The assistant came back smiling. 'It was going on sale in the new year and, with the missing button, we've marked it down a bit more. Would you like it at half price?'

'Half price?' Had she heard her correctly?

'Yes, we pride ourselves on the perfect outfit for all occasions and, as we can't find the button, this can no longer remain in stock.'

'I'll have it!'

'Is it for something special?' the assistant asked as she wrapped the garments in tissue.

'A wedding... mine,' Rose confided.

'In that case, you really should try this.' She crossed the shop to the hats and came back with a matching wide velvet band with a short veil that partly covered the face or could be swept back. Rose tried it and it held her hair back perfectly. She closed her ears to the sums her brain was doing and added it to her buys. Rose danced out of the shop with the lustrous Hannah's bag swinging from her fingers. She'd saved a fortune because she could sew a button or two on.

Once she got home, she hung the outfit on the outside of the cupboard of her room and gazed at it every few minutes. She loved the crimson band for her hair and she'd carry Mam's favourite cream Christmas roses to lighten the outfit. Tears stung her eyes and she wished her mam could be here. She thought she heard, 'I am pet, I am.'

Rose dried her tears. No, you're not Mam and you left me with Dad to deal with too,' she sniffed. This wedding was making her so emotional. She had to try on the jacket once more to see if she still loved it. As she pushed her hands into the deep and roomy side pockets, her fingers clasped something round and she pulled the missing button out of the pocket. How strange, the assistant had felt in both pockets.

Never mind strange, what good luck! She'd take this as a good omen.

56

On the morning of her wedding, Rose lay in bed and didn't want to face the day. From the tiredness and heavy feeling in her chest, you'd think she was going to a funeral today. What was wrong with her?

She sat up and there, hanging on the back of the door, was the red outfit that she had chosen with care. She crossed her arms and held onto her shoulders as she turned away from it.

Today, it seemed all wrong. Her chin wobbled as she thought of how her mam would have insisted on a long white dress and would have had a hand in the making of it. She bit her lip but tears flowed down her cheeks. Mam wouldn't be there, her dad wasn't walking her down the aisle and she wasn't saying her vows in her own chapel. What was she thinking of?

Lottie arrived and Rose gave her a quivery smile before bursting into tears. 'I love Danny but I can't do it.'

'It's the wedding nerves, that's all,' Lottie put the kettle on as Rose listed all the reasons why she couldn't go through with the wedding.

When she'd exhausted her list, Lottie handed her a hot cup of tea. 'No more excuses and no more crying after this bout mind you. Your face is all blotchy and your eyes will swell up.'

Rose looked in the mirror and ran a basin of cold water to bathe her eyes. She was lucky to have a pragmatic maid of honour who ignored her misgivings. She had made her choice and she loved Danny Dodd so she'd better get ready to be his bride.

Andrew played Wagner's Bridal Chorus on the organ and Danny, looking debonair in his dark suit, turned towards her as she was walked down the aisle by Bella.

'You are beautiful,' he whispered when she reached his side and her doubts were gone.

Andrew left the organ to conduct the service and afterwards Lottie and Dennis signed the register.

The four of them left the chapel to the sweet sound of 'The Waters of Tyne' and were met by Bella with a camera. 'We must take a photo or two to commemorate today,' she insisted.

Bella laid on a delicious spread of cold meats and cheeses with bread and pickles and there, in pride of place on the table, was a small but perfect wedding cake.

'Bella, you shouldn't have!'

'It was a pleasure, Rose. I bought the fruit cake from Greggs of Gosforth, sorry Danny we don't have a Williams, and I iced it on Boxing Day. The figures were the two we had on our cake… something borrowed.'

'I run a baker's shop and didn't even think about a cake, thank you Bella,' Danny said.

After an hour, Danny took her hand and murmured in her ear, 'Time to go, shall we say our goodbyes?'

They weren't having a honeymoon. It was New Year's Eve and they wanted to celebrate alone in their new home in Alnwick. 'Hang on Rose.' Danny stopped her as they walked along the side alley to their door. He went ahead, unlocked the door and strode back to sweep her into his arms. 'I haven't forgotten this tradition. A whole staircase to carry you up, I hope I'm up to this.'

When they got to the top, he lowered her gently onto her

feet and kissed her before turning on a switch. The room was lit by coloured Christmas fairy lights strung along the mantelpiece. On the table, was a bowl filled to overflowing with the Roses chocolates he always bought her.

The fizz of happiness that had grown ever since she got over her morning wobble threatened to overflow. She turned and kissed him before he led her along to the bedroom where another string of white lights ran along their headboard. They illuminated a sprinkling of red and white rose petals over the bedspread. 'Danny, this is… it's magical.'

He swirled her in a circle and there was a huskiness in his voice as he said, 'I love you, Rose.'

'I love you too, Danny.' She took off the crimson band holding back her hair, shook it loose over her shoulders and stepped out of her shoes. They both took off their jackets together, their eyes never breaking contact as they hung them over a chair by the dressing table.

Rose gave an intake of breath as Danny stepped towards her, turned her around and slowly unzipped her dress. He carried it carefully to the chair before facing her and taking off his tie. She stood before him, aching to be in his arms. 'Come here, my beautiful Rose.' She didn't need to be asked, she went to him and unbuttoned his shirt as he unbuckled his belt.

Flames of passion licked through her body and he hadn't kissed her or touched her yet. He stepped out of his trousers and slipped the straps of her slip from her shoulders so the garment fell in a puddle at her feet. His arms wrapped around her and, for the first time, her skin touched his. His taut belly pressed into hers and she pushed against him, needing the connection. His hands stroked down her back past her knickers until he reached for her buttocks. He clenched her to him.

'Danny,' she was breathless, her legs were molten and a longing to be all his raged through her. This was why he had always stopped before. Now there was no going back.

He kissed her slowly; she kissed him hard. 'I want you,

Danny.' He led her to the bed and she lay down on the strewn rose petals. He turned her onto her belly and removed her brassiere stoking the fire and need inside of her and making her want to turn and cling to him. All hesitation and shyness gone, she turned and arched her back as he kissed her nipples. She reached down past his belly and, with a ripple of excitement, she found how hard he was. He wanted her and she wanted to be his.

57

1955

After a whole day together in their own world above the baker's, they were ready to face reality. January the second fell on Sunday so they called into the farm to see Stanley.

Rose visited Stanley often and Dad had left it to her to explain the reason for their fall out. He had been shocked and upset to learn about Joy but he'd not held it against Rose. 'I'll try to find the right time to talk to Dad. You were fourteen when you found out. What could you have done. I'm glad you kept Mam's secret and I didn't find out then. I was still raw from losing David.' If only Dad could think along those lines.

Rose couldn't wait to wish Stanley a happy new year and tell him their news. Brenda was at home and, as Stanley took Danny to see a piece of new machinery, Rose and Brenda had a cup of tea and sampled some of Rose's wedding cake.

'That Greggs of Gosforth is a good bakery, really tasty. I bet they'll do well, Williams had better watch out.' she said through a mouthful of crumbs. Rose caught her looking wistfully at her wedding band. 'I wish I could be married and give up work. I'm fed up with that solicitor's office and would rather raise children and chickens.'

'Is there anyone you fancy for the husband role?' Rose asked and Brenda blushed crimson.

'No. Nobody on the horizon so I'll just have to keep working.'

Rose tactfully ignored Brenda's flushed cheeks. 'I want to keep working. I'm not giving up just because I'm married, that's old-fashioned nonsense. I love being at Campbell's and I'd hate to be stuck at home.'

'What about children?' Brenda's cheeks had cooled down and she poured them more tea.

'Not for ages. We have plenty of time.'

Roger was surprised to be greeted from his annual trip to Scotland for Hogmanay by the new Mrs Dodd. After hearty congratulations and a toast in whisky, he insisted on giving her some beautiful glasses that were still boxed and he hadn't used. 'They were a wedding present, Edinburgh thistle crystal from my side I believe but Mrs Campbell kept things for best.'

'I will too, Roger.'

'Don't lassie, don't. I'd like you to use them and enjoy them and if they break then they break but they've been used.'

'Now what will I do if you're not going to be above the shop making my life easier? Saturdays I can manage but I can't imagine being on call again.'

'I'll brew a pot of tea and we'll think it through.'

Rose and Danny had a phone in their hallway for the baker's shop so it was decided that Rose would drive Roger's Land Rover to Alnwick and be the one on call if there was an emergency.

'Alnwick is central and, if it's nursing and I'm not needed, you can go on your own. I'm getting old for night disturbances. You're a vet in every way but the name and papers. If it wasn't for you, I'd retire.'

'Don't say that.' Rose objected but he'd grown more stout and less agile and he did like a whisky at night so perhaps it was better if she became the main driver.

Lottie had their number and used the box on the corner of First Row to phone Rose. Rose then called her back so she wouldn't use too many coins. 'Hi Rose. Is it Terry's week to visit you this Friday?'

'It should be.' She had wanted to spend every weekend with Terry but he'd hinted he liked to go to the match and play out with his pals on Saturdays so, over Christmas, they'd settled on every other weekend.

'Are you taking him to Morpeth as usual or taking him to Alnwick and telling him you're married? I'm dying to tell Mam about the wedding but I want you to tell Terry and for your dad to hear your news first.'

'I'm telling him straight away on Friday. He likes Danny and he'll like having that little room.'

'Great. I'll tell Mam on Friday night.'

Rose smiled. That Lottie was turning into a Linwood gossip but at least she'd checked.

The news travelled faster than that. Dennis's mam had 'found' a ring box that had 'dropped out' of Dennis's suit pocket onto the bedroom floor and she questioned him about it. Lottie phoned and told Rose at work on Thursday.

'More like interrogated him, Rose. Poor Dennis canna lie. She was snooping in our room. No wonder I want to move out, she stole my news from under me. After that, I told Mam and she sends her congratulations.'

Lottie confirmed that Dad, Terry, Gracie, Mrs Dodd, the whole of the rows knew before Rose had time to see Terry and before Danny had called to tell the Dodds. The pair wouldn't be popular with the Dodds and rumours about why it was a hasty marriage would vie with the ones about why Rose had moved from her dad. They'd be racing each other all over the rows for first prize.

'I'm not going to Linwood to pick up Terry on my own,

Danny. Your lot will be gunning for me, Terry might be in a huff and I don't know what Dad'll say.' Rose had developed a rash around her neck and bitten her nails right down whilst waiting for Danny to come home and hear the news.

'I can't leave the shop before six. I'll go over and talk to Mam and Dad and Gracie after that. I'll go and speak to your dad too. I think you should go and collect Terry from school as planned though and bring him here. He loves you. A wedding? It's nothing to a laddie.'

'Suppose you're right.'

Rose tossed and turned and didn't sleep at all well but Danny slept soundly. It's alright banging on about equality but women are the biggest worriers, Rose decided, as the church bells struck three.

58

Rose was kept busy all day dispensing liniment and advice until it was time to pick up Terry. January at the vets was a busy time with new puppies needing jabs and older pets who were feeling the winter cold and developing stiff hips or aches and pains.

When it was time for her to leave, she decided that, as she didn't want to bump into anyone, she would park the distinctive Land Rover at the far end of the village and walk to the school only when she heard the bell ring. Her plan might have worked but Mrs Dodd was there at the gates looking left and right along the road and it could only be for her. At least there wasn't a gaggle of mams waiting.

'Hello Mrs Dodd, would you be waiting for me by any chance?'

'Don't be hoity toity with me, by any chance indeed. It just so happens that I am waiting to catch you. Fancy marrying our Danny and not inviting us to the wedding!'

'He's coming to see you tonight. We had our reasons.'

'Just because you're not speaking to your father, you kept us away too. First you chase my lad away to Alnwick and now he's parted from his own family.'

Rose didn't know what else to say. She would be blamed whatever she said. 'He'll see you tonight and it wasn't meant to insult you. We just wanted it to be quiet.' Rose scanned the group of youngsters pouring from the building into the yard and hoped Terry would be one of the first so she could make her getaway.

'We're sure you're expecting, Rose Kelly.' Mrs Dodd, hands on hips. threw at her.

'And if I was?' Rose threw back at her. Their eyes met and Mrs Dodd seemed to have run out of steam. 'And if I was, then *you* of all people should be thankful that Danny would stand by me.' Maybe that remark was a bit harsh but Rose wouldn't be browbeaten by Mrs Dodd. '*But*, Mrs Dodd, I'm not.'

Terry came running up and looked at Mrs Dodd then back at her. 'Are we going along to Mrs Dodd's for some of Gracie's fruit loaf?'

Mrs Dodd ruffled his hair 'Not today, pet. I'm off home now. Have a grand time with your sister.'

'I'm starving, Rose.'

Rose watched Mrs Dodd waddle off. She was volatile but she seemed fond of Terry. Turning her attention back to her brother, she said, 'We'd better get in the car and think about what we'll have for tea, then.'

As they were driving north, Rose told Terry all about the wedding, and where she was living. She described the flat.

'So do I get to have that spare bedroom to myself?' Terry asked

'You do.'

'And Danny will be around on Saturday morning for a kick about?'

'He will.'

'Can we have bacon and egg with fried bread in the morning?'

'You can.'

'Promise not to cook the egg until it's hard?'

'That's asking too much Terry Kelly,' she laughed.

Terry and Rose ate fish and chips fresh from the paper and she put a portion on a plate in the oven for Danny. Excited about being in the guest bedroom, Terry was eager to get ready for bed. Rose gave him a torch to read a book for a while but, when she peered in at eight o'clock, he was already asleep.

She put the torch to one side and sat on the edge of the bed. After brushing his shock of blonde hair out of his eyes, she traced her hand around his brow and chubby cheek until it rested by the dimple. He needed a haircut; Dad never remembered such things. Maybe Danny could take him tomorrow. From the light of the hallway she watched him sleeping. He was such a bonnie lad with long lashes and that cute dimple. Rose tried to push the thought away but it surfaced before she could stop it; was his sister, with her matching dimple, still bonnie and sleeping as peacefully? Where was she?

Danny opened the door a few minutes later when she was about to throw the dried fish supper in the bin. One look at his face and she cried out, 'What's happened?' He had a fat lip and the beginnings of a black eye.

'Don't throw them away, I'm starving.' He walked over and gave her cheek a kiss.

'Danny, answer me. Who has done that to you?'

Danny grinned. 'I've survived the rage of the rows. I walked into Third Row and my dad gave me the shiner on the eye for upsetting my mam and Gracie. After a bit of a barney, they came around to the idea of us being a couple and I've invited them to come next Sunday. I hope that's alright?'

'Of course it is, but fancy your dad doing that.'

'He took me to one side as I left and said he was sorry but he had to do it or my mother would've gone for me and, believe me, she has a harder hand. He also said to tell you he thinks you're a grand lass and hopes we'll be happy together.'

'The lip? What happened there?'

'I went to your dad's allotment and he was painting. I pulled up a cracket to sit beside him and said how I knew he'd have heard our news due to Dennis's mam. I explained that we wanted a quiet wedding because he wasn't speaking to you and I hoped he'd be happy for us.'

'What did he say to that?'

'He never spoke at all. He just got up, pulled me up by my shirt and butted me in the mouth. Then he walked away from the allotment leaving me and his painting.'

'Two dads in one night. What did you do then?'

'I was so vexed that I looked for a pen or something to write "doylem" over the canvas.'

Rose clapped a hand to her mouth. 'Had he almost finished it?'

'Damned if I know. He *is* a doylem for not speaking to you and he could have knocked a bleedin' tooth out. Anyway, I said I was about to… I didn't because the picture, when I took a look, was it's so beautiful. I think it's of your mam when she was younger with her head back and laughing.'

He was painting her again. He was painting Mam! It was a copy of the painting he'd thrown on the bonfire. Thank the lord that Danny hadn't ruined it. 'I have some TCP. Let me bathe your lip and check that eye.'

'Let me eat this supper before it gets cold and then you can fuss over me all you want.'

Rose knew her dad was hurting to behave like that but she was in pain too. Maybe that painting was a sign that he was ready to accept Mam's goodness along with her mistake. It was a mistake, giving away Joy but it was done. Losing Mam had been painful but knowing that she must stay away from her sister, and being rebuffed by her dad, these things broke her heart.

She had a wonderful new husband and a lovely place to live and she enjoyed her job but, all the time in the background, her heart felt torn to pieces because she loved her dad and wanted him in her life. She tried hard to keep her sadness from Danny. He could cheer her up, make her laugh like nobody else, and he was a balm to her battered heart. Maybe in time it would mend.

59

The first few weeks of married life passed in a whirl and, before she knew it, Rose was checking the calendar and feeling queasy. So much for Danny saying he'd take care of things, she was very definitely pregnant. She couldn't blame Danny totally. They'd both been careless about using condoms that first weekend and Rose still hadn't gone to the clinic to check out other methods. She was pregnant, bloated and sick and Danny was proud, loving and wanting to broadcast it to the world.

'Don't go telling Dad and risk another dust up, Danny. I don't want that. You can let Gracie know and I'll explain to our Terry then Dad and the rest of the folk in the rows can find out from them.'

'Shall we break the news to Dennis and Lottie and ask them to be godparents?' Danny asked.

'What about Stanley and Brenda as godparents? You don't have to be a couple.'

'Either. We can keep one lot for next time.' Danny looked serious.

'Danny Dodd you're way ahead of yourself. Let me get over the shock of having *this* baby first.' She kissed him and he held her in his arms.

'Shall we have an early night?' he whispered. 'And we won't have to worry about you getting pregnant.'

'I'm retiring, Rose. I canna train another assistant to do what you do and I'm getting on in years.' Roger sat nursing a cup of tea in the kitchen above the surgery. He hadn't taken the news of Rose's pregnancy well.

'Rog! I can work for a few months yet and then—'

'And then I'll be left doing night calls, cat fur balls, anal glands and all the stuff you've taken on and I canna go back to all that.'

'I was going to say that I'll work part-time. I'll train somebody up, I've started writing pages of guidelines already.'

'You canna possibly write down all you know and you canna work part-time with a little bairn, Rose. Audrey does a few hours but she's got her mother at home.'

'I'll work something out Roger. I hate the idea of giving up the job I love.'

'You canna have it all ways, lassie. What does Danny say?'

'We haven't discussed it, yet.'

'You have your bairns and look after your man and maybe you'll get back to work when they are grown up, Rose. It's a worthwhile job, keeping a family happy.'

There was no moving him and Rose felt frustrated. She *could* write a book for veterinary assistants that would outline all of their roles and what to do in most emergencies. She had already made a start.

The day after Roger put the premises up for sale, Mr Maxwell senior called around. 'I hear congratulations are in order, Rose.'

'Oh yes, the baby,' she said.

'I did mean on your marriage. Frank told me about it but of course, a baby too, congratulations about that.'

Rose blushed. He'd think they'd rushed into this because of a baby.

'I'll just tell Roger you're here.'

Roger returned from the lunch alone. 'Maxwell is taking over the practice Rose, but don't get your hopes up. He agrees with me that you should take a break and enjoy your family and he's bringing his own staff. His son will run it when he's qualified.'

Rose knew when she was beaten. It would be difficult to work with Frank anyway because... well because they were both fond of each other and working closely together would be wonderful but it might not be fair on Danny.

She'd resign from her post but she'd continue to write that book for veterinary assistants and, one day, it might just get published.

60

They were helping Lottie and Dennis to move into number two. 'At last. I can't believe it's taken them so long to hand over Mary's keys.' Lottie linked arms with Rose as they walked from Lottie's mams to number two in aprons and with scarves around their heads ready to sweep, scrub and clean.

Larry was waiting by the front door as they walked along. 'What the hell is he after now?' Lottie whispered to Rose as they approached him.

Larry looked sheepish. 'I'm sorry you've had to wait, Lottie, but there was a lot to go through. We've left quite a bit of furniture though and, if you don't want it, I'll take it to the second-hand shop in Ashington.'

'Kate said as much yesterday. I think we'll need it all, thanks. You didn't have to come to welcome us.' Rose sensed that Lottie was eager to get in. She'd been telling Rose about her plans for number two for weeks.

'I left our Tom and Jackie's medals on the sideboard and hoped I could catch you and get them back.'

'Ah, I see. Of course you can. Come in.' Lottie opened the front door and let Larry go in first.'

Larry picked up the medals. 'Two brothers lost and only me left now. We've looked for Mam's nest egg but couldn't find it. If you do come across a long brown envelope stuffed somewhere in here, would you let us know, Lottie?'

Lottie rolled her eyes and sighed. 'All of the rows know about the lost nest egg, Larry. Kate's demented about it and I'm sure she's covered every hidey hole but you can trust me, I would tell you if I found it.'

Larry nodded. 'Aye you would. Thanks, Lottie.'

As he left, Rose sat down feeling faint. A long brown envelope? It sounded like the one she'd taken from Mary. The one that clearly said 'For Rose, for Danny'.

'You look peaky. These early days are the worst, hinny. You sit there and I'll put the kettle on. You needn't do much cleaning, I just wanted some company.'

Danny helped Dennis to carry a bed and a wardrobe from Dennis's mam's.

'Danny can we go home, soon? I need to lie down.' Rose was in a turmoil just thinking about that envelope that she'd had for months.

He nodded, 'As soon as we get these up the stairs, I'll take you home and then I'll come back to help.'

As soon as they were alone in Danny's car, she told him.

'You think the envelope you took for me is the bleedin' nest egg that they've searched high and low for?'

'I'm sure of it, Danny. What'll we do?'

'I'm damned if I know but let's check first.'

'I knew it would be.' Rose felt sick to her stomach as she looked at the neat wad of notes lying on their kitchen table. More white five pound notes than Rose had ever seen, even in Mr Campbell's till, and some green pound notes too.

'I daren't count it, Rose. How did Mary save such a fortune?'

'She was careful and so was Mr Elliot. They ate from their allotment and she was great with a needle. She didn't take much, but folk paid her for delivering their bairns too.'

'What'll we do?' Danny looked as stunned as she felt.

'Crikey Moses, Danny. They'll never believe that I took it and we didn't open it until now. I wish my Dad was speaking to me, he'd know what to do and how to put things right.'

Danny stood up. 'You're right, Rose. Your dad has brains and common sense. Mine would ask for a sub then go and tell all of the 'tute about it.'

'What do you mean, I'm right?'

'I'm going to call in on your dad and ask him what to do. I'll say I'm asking for a friend.'

'So you'll ask him, hypothetically, what he'd do?'

'Is that what you call it?'

'Yes it's a hypothetical question, not real.'

Danny kissed her brow. 'Wish me luck. Maybe I should put a mouthguard in before I knock on the door?' He was off down the stairs leaving Rose with a fortune on the table.

Twenty white notes and ten green; a hundred and ten pounds went back into the envelope along with the slip of paper that stated for Danny Dodd from Mary Elliot and was dated the previous year. The bolder script told Rose that Mary hadn't decided to leave Danny her money on the spur of the moment when she was ill. Mary had planned this.

Rose studied the envelope that Mary had held in her hands as she slept. Mary had got it out from its hiding place and written on it whilst Rose was chatting to Kate. 'For Rose, for Danny.' It had seemed clear to Rose that she should take the envelope and give it to Danny. She hadn't dreamt it would be her nest egg; so much in an ordinary brown envelope.

Danny was her grandson, she'd confessed that to Rose. Could it be that she had always wanted Danny to have her savings? If that was so, Larry and Kate would be livid. What advice would her dad give Danny? Would he even talk to him? Rose put the envelope back in the drawer and got ready for bed.

She sat reading but kept reading the same page. It stopped her from worrying too much about Danny but she was glad to hear his key in the lock. Jumping out of bed, she was at the top of the stairs as he came up.

'Let me look at you. Are you alright?'

Danny kissed her. 'No bruises this time and he took me down to the allotment and we chatted, man to man, like. He's a wise man, your dad.'

'At times he is, when he's not stubborn and ignoring his own daughter,' Rose said.

'He did ask how you were and if I was looking after you.'

'He did?' Her heart leapt.

'Don't get your hopes up. He didn't say owt about seeing you or anything.' Danny walked into the kitchen and sat at the table. 'I'll tell you what he did say, as you're making me one of your cheese sandwiches with brown sauce and a cup of tea.'

'I'll make one for myself too. I'm famished but couldn't eat for fretting about you.'

Rose set to work slicing bread as Danny explained, 'He saw right through my hypothetical problem.'

'Did he?' Rose grinned. It was a treat just to hear about Dad second-hand and know he was still the same clever John Kelly.

'Aye he just came out with it. "This friend of yours, it's you isn't it, Danny?" So I told him the lot. You and Mary Elliot, the envelope, the way you and Mary had talked about me and Larry and her being my granny. He's a good listener. your dad.'

'You are too, Danny.' Rose handed him his plate and mug then sat opposite.

'We sat in silence for a bit because I knew, I could tell like, that he was thinking it all through. Then, what he came up with, I was shocked.'

'What did he say?'

Danny repeated her dad's words in the tone she knew he would've used.

"'Danny, I think that Rose was right to take the envelope because it was addressed to you both. 'For Rose, for Danny' the fact that it is in Mary's own script will prove that.

"'I think that Mary Elliot was of sound mind and she admitted you were her kin to Rose, because she wanted to make amends to you. She willingly left you her savings. You don't need to let Larry know but, if you want to be open and honest about it, you can do that.

"'First of all, I would go to a solicitor to have this checked out and ask the solicitor to inform Larry Elliot of Mary's wishes by letter.'"

Rose thought through what her dad had suggested. 'I'll ask Roger for a good solicitor tomorrow and we'll do it straight away.'

'Rose, to think I might have some money to put away. I'd like to be a partner in Williams bakery one day. This will be a start.'

The solicitor looking into their case did not think they needed to send a letter and he certainly didn't think that Danny should offer half of the money to Larry. 'Mary Elliot addressed the letter to the two of you and the note inside is clear. It's a gift and the only ambiguity would be whether it was meant for two people, Rose and Danny, or for Rose to hand it over as it was "For Danny"'

'We share everything, so that's not an issue,' Rose assured him.

'I'd feel better if you sent Larry Elliot a letter and explained the money was left to me,' Danny insisted.

'Do you want me to name you in the letter?'

'Aye, why not? Write that she left her savings to her eldest grandchild, Danny Dodd. See if he argues with that.'

Rose could sense the relief and the weight slide from Danny's shoulders when the solicitor agreed.

When they got out he said, 'I've had to live with rumours all my life and they washed off me because I was loved by my mam and dad and Gracie. Let him tell the rows, and Kate, *who* got Mary's money and why, or live with his secret a bit longer.'

Nothing more was heard of the lost nest egg and Rose was sure that knowledge of the whereabouts of Mary's savings stayed with her dad, Larry, Danny and her.

Dad had helped Danny out but he still didn't stay in the house to see her when she dropped Terry off. Was her baby going to miss out on a grandad?

61

Rose accepted a gift of a beautiful thistle brooch from Roger and an outfit for the baby. 'Audrey chose the baby's clothes so, don't worry, it's not a kilt.'

'Thank you, Roger. I've loved every minute of being here.' Tears rolled down her cheeks.

'Aye, it was the moggies and the pups you loved, not being with a grumpy old Scottish beggar like me.'

'I enjoyed learning from you,' she sniffed and wiped her eyes.

'I enjoyed your company, lassie, but now, I'm going to put my feet up, drink a good malt and start packing for Scotland. My sister is looking forward to having me there. She's coming tomorrow to help me pack up because I don't know where to start.' He blew loudly into a handkerchief.

She waved Roger off the premises, closed the door and howled. She loved this place and didn't want to say goodbye.

After checking the filing was up-to-date for the umpteenth time, the surgery was immaculate and the stock room and the little flat upstairs were in good order, she waited for Danny. No more Land Rover or driving off to farms and no more night calls. What would she do with herself?

Danny beeped and she carried her belongings to the door. One last look around and then she locked up and put the keys through the letterbox. Her dream of working with animals was over, but just for now. She'd come back to it, one day.

A week of dusting, cooking, washing and preparing Danny's meals was enough for Rose. She could have all these jobs done by lunch-time and reading all afternoon was only a treat if you only did it every now and then.

'I'm bored Danny and I've got months yet before the baby keeps me busy.' She sat with her legs up as they watched the news.

'Find something that'll interest you. Why don't you knit a few baby things?'

'Danny, you didn't see my knitting when Mam was pregnant! And then I had Mary-from-next-door to find the dropped stitches.'

'Study a few recipe books?' he suggested.

She threw a cushion at him and laughed. 'You're no help. I'll find something myself.'

The idea came to her when she was boxing all of her notes from the surgery. She couldn't bring herself to discard them and was going to keep them in the cupboard under the stairs. That handbook she had started before Roger decided to sell up, she would write it now whilst everything was fresh in her mind. She'd look out for an old typewriter, read through her notes and write chapters on everything she had learned over the past few years.

'A great idea,' Danny said when she told him at lunch-time.

'I just need to scan the small ads and look in second-hand shops for a typewriter and I'll make a start.'

The next day, Danny came upstairs with a parcel. 'For you, Mrs Dodd, to keep you happy.'

Rose opened the box to find an Imperial typewriter. 'Danny, this is wonderful, it's almost new. Was it expensive?'

'I want you to be happy and you're happy when your mind is beavering away at something challenging. Anyway, look at it as a gift from Mary Elliot.'

With a silent thanks to Mary-from-next-door, Rose settled down to write her handbook. She worked at it every afternoon. More and more ideas for chapters came to her and her daytimes had a meaning once again. She finished half an hour before Danny shut up shop then rushed around making their evening meal.

Life couldn't be better, except for the continued silence from Dad. He had painted Mam's picture so, if he could forgive Mam, why couldn't he get in touch with her? Maybe he just couldn't stop loving Mam, but maybe he could stop loving her because she'd kept him away from his other daughter?

She didn't talk about it with Danny anymore. Danny thought she was overthinking things and that her dad would come around by the time the baby came.

'He's getting on fine with Gracie looking after Terry and him, and he talks to me if I stop by.'

'Does he ask after me? Ask how I'm doing, though?' She wanted her dad to care.

'He doesn't need to because he hears what I tell Gracie and he hears about how tubby you're getting from Terry.'

Danny could joke all he liked but she knew her dad and he was like her, he overthought things too.

Rose sat down as usual at her typewriter. This afternoon, she was starting a new chapter on dealing with overwrought pet owners in a kind but firm manner with a few examples, names changed of course. She typed the first sentence when the phone rang in the hallway downstairs. Should she go down and answer or wait to see if someone from the shop came through? It would be for the shop at this time of day.

Sure enough, the door from the bakery opened and it was Danny's voice she heard. 'Williams the Bakers, can I hel—? Oh no! How bad?'

She froze, she heard murmurs, he'd lowered his voice. It was bad news but she couldn't hear clearly. Getting up from the chair, she made her way to the top of the stairs. Danny must have come up two at a time because he was there before her, his face ashen. 'There's been a fall of stone at Linwood. Your dad's hurt, Rose. They've brought him up to the pithead and he's in an ambulance heading for the Royal Victoria Hospital.'

Rose felt a rush of heat through her body then blackness.

She came around with a pounding head and a sickly feeling. Sitting up, she asked Danny for a bowl. He rushed out and brought one for her. It all came back, he'd told her that Dad had been hurt, in hospital. She retched and Danny held her hair back. When she'd finished he wiped her face with a damp cloth and she lay back. 'Take it easy, love. You've had a shock.' He patted her hand.

'What else do you know?'

'Nowt. You keeled over and it was lucky I was at the top of the stairs. You've just been out for a few minutes'

Minutes? She felt like she'd been out of it for hours. 'I must get up and we must go, right now.'

'Rose love, Gracie told me he was on his way to the RVI. She is going there now to sit by him and phone as soon as she has news. We'll just sit here and wait and you can get your rest.'

'Rest? Rest! Danny, I can't possibly rest when my dad's been hurt and I don't know how he is. Why should your bleeding Gracie be there when I'm not and I'm his daughter? I'm going whether he will speak to me or not and if you don't take me I'll… I'll just get a bus.'

'Calm down. This canna be good for the bairn.' Danny's soothing voice irritated her.

'Good for the bairn? What about my dad? What if I lose him and we're not even speaking?' She flung the blanket off her.

'Okay Rose, I'll drive you to Newcastle but you'll have to calm down or your blood pressure will be sky high.'

Danny was keenly reading the baby books she'd borrowed from the library. Too keenly the way he was going on. 'I'll stay calm if I think I'm doing something, let's go.'

Gracie met them in a corridor just off the ward to say that her dad had recovered consciousness and was confused. He'd been taken straight into theatre for an operation on his crushed hand.

'Is it bad?' Rose held back the tears.

'I don't know, hinny. They had it all swaddled in bandages and he was still black from the pit so it's hard to say.'

'Which one?' Rose dreaded the answer.

Gracie thought for a moment. 'His left'un. That's not so bad is it?' she smiled.

Rose shook her head in disbelief. 'Haven't you even noticed Dad's left handed? It's his painting hand they're operating on.'

'No need to be sharp with our Gracie, Rose.' Danny put his arm around her and she shrugged him off. 'It's not your dad who is lying there being operated on so leave me be, Danny Dodd.'

Gracie raised her eyes at Danny and Rose saw. She felt awful because she knew she was behaving badly but these two had each other. Her dad had to come out of that operating theatre so she could tell him she loved him.

62

The RVI had strict visiting times and all three of them were ushered out and told to come back for evening visiting. 'Mr Kelly is in good hands and we can't have patients' families cluttering up our corridors.'

Danny drove them back to First Row and Lottie immediately came rushing out of number two to give her a hug. Terry followed her and hugged Gracie. 'I'll come and make the tea,' Lottie said. 'You lot just sit down. How is he?'

Rose felt too weary to speak but Gracie chatted away. She could tell that she got on well with Lottie. Gracie was almost a permanent fixture at number one, it seemed. She stayed to watch Terry when dad was working nights and was there every day. Rose tried to stop her jealous thoughts. She couldn't be here anyway now that she was married but there was no getting away from the fact that she was envious of Gracie for taking her place here.

Gracie served them soup with homemade bread and Rose felt better. She went to lie down in her old room for a while and she heard muttering downstairs. Were they talking about her and thinking she was rude? Her tears fell onto the pillow and she slept.

Danny woke her. 'Wake up sleepy head, I'm taking you to the hospital for visiting and Gracie is staying here with Terry.'

Rose sat up. 'Does Gracie not mind?'

'Gracie just wants to be where she's needed,' Danny said.

Rose felt ashamed of her behaviour. 'I'll get ready and, before we go I'll say sorry to Gracie for being so sharp.'

Danny nodded. 'I think you should. She's been nothing but kind to you.'

Rose came down and gave Gracie a hug. 'Don't worry yourself about me, pet. I can see you're upset about your dad and I just hope this brings the pair of you together.'

Gracie's words reminded Rose that her dad might not even want to see her. What would she do then?

The ward reminded Rose of the isolation hospital. Rows of beds on two sides of a long room, some with curtains closed around them. Danny was waiting in the corridor just outside of the ward. 'You go yourself and I'll come in in a few minutes,' he whispered. Everybody seemed to whisper in these corridors.

Rose walked slowly along the row looking left and right.

'Over here,' a familiar voice called.

Two beds further up and to the left sat her dad with his left arm hanging up in a swing contraption.

'Dad!' She rushed over and then stopped, unsure of what to do.

'Come here and give your dad a kiss then, hinny. I didn't think I'd see your bonnie face again when that stone came down.'

Rose kissed her dad then burst into tears. 'I couldn't lose you, Dad. I couldn't bear it.'

'I'm here for a long time yet. I hear I'm going to be a grandad and I want to be around for that.'

Danny came in and they heard how the fall of stone had just caught her dad and his marra. His marra was further up the ward with a broken leg. 'My own rescue team got me out. They did a grand job and the morphine they gave me was what had me out for the count until I got here.'

'Was the operation successful, Dad?' Rose looked at the thick wadding around his hand and arm.

'I don't know, Rose. I'm keeping it high like this for circulation, I think. They've patched it up but I won't know how the hand will work until it heals.'

'Your left…'

Dad nodded. 'Aye, it might put a stop to the painting but at least I'm here. Don't you fret, lassie.'

He joked with Danny about how he'd gone into the operating theatre black with dust and come out scrubbed clean. 'I'm glad I was asleep for that. Whoever soaped me down did a good job, though.'

As they were leaving, Dad said, 'Can we have a minute, Danny? Me and Rose.'

'Yes, of course Mr Kelly. I'll be in the corridor, Rose.'

She watched Danny walk away and swallowed hard. What was Dad going to say? It had been wonderful to sit and talk.

Dad took her hand with his right hand. 'He's a good lad. He turned out well and I'm glad to have him for a son-in-law, Rose.'

'Thanks Dad, that means a lot.' She smiled and got up to go.

'That's not all, pet. I have to say how sorry I am that I took all my bitterness out on you. Deep down, I knew you couldn't go against your mam but I was that vexed and couldn't get at her so you took her share as well.'

'Oh Dad. It's all a mess but we can't do anything to put it right with Joy. She has a family and we have to let her go and be happy.'

'I know, I know that. I didn't make a scene you know. I didn't go to their house but I think Mrs Fletcher got wind of something from the school because they've left the Gloria.'

'Poor woman, she'll always be looking over her shoulder. I'm glad you didn't go, Dad.'

'I've got one lassie back and that'll be enough for me until you have yours.'

'I might have a boy, Dad.'

'We'll see.' He lay back on the pillows looking tired. Rose kissed him. 'Try and get a good night's sleep, Dad.'

'I'll sleep better tonight because I've seen you and said sorry.'

'I'm sorry we didn't speak sooner,' Rose said before she left.

Dad's rehabilitation started as soon as he got out of hospital. He gained some use in his fingers and could feed himself but he couldn't use his cut throat razor and he didn't try to paint.

It was time the family had a celebration together and Dad decided they would have a party at the 'tute for Rose's twenty-first in the middle of August. He insisted on paying for it and invited all the rows and everyone they knew.

The day before, he gave her his present and she gasped as she opened it. The painting of Mam, her head back laughing and it was just as striking as the original. 'This is the last painting I completed and I want you to have it. It helped me to paint it but it hurts me too much to look at it often.'

Rose hugged him. 'Thanks Dad but please don't talk like that about your painting. It's early days and you might improve. Your fingers will become more flexible.'

Dad nodded but didn't look convinced. He was back at work and could grip a shovel. He could tend the garden and he could shave using a safety razor so surely he could try to paint?

On the night of her party, Rose was four weeks away from her due date and felt heavy and hot. Dancing was out of the question. She watched everyone else on the dance floor and just wanted to go home. Her dad and Gracie were dancing and having fun and those uncomfortable prickles of envy flared again. Mam had been dead for years, she wanted Dad to be happy and she liked Gracie but… she just didn't like to see her in Mam's place.

'What are you frowning at Mrs Dodd?' Danny came over with a cool lemonade for her.

'Thanks Danny.' She took a sip. 'I just feel like a pet rhino and I can't join in the dancing.'

'Who can't?' He pulled her to her feet and took her in his arms to glide onto the floor. They were a massive baby bump apart and not as graceful as usual but Rose loved being there on the dance floor in Danny's arms.

She swirled past Mr and Mrs Norris who had been part of her life for so long, Lottie and Dennis who were chatting to Robbie, Betty and the rest of the gang, she spotted Mr Maxwell and Frank having a pint at the bar with Stanley and Brenda and then she came to a stop by Bella and Andrew who were talking to Eddie-who-plays-the-accordion. 'Thank you so much for coming.' She hugged Bella.

'I wouldn't have missed this coming of age for the world. Your mam would have been so proud of you, Rose.'

Rose swallowed and nodded. 'Thanks,' she managed.

Perry Como singing 'I've Got the World on a String' started and, as Danny led her off onto the floor, she enjoyed being held in strong, loving arms as Perry sang about love.

63

The first week in September, Rose finished her book. She wasn't sure what to do with it.

'Why don't you ask that vet pal of yours, Frank?' Danny suggested. 'I chatted to him at your birthday and he seems decent. He'll be able to pass it on to the right folk, I'm sure.'

Rose felt too bulky to call around to the practice so she wrote a note to Frank explaining how she'd written the manual and sent it off for his opinion. He'd tell her if it was any good or not.

Now I'll have time on my hands again, she thought.

She was wrong, she didn't have any time at all. It was happening!

After getting up early, at five o'clock, because she felt uncomfortable, she sat down with a cup of tea and, woosh, her waters broke. 'Danny! Danny! It's time.'

They were booked into Morpeth Cottage Hospital for the birth and Danny got them there in record time.

Then there was a wait. The contractions seemed to have stopped. Rose went through the indignity of a shave by a midwife then an enema. Things couldn't get worse, she was sure.

Then they did, a lot worse. Pain after pain until she seemed to be on a crescendo of pain. This couldn't be right?

Then the urge to push. The midwife encouraging her and hearing her cry out, 'I see the head.' Another tremendous push and she heard a high pitched wail. 'You've got a little girl, Mrs Dodd.'

The baby was placed in her arms. She was red, wrinkled and screaming. Rose watched her little fists as they struggled to get free from the blanket and fell in love with her.

Danny, eyes wide with wonder, took the baby from her. 'She's beautiful, just beautiful, Rose.'

Rose looked at her daughter, quiet now in her daddy's arms and saw the redness recede and her eyes open, dark blue like Danny's. Yes she was beautiful.

Rose learned that babies are hard work and sleep is a precious thing during the first few weeks of having Lily. Danny chose the name and Rose liked it. Every time Rose got into a routine, Lily changed it.

She was a hungry baby who wanted to be fed at all hours and the house looked like a devastation area by the end of the day. Danny would come in to help her to restore order and help her to cook their supper and sometimes she got to eat it before Lily woke up again.

It was a particularly bad Monday afternoon when the doorbell rang and Rose rushed to open the door before the caller rang again and woke Lily. There stood Frank Maxwell with a bunch of flowers.

Rose wanted the ground to open up. She hadn't untied her hair for days, she was wearing a dressing gown splattered in colicky baby sick and she was barefoot.

'Hi Rose, I heard the news and thought I'd call to see your new arrival.' Frank kissed her cheek and didn't seem to notice she was a complete mess.

She couldn't keep him at the door but upstairs was a bomb-site. She led the way and couldn't decide whether the kitchen or the living room was worse. As she hovered, Frank entered the kitchen.

'Whoa!' he backed out. 'I can see it's not the best time to call,' he said.

She shrugged. 'It's never the best time. Come into the living room, it's almost as bad.'

Frank grinned. 'You never were keen on domestics yet you could run a surgery so efficiently. You'll have to take a few tips from your own guidebook. "Leave each room clean and tidy and ready for whatever the next day brings."'

'Shut up, Frank Maxwell. And talk quietly or you'll wake Lily.' She couldn't help smiling.

'I'd love to see her.'

'I'll get her up soon. Do you want a cup of tea first?' she asked.

'No, no, honestly I don't want one, I came with these.' He handed over the huge bouquet of roses. 'And I came to tell you that your handbook is brilliant. I've shown it to Dad and a few of his colleagues already and they agree.'

Really? Rose smiled. Did he mean it?

'There's a good chance it could be published, Rose. But… there's a snag.'

'Published? What's the snag?' She was aware of sounding like Frank's echo.

'It's you.' He rubbed his face the way she knew he did when he was embarrassed.

'Me?'

'You haven't the credentials that would give you clout among the publishing world.'

'Veterinary assistants don't *have* credentials. They don't have any training, that's why I wrote the book.'

'I know. I think I have an answer but it's up to you.'

Rose lay the bouquet on a side table, sat opposite him and drew her dressing gown around her. 'Go on.'

'Dad has written a few papers and he's a well-recognised veterinary surgeon. I'm sure if he edited the guidelines and added a few footnotes from a vet's point of view and you published it together, it would be taken up. What do you think?'

Rose pursed her lips and gave the matter a moment's thought. 'What do I think? I think I don't want a veterinary surgeon interfering with a veterinary assistant's manual and then adding his name to all my hard work.'

Frank looked down at his shoes. 'Sorry Rose. I didn't mean to upset you. I do see your point and I was only trying to help.'

She immediately felt sorry she'd said that. She'd been teasing, well half-teasing him. 'On the other hand, if I'm too precious about it, it won't go anywhere.'

Frank nodded. 'That's what I mean. Dad said you could have all the royalties of course.'

'Royalties? You mean we'll *sell* it, not give it away?'

'Of course.'

'Wow, Frank. Let's do it. We can give the royalties to an animal charity, I just want my handbook to be used.' She grinned.

Frank stared at her. She smoothed her hair back, she must look a real mess.

'You look lovely, Rose. Motherhood suits you,' he said.

A wail sounded from the bedroom. 'You're going to meet Miss Lily Dodd and hold her whilst I wash some cups and make us a cup of tea to celebrate.'

'Why don't you get dressed and I'll take you both to that nice tea shop around the corner?'

'Okay but I'll hand Lily to you while I get ready. You don't know what you're letting yourself in for.'

She told Danny all about it that night. He was as excited as she was that her book might find a publisher and he wasn't jealous of her friendship with Frank any more or she would have been able to tell. Their love was secure.

64

December arrived and Rose had very little Christmas shopping done. She left Lily with Gracie and her dad to go into Ashington and, all the time she was away, she wondered how they were coping.

When she returned, Gracie was cooking in the scullery and Dad had a sketch pad on his knee. He'd drawn several sketches of Lily kicking her legs on a blanket on the floor. 'I could sketch this little miss all day. She's entrancing like you were.'

Rose picked up the sketch pad. 'Dad, you haven't lost it. These have captured her beautifully.'

He stretched his fingers, 'They're stiff and a bit numb but they're working. I'm a lucky man in many ways.' Dad looked at her and the baby and his glance flicked to the scullery where Gracie was cooking.

Rose and Danny spent Christmas Eve at home and marvelled at how, at three months, Lily's colic seemed to have disappeared. She slept through until six the next morning. After feeding her, Rose dared to put her into a pretty white dress and risk that a bib would be enough to keep the outfit sick free until they got to Linwood.

She handed Danny the new sweater, deep blue to match

his eyes, that she'd chosen for him. 'Thanks Rose,' he put it on straight away.

'This is for you.' He handed over the familiar shaped box.

No surprises here, Danny had bought her roses chocolates for every occasion since she was fifteen. She smiled. 'Thanks Danny.'

'Open the box!'

His excitement was contagious so Rose ripped off the paper, opened the box and poured the Roses chocolates onto the table. Her heart skipped a beat; there in the centre was a gold chain with a delicate rose charm hanging from it. 'It's beautiful, Danny. I'll wear it always.'

After they packed the many things needed for Lily to leave the house, and the presents for all of the Elliots and the Dodds, they set off to spend Christmas Day at First Row.

Gracie and Rose cooked Christmas dinner on the range, using fresh vegetables from Dad's allotment and roasting one of Mr Dodd's chickens. 'Dad said it was my Christmas present. Aren't I the lucky one?' Gracie gave a wry smile.

Rose couldn't help but laugh. She was getting more used to Gracie being around. She'd always liked her and was trying to stop those green twinges when Gracie shared a joke with Dad or received a hug from Terry.

Dad gave his visit to the 'tute for the usual Christmas drink a miss and seemed happy to sit back from the range, out of the way of pans and roasting trays, and entertain Lily with songs and rhymes. Rose paused as he sang one of the old songs he'd taught her then Stanley and then Terry. 'Clap your hands for Daddy coming down the wagon way with a pocketful of money and a cartful of hay.'

Lily was all smiles, waving her hands and kicking her feet for her grandad.

Today the house seemed to be full of memories. She could

picture Mam cooking with Mary-from-next-door whilst she was sent off to chapel with Stanley.

Lucky dozed on the rug in front of the range with one eye on the tasty treats coming in and out of the oven. His muzzle had more than a few grey hairs but he'd bounced about like a puppy when Terry took him for a walk earlier. Terry had his nose in *The Guinness Book of Records* that Rose had bought him for Christmas and every now and then he'd read one out.

At last, the lunch was ready to serve. Lily slept, Danny came in from the 'tute and Dickie Valentine sang out 'The Christmas Alphabet' as Gracie and Rose served up dinner. 'Rose listen to what's on the radio!' Terry knew all the words and his clear voice sang along.

'That voice should've been singing in the chapel before your dinner, Terry Kelly.' Rose couldn't resist telling him. He was sporadic about going to Sunday school nowadays but, if Dad and Gracie didn't insist, what could she do? Her mam would've insisted on him going but she wasn't here. Did the Fletchers encourage his sister go to chapel? Rose pushed the thought away, Joy often popped into her head. Was it the same for Dad?

Terry pulled her back to the present. 'Do you know that Dickie Valentine has topped the charts with this? He's number one! Do you think our Stanley will bring this record with him this afternoon? I'm fed up of him playing 'Unchained Melody' whenever he comes. I think he plays it and thinks of Brenda.'

'He'll bring some new ones but I'm not sure if he'll have this one. And don't you go making comments about him and Brenda.' Stanley still loved his music and he was driving over for tea later on with Brenda. He was a couple of years younger than Brenda but they seemed to be very taken with one another. With Stanley working on the farm and Brenda living there, they weren't exactly dating but spent part of every day together and seemed more than happy to do so.

Rose missed working with animals. Life was busy with a

baby, a husband and a flat to look after but she still hankered after her work with sick animals and the adventure of travelling out to farms when there was a difficulty. Would she get back to it one day? Yes, she'd make her dream happen eventually.

She was excited about *The Veterinary Assistant's Handbook* by F Maxwell VetMB RCVS and R Kelly – she'd used her maiden name – coming out in 1956. She was sure it would be a well-thumbed book in a lot of surgeries and wouldn't just sit gathering dust on the shelf like some of the weighty veterinary tomes she had waded through. She was proud of being published and so was her dad who wanted his own signed copy. One day, when Lily was bigger she would go back…Crikey, the Yorkshire puddings!

A burning smell pulled her out of her daydream. She'd taken her mind of her cooking chores again. In the rows, Yorkshires were served whether the roast was beef, chicken or pork, and now these would be overdone.

Clear plates proved that Gracie and Rose had made a good effort. Danny provided a Christmas pudding from Williams the Bakers and it was delicious but not quite like the plum duff that Mam and Mary-from-next-door served up. There was no silver sixpence in it for Dad either; some traditions fell by the wayside but they'd make new ones.

Dad stood up after they'd eaten their pudding. 'You and Danny go for a bit of air while Lily is asleep. I'll help Gracie with the dishes before all of the others arrive and then we can settle down to listen to the Queen's speech.'

That was a new tradition that Rose wasn't going to argue with. She grabbed her coat from the scullery door. 'Come on Danny. Don't just lounge back on the chair, you need to whip up an appetite for tea. Your mam and dad are coming over with a trifle and fruit cake and Stanley and Brenda are bound to bring some farm goodies.'

Danny linked her arm as they left the back yard. 'Isn't it nice to get out for a bit?'

She nodded and kissed his cheek. 'It's so nice to have a few minutes to ourselves.'

They reached the corner. 'Were you wanting to go into the chapel? There isn't another service until six so it will be quiet.'

She considered it for a moment before saying. 'No, I've got somewhere else in mind.' Taking his hand, she led the way towards the allotments.

At the fence near the allotment gate, they paused. 'I remember sitting right here when I was almost five years old and you were the big lad showing off about what you knew about the war.'

'Was I? I was all of seven and thought you were like a princess so I always showed off around you.'

'Really? I was just the pitman painter's daughter from First Row and didn't think you noticed me at all.'

'Oh yes, I did. I brought you Lucky to fix because you were good with animals and remember that Christmas when you were in hospital? I got a clip around the lug for being out all Christmas afternoon but I had to see you. I was so worried you'd die.'

'Oh Danny.' She hugged him.

'Yes I was worried you'd die and I hadn't kissed you.' He laughed as his eyes locked with hers and she gazed into their inky blue depths. They hadn't changed, serious one moment and dancing with laughter the next.

'Those cards and letters you brought for me, I wanted to keep them but I couldn't take anything from the hospital in case of infection.'

'I'm just glad you came out. Some didn't.' He crushed her in a hug and buried his face in her hair

'I remember you reaching your hand to the window.'

'You put your hand over mine and I swear I could feel the warmth through the glass. I thought of that all the way home; no kiss though.'

Rose took Danny's face in her hands and kissed his brow,

both eyes and his nose before her lips met his. He could still start up a flock of cabbage whites in her stomach when they kissed, a long kiss that they were in no rush to end. Eventually, Danny released her and she said, 'Christmas makes me nostalgic, that's why I wanted to come to Dad's allotment.'

She pointed to a cluster of milk-white flowers sheltered by the south facing side of Dad's shed. 'These were Mam's favourites, Christmas roses.' She slipped away from Danny and searched for garden scissors in the shed before snipping off three stems to carry home. 'They don't last long indoors but I've picked these to take home, one for Mam, one for David and another for...'

Danny took her into his arms, he knew exactly who she was missing today. 'Wherever that young sister of yours is, I'll bet she's having a happy family Christmas. Who knows the future? One day you might be reunited.'

'I hope so, Danny. That'll be a day to remember.' Rose reached up and kissed him.

'Let's go back and celebrate everything we do have.' Danny held her tightly. He had the knack of saying just the right thing.

Today she missed Mam and David, gone forever, and her little sister who was goodness knows where, but she had such a lot to be thankful for and a houseful of love waiting for her in First Row. She was blessed with Lily and, best of all, the heart of this wonderful man.

Flakes of snow began to fall as Rose reached for Danny's hand, 'Let's run!'

Together, they flew back down the lane their feet familiar with every step of the way home.

GLOSSARY OF
LINWOOD LANGUAGE

Adam's ale – a glass of water

Bait – a packed meal for taking to work

Bevin boy – a conscripted miner named after Ernest Bevin

Clout – a smack or thump

Cloot – a rag or cloth

Clootie fruit pudding - a pudding filled with fruit and boiled in a cloth then left to dry by the fire before serving

Connie – conscientious objector shortened from consecientious

Cracket – a low stool with a hole in the middle for carrying it.

Doylem – a foolish person

Gallowa – any pit pony not just a Galloway pony.

Hinny – a term of endearment like 'honey'

Hintend – hind end, backside

Linties – fast running birds so used to describe anyone rushing about.

Lowse – finishing time, the end of a miner's shift or drinking up time at a bar.

Lug – ear

Marra – a workmate or friend

Masting – the brewing of tea in a pot

Netty – lavatory. Some say it is a shortening of 'necessity'

Nowt – nothing

Owt – anything

Plum duff – a spiced, steamed or boiled pudding

Pig's ear – a mess – you've made a pig's ear of that.

Proggy mat – a homemade mat made from pushing strips of cloth into a hessian backing with a progger

Progger – a tool for making a proggy mat

Scullery – a room off the kitchen with a sink and bench and some shelving and sometimes a larder

Singing hinny – a scone cooked on a girdle

Taties – potatoes

Tats – tangles or knots, in hair or wool

Yammer – to moan and groan

RECIPES

Ginnie's Stand-Your-Spoon-Up-In-It-Soup

This is a thick hearty soup that can be made using vegetable, chicken or ham stock

Ingredients:

- Yellow split peas – use half a pack or four good handfuls

- Ham bones, a ham hock or 2 pints of stock from a chicken carcass or cubes. (Ginnie's tip -Norris's shop will give you a free ham knuckle bone if they have one.)

- One large leek or onion- chopped finely

- Three large carrots -grated

- Salt and pepper to season (Ginnie's tip - Always leave the seasoning until the end as ham bones and hock can make the soup salty enough.)

Extra advice from Ginnie - Get the veg from John's allotment or ask around to see who has veg going spare. If you like them, add either a stick of chopped celery, a grated parsnip or diced potato or any vegetable in season at the allotment. You don't need to add anything and don't add the lot. John likes parsnip added and Stanley hates celery. Everybody likes a bit of chopped potato.

Method:

1. Place yellow split peas in a large bowl and cover with boiling water leave to steep overnight. If you forget, leave them at least four hours or make the soup the next day. The split peas must be steeped to be soft.

2. Take your largest pan and place the drained split peas in it with two pints of boiling water

3. Allow the peas to simmer for half an hour and remove any 'scurf', the grey bubbles that form when it is boiling, from the top of the water.

4. If you have stock, add 2 pints of stock to the split peas. If you are using ham bones or a hock, add them now with two extra pints of water.

5. Prepare the veg as mentioned above. Grate and chop finely.

6. Add all of the veg and cover with a lid. If there's too much liquid, drain a bit off. Leave the lid slightly open

7. Simmer on a low heat until all of the veg is soft and the soup is as thick as you like it. (Ginnie's tip - Don't be in a hurry and keep giving it a stir so it doesn't stick to the

bottom of the pan. Ginnie leaves this to simmer on the range all afternoon until it is (almost) thick enough to stand her ladle in it.)

8. Remove the bones, flake the ham into the soup

9. Go easy with the salt and pepper. Taste first before you add any.

10. Serve with freshly made bread or a national loaf from Norris's shop

The Loudest Singing Hinnies in the Row

Hinny (honey) is a term of endearment used in the colliery rows to address people. The singing part of the name comes from when the cakes are cooked in the hot pan because, as they hit the pan, the butter and lard start to sizzle and the hinnies 'sing'.

Ingredients:

- 450 grams /1 pound plain flour

- 1/4 teaspoon baking soda

- 1/2 teaspoon cream of tartar

- 1/2 teaspoon salt

- 110 g /4 ounces chilled butter – sadly must make do with marg when there's a war on

- 110g /4 oz chilled lard

- 175 g /6 ounces any dried fruit (currants, sultanas or raisins)

- 4 to 5 tablespoons milk (to mix)

Method:

1. Add the flour, bicarbonate of soda, cream of tartar and salt into a large mixing bowl.

2. Cut the cold butter and lard into small pieces, add to the baking bowl and rub together with the flour until it turns into fine crumbs Work quickly, and lightly and make sure the equipment and ingredients used for making

the hinnies are all as cool as possible, including your hands. If the fat melts into the flour now, the scones will be dense. (Ginnie's tip -Run the bowl and your hands under cold water just before you start.)

3. Stir in the mixed fruit. Once thoroughly mixed, add milk, a little at a time, until the dough comes together. It should be soft.

4. Dust a board or work surface with a little flour, and roll out the dough thinly to around the depth of a coin)

5. Cut the dough into 8 pieces with a sharp knife or use a scone cutter. (Ginnie's tip -When cutting the hinnies using a scone cutter, avoid twisting the cutter, just press down then gently shake the hinny onto the prepared tray. A blunt knife or twisting the tart cutter tears at the edges of the hinny and that stops them rising as they cook.)

6. Heat a girdle over the range or use a heavy-bottomed frying pan on a stove.

7. Tear of a little piece of the lard wrapper and smear it with lard to grease the pan lightly. Once hot, cook the hinnies a half a batch at a time for approx 5 mins on each side. Listen to them sing and watch them turn a golden brown.

**Serve warm with a sprinkling of sugar
or some homemade jam.**

Delicious with melted butter when it's not rationed.
Eat them fresh. They'll keep for a day if you're
lucky enough to have some left.

THE PITMEN PAINTERS
1934-84

The pitmen painters were a group of artists who formed in the 1930s. In 'Rose's Choice', John Kelly is a fictional character from the group. The group began as an evening class of Northumbrian pitmen keen to learn about art. Within weeks they were producing their own work and, over the years, their paintings amounted to a complete record of life in a mining community: work at the coal face, the pithead baths, allotments, the pit ponies and scenes from the colliery rows. They were exhibited in London and Edinburgh as well as locally. William Feaver's book 'Pitmen Painters: The Ashington Group, 1934-1984' covers the fifty year history of the group and contains illustrations of dozens of paintings, drawings, prints and sculptures by the pitmen. Lee Hall of 'Billy Elliot' fame has written a successful play, 'The Pitmen Painters'. It has toured nationally and internationally. A large collection of the group's work is on display at Woodhorn Museum in Northumberland. As well as holding a fascinating exhibition of the pitmens' paintings, this old colliery site is packed full of the social history of mining and well worth a visit.

BOOKS IN THIS SERIES

THE COLLIERY ROWS

A series of family sagas set in Linwood Colliery rows

The Unwelcome Angel

A gripping emotional novella for readers who would love to read more about how the women coped in the winter of 1944 when the strangling angel visited Linwood. You'll learn more about the epidemic from Ginnie Kelly, Edna Simpson, Dorothy Fletcher and a new character, Nurse Helen Tweedie as they battle diphtheria, pit dust, the Germans and prepare for a World War 2 Christmas.

Rose's Choice

Rationing, bombing, disease and pit disasters are part of Rose Kelly's World War 2 childhood. When the spirited coalminer's daughter discovers a family secret, she makes a choice that overshadows her teenage years. Rose tries to make the most of post-war opportunities but family tragedy pulls her back to a life in the colliery rows. She relinquishes her bright future for domestic duties because her family comes first. Will family ties get in the way of her dreams?

Rose's Ever After

Coming out soon. A return to the colliery rows to meet Rose and the Kelly family again, including Joy. There are tears and triumphs in this moving saga of love and belonging.

OTHER BOOKS BY CHRISSIE BRADSHAW

A Jarful of Moondreams - Cleo has always strived for success and enjoys her independent lifestyle but she is about to lose control of her life and discover how tough that can be. Alex hates the crazy idea that she should be uprooted from her home and friends to live with Cleo, her bossy older sister. Teri is desperate for her two daughters to bond but worries that she has left it too late. Love and change is in the air and the 'Moondream' jar that has held their wishes for many years is about to spill shocking secrets. Follow Cleo, Teri and Alex as they face a summer to remember and discover just what it takes to make their dreams come true.

The Barn of Buried Dreams - Erin and Heather Douglas are struggling. Their mother's death has left a void in their family and everyday life has side-lined their dreams. Erin has buried herself away in the family home and left her stage career. By hiding away, she is avoiding the pain of returning to London and the acting world where her ex-fiancé is enjoying success and a new relationship. When she meets charismatic Texan Jackson McGee, she wrestles with her feelings for him. Should she trust another man? Heather is juggling babies, work, a rocky marriage and running on wine. An overheard conversation makes her ask, would Mark cheat on her? Can the sisters help one another to face their fears, dust off and revive those dreams and find joy in life?

PRAISE FOR AUTHOR

"A Jarful of Moondreams spills over with longing, love and life. The exploration of sibling rivalry will make sisters all over the world laugh and cry....at the heart of this novel is an issue that will resonate with many women-what does it mean to be a mother?" - ' MAGS' 5 star review.

" ...lovely storyline and likeable characters. It will make you laugh and cry in equal measure. This is a very accomplished debut novel. I am really looking forward to her next book." - Book literati 5 star review.

"I knew, as soon as I started talking to the characters, I was hooked. The story was great with twists and turns. It made me laugh, it definitely made me have a tear or two. Bring on the next one, Chrissie. a great read." - 5 star review Verified purchase.

ABOUT THE AUTHOR
CHRISSIE BRADSHAW

Chrissie, 2016 winner of the Romantic Novelist's Association Elizabeth Goudge writing trophy, is a seasoned tea drinker who writes contemporary and historical family sagas.

Chrissie has always loved match-making a book to a reader. Writing the kind of book she loves to read takes this a step further. When Chrissie is not writing or reading, you will find her walking her dog on the beach, travelling or spending time with her family and friends. She would love to hear from readers.

Chrissie enjoys tweeting on @ChrissieBeee

Her instagram account is chrissie_bradshaw_author

Her blog is www.chrissiebradshaw.com

and she has a Chrissie Bradshaw author page on Facebook.

To join her mailing list, email-
chrissiebradshaw@hotmail.co.uk

ACKNOWLEDGEMENT

I couldn't write without the support of my family and my writing friends. Writing has put me in touch with other authors who keep me going when the writing doesn't flow and celebrate with me whenever I have a success.

Thanks to you all!

Lightning Source UK Ltd.
Milton Keynes UK
UKHW021258020720
365868UK00002BA/22